AN ACCIDENTAL LIGHT

Elizabeth Diamond spent many years writing poetry and working, amongst other things, as a home help, a shop assistant, a typist, and a special-needs teacher, and dreaming of being a published author, until a chance place on a writers' development award, followed by an arts council grant, gave her the time to write her first novel – just to see 'if she could'. The result was her debut novel, *An Accidental Light*. She lives in Devon, and has two grown sons and three granddaughters.

elizabeth diamond

An Accidental Light

PICADOR

First published 2008 by Picador

First published in paperback 2009 by Picador
an imprint of Pan Macmillan Ltd
Pan Macmillan, 20 New Wharf Road, London N1 9RR
Basingstoke and Oxford
Associated companies throughout the world
www.panmacmillan.com

ISBN 978-0-330-45352-3

A CIP catalogue record for this book is available from
the British Library.

Typeset by SetSystems Ltd, Saffron Walden, Essex
Printed and bound in the UK by
CPI Mackays, Chatham ME5 8TD

To my granddaughters, Emily, Jessica and Sophia –
and to the memory of Sister David, who sowed the seed.

An Accidental Light

I

JACK

A life can change in an instant. That's all it takes. Then be haunted by 'what ifs'. What if I hadn't gone for a drink that night, or had taken a different route home? What if it hadn't been raining? What if I hadn't been there at all? Someone else, with a different name, living another life.

She came at me out of the blue, I said to the coroner. I'd never known what it meant before. She came at me out of the blue gloom, the blue rain, the blue shadow of the red bus. A smudged shape moving in a royal-blue school uniform between the rear of the bus and my moving car.

I didn't see her. I didn't have time to brake.

'Why didn't you have your headlights on?' he'd asked. He had a thin angular face, eyebrows that met in the middle, thinning grey hair.

I couldn't tell him about the light in November. When it's easy not to notice the first signs of dusk. When shapes suddenly lose their edges and a girl moving quickly from behind a stationary bus, moving in the fading light, in the rain, in the November gloom, may be a ghost, a spirit, something from the Underworld, a phantom from out of my own mind.

'It would have made no difference,' I had told him. 'I wouldn't have had time to stop.' *She came at me suddenly out of the blue.*

'You can't be sure,' he'd said, his mouth a thin line of disapproval. 'Even a second could have made a difference.'

He was right, of course: I can't be sure. I can't be sure of anything anymore.

I couldn't tell him about time either; how there are two sorts. There's clock time where seconds mount up to minutes and minutes to hours. Where day changes to night and weeks build to months and months to a year, and the years play out on your face and in your thickening waist. The time most of us live in.

Then there's the other sort. It has no limits. It reels you backwards without warning, spins you young again on a whim. It can be triggered by anything: a fragment of music, a scent on the air. Or a child moving in a blue school uniform in the rain. It claims you in dreams, on the borders of sleep, even in your waking moments when you think you're safe.

A child moved out suddenly from the rear of a bus, ran in a blue smudge of uniform through the misted rain, moved out from that forward linear tick-tock time into the other, where she's caught forever, like a broken leaf in a whirlpool current. I've seen her a thousand times. Running through the blue shadows in the rain. Stopped by a screech of brakes and my voice shouting. Stopped by the sudden boom of my heart.

Her name was Laura. I found that out later in the station. Bob Lees was on duty that night. He sat me down in the interview room, fetched me a coffee and handed me a cig-arette. I'd given up months ago but none of that mattered now – my old life wiped out now like a cloth wiping a smudge from glass. My hand trembled when I held the cigarette and put it to my mouth. Bob lit it for me and I inhaled. It tasted bitter; I was thankful for that, needing the bitterness.

'Jack, you know that Laura is dead.'

More a statement than a question. He said her name gently. He could have been naming someone I'd known for a long time, even someone I loved. His voice made her name sound intimate. *Laura. Derived from Laurel, meaning victory.*

When I knelt over her in the road she lay as still as a doll, her pale face like wax, not a mark on it. There was a bubble of saliva in the corner of her mouth. I'd touched her then, but only lightly, my hand brushing the top of her head. She could have been my own child lying there, her blue school skirt hitched up above the thin bones of her knees, books spilling out from the school bag by her feet. My hand, resting on the top of her head, felt damp. When I pulled it away my fingers were dark with blood.

I've seen dead bodies before. Often. I've seen them in the morgue and in the autopsy room. It's part of the job. I've seen them encased in plastic, like a joint of meat. The zip's pulled down and I've breathed in death, musty, like rotten leaves. A dead body has no name, although on the records a name might be assigned to it, surname first. But it's just a word; there's no music attached to it, no essence.

I've seen casualties of road accidents before, like Laura. I've been first on the scene a few times, waiting for the ambulance. I've done the stuff you're supposed to do. Check for consciousness, for breath, for a pulse.

'Can you hear me?' I've said. 'Can you hear my voice?'

I've tilted my head towards their nostrils, hoping to feel the warm tremor of a breath on my ear, watched for the rise and fall of their ribcage. I've even had to do CPR once. He was an old man, a derelict. He died with the bottle still clasped in his hand. I'd felt his whiskers in my mouth. It did no good; he'd gone anyway. But you have to try.

When someone dies suddenly, within seconds, within minutes, they're not like those corpses on the mortuary slab. There's a touch of colour in their cheeks still, a suggestion of light in their eyes, as if the soul – if you believe in that stuff – is uncertain where it should be.

Did I know Laura had died? Yes. But she wasn't dead then, lying on the gritty tarmac, a drizzle of rain on her face. I saw her lips move slightly. A faint sigh, a low moan beneath the breath.

I dipped my head towards her face and listened to her breath and felt a faint fan of warm air on my cheek.

'Sweetheart,' I said, as if she was my own child and I loved her, 'it's OK. You're going to be OK.'

Her eyes stirred beneath their closed lids. I kept my eyes fixed on her face and noticed little else. Not the froth of blood that welled up from her chest wall and seeped into the royal-blue blazer. Not Dave's voice behind me on the mobile. A curl of blood leaked slowly down from her hair-line. I took my handkerchief from my pocket and stroked it gently upwards towards her brow-bone so it wouldn't get into her eye. I held her hand. Her fingers lay cold and still in my own.

How long? Seconds. Minutes. I don't know. What's time? Sometimes it stops all together.

Dave's voice breaking in, restoring me to clock time. Its forward motion.

'The ambulance is coming, Jack. I can see it.'

I could hear it too. Shrieking down the road towards us, the road emptying suddenly, making way. Within seconds, the paramedics were leaping out, their brisk urgency nudging me back. Checking her pulse, clamping an oxygen mask over her mouth. Her body slid from me onto the stretcher and they lifted her up. That's when it happened. I felt a cold rush of air come over me and pass me and that's when I knew she had died.

Although I didn't know her name then. *Laura*.

'Jack, you know that Laura is dead?'

More a question, than a statement. Bob was ten years younger than me. He looked at me like I could have been a brother.

'Yes, I know,' I said softly.

Sam picked me up from the station about nine, maybe ten. After I'd made a statement, had a blood test. I came out of the door and she walked right up to me through the thin cold rain. She was wearing a light-coloured raincoat that fell open at the front. She buried her head onto my shoulder and curled the fingers of her right hand against my neck. Her fingers were cold from the rain. I slid my hands under her raincoat and around her waist. Her body felt warm and soft under her cashmere sweater.

'It'll be OK, darling,' she murmured.

But it won't, not now.

'Laura's dead,' I said, flatly. I used her name; it sounded like I could be talking about my own daughter, someone I loved. I felt Sam's body flinch slightly at my words. We stood together in the rain for some time, holding each other. She broke the spell. She moved away.

'Where are the girls?'

'Sarah's babysitting.'

I've seen people in shock before. I've seen their eyes blur and the colour drain from their face. I've seen them shuffle as if they've suddenly grown old, as if they've forgotten how to move their legs. I wanted to bury my face in Sam's hair for ever. I didn't want to think.

She took my hand and led me slowly towards the car park.

Laura's father was at the inquest. I couldn't look at him, but all the time I was giving my evidence I felt him looking at me. His eyes were stripping me bare, flaying the skin from my face.

You killed my daughter. My daughter is dead because of you.

I could hear the words in my head, as if he was transmitting them telepathically.

What's it like, to lose a child?

One day she's there, giggling over some adolescent secret at the dinner table, leaving towels on the bathroom floor, her

room in a mess. Thirteen years old. A worrying age. He
would have worried about what she was doing after school,
who her friends were, how much she was discovering about
boys. The worst still to come. Would someone pass her a joint
one evening at a party, when she was older, an E, a snort
of cocaine? Would she take it? Would she get drunk, off
her head on gin or vodka, let some acne-faced boy with one
thing on his mind go 'all the way', lying amongst the coats
on some stranger's bed upstairs? Would she get pregnant
one day, have an abortion? Would she fall for some nonce
he'd hate? (He'd hate them all, of course.) Would she scream
at him to leave her alone? Had she already? How many
ways would she break his heart? He'd never know.

Of all the things he worried about did he worry about
this? That late one Tuesday afternoon in early November,
two police constables with poker faces would knock on the
door and say, 'Mr Jenkins? May we come in for a moment,
sir? I'm afraid we have some bad news.'

Who opened the door? Did his wife open it? Did he call
out from the kitchen – 'Who is it, dear?' Or was he working
late. Or maybe driving home through the blue gloom, through
the blur of rain, anticipating the evening. A hot meal, a
film on the telly, maybe sex with his wife.

Or maybe they'd already been pacing the floor, wondering
where she was, why she wasn't home. They might have
phoned Chloe's house – the friend she'd gone home with
after school – 'No, she isn't here. She left some time ago. To
catch the bus, she said.'

And then the knock on the door.

Mr Jenkins? May we come in?

A life can change in an instant. That's all it takes. I should know.

He would have gone to the mortuary later. Maybe the next day. Give them time to clean her up, make her look presentable. They knew who she was but you need the formal identification. What is *that* like? To see the sheet pulled back to reveal the face of your dead child.

I've accompanied parents to identifications a number of times. Mostly they're just numb, as if a shell has blasted in their face. You sit them down afterwards, have someone make a cup of sweet tea. What did *he* do? Mr Jenkins. Laura's dad.

The inquest found that Laura had died from a punctured lung, coupled with a haemorrhage in the brain when her head had hit the road. No one was to blame. An unavoidable accident, that's what the coroner said.

We walked out from the court into a sudden spell of sunshine, a low winter sun slanting in our eyes. There was a gust of wind and yellow leaves scuttled around our feet and I saw him standing several yards away down the road with his wife. They looked lost, the two of them. Like they had lost their way. For an instant the wife caught my eye. I was the first to look away.

2

Why did I join the force?

Because it made things easy. It made knowing what to do easy. You learn the rules and then you apply them. Wearing the uniform was part of it. Some people say it's dehumanizing, but I liked that part. I wore the uniform and I learnt the rules; it was easy.

But it has its drawbacks. People see the uniform and not the bloke that's wearing it. Some people hate it; it's like a red rag to the bull.

'Fucking pigs – you're all the same!' some bloke screamed in my face. I felt his spittle on my cheek. He was pissed. I had pulled him over for careless driving and now I had to breathalyse him. But he wasn't having it. He swung at me like a punch-drunk boxer, missing with every jab.

Fucking pigs – you're all the same!

It was the uniform he hated. It makes it easy and it makes it hard.

In the end I had to arrest him for attempting to assault an officer and for resisting arrest. He got three months inside for all that, in the end.

Are we all the same?

I guess we are. It works that way. They don't like you to think too hard, to question things. You learn the rules and you regurgitate them and you end up talking the same way. Even and flat, a bit of a monotone. You keep the muscles of your face under control and your emotions buttoned up under that thick uniform.

You arrest kids for fucking up their lives with drugs and old ladies for shoplifting and drunks for being disorderly. You cut down a suicide from a rope and watch forensics take DNA from the body of a child found half buried under leaves and you knock on some poor sod's door and tell them their son or their daughter is dead.

The uniform helps then. The uniform does the talking for you.

Since Laura, I don't know if I can do it anymore.

The mornings are the hardest. Sam's curled in the bed, away from me, sleeping. Her breath puffs slightly on each exhalation. It's funny how the bedroom can look unfamiliar in the dark, like it needs light to make it real. I stare into the dark, watch the grey light building at the window. I can hear the clock ticking on the dresser, Sam's puffing breath. My own heart beating.

I wanted them to throw the book at me. I wanted to do time.

There was no case, they said. I'd done nothing wrong.

They'd breathalysed me at the scene, a blood test later down the station. I was well under the limit. We had stopped for a pint on our way home. It was what we often do. Dave had two but I'd stopped at one. There was no evidence to say I was speeding. Dave made a statement.

I have no reason to believe PC Philips was exceeding the speed limit, he'd said. *PC Philips was driving with due care and attention. The child ran out suddenly from behind the bus. In my opinion it was not possible to avoid hitting her.*

They took witness statements from the scene. Someone sitting at the back of the bus had seen it all. The blurred blue shape of the girl in the royal-blue uniform running out in the rain. My grey BMW. A screech of brakes. The girl's body flying up then crashing down like a rag doll. The smack of her head on the tarmac. The woman coming out of the Spar on the corner had seen it, and someone at a cash till down the road. They had checked my car for faulty brakes, made sure its MOT was current, measured the skid marks on the road.

The post-mortem had said the injuries were in line with my statement and Dave's. There was no case, they said. I'd done nothing wrong.

But when I wake up in that room in the darkness I see her pale face, the way her lips moved, her eyes stirring under their lids, the blood that curled from her hair. I see her parents looking lost outside the coroner's court.

I hear their thoughts, their words in my head. Or maybe my thoughts, my words.

Laura is dead. You killed her. Laura is dead because of you.

'Maybe you should think about counselling?'

Sergeant Connor's voice testing me out, watching my reaction. He's good at that.

'You've been through a stressful time. It could be arranged, you know, with Occupational Health.'

His eyes on my face. They meet mine for a moment. I look away.

'I dunno . . .'

'You're not yourself. You know that. Maybe you need some more time off . . .'

I had three weeks' sick leave after the accident. Stress and anxiety, the doctor had said. And a slight whiplash injury.

The whiplash was nothing really. A feeling of stiffness around my neck and shoulders, some shooting pains up the back of my head. Gone after a week or so.

While I was off they were carrying out the investigations at work. The checks on the car, witness statements, the post-mortem report.

Connor himself had come to see me at home.

'It's going to be all right. There's no case to prosecute.'

He was on his way home. He was in uniform still. The girls had finished their tea and Sam had taken them up to the bathroom to get them out of the way. I could hear them shrieking up there, having fun in the bath. Connor took his hat off and put it on the table and I remember I was on edge about that. The girls had had spaghetti hoops for tea and I was worried he'd put his hat on some splodge of mess and when he put it back on again there'd be a stain of tomato sauce in his thinning grey hair.

'How you feeling in yourself, Jack?'

'Fine. I'm fine.'

I wasn't lying. The bad nights hadn't really started yet, the repetitive thoughts. The doctor had given me something for anxiety. Mostly I just felt numb, as if life was passing through me, not me through it. I could press a button and turn it off any time I wanted. I would watch Sam doing stuff with the girls – brushing their hair, pulling jumpers over their tousled heads, rubbing sticky jam from their hands and think:

That's funny. Why's she doing that?

It was like I was seeing things from a different angle. Like in those cognitive tests. An aerial close-up of the top of an umbrella, for instance. You don't recognize it at first, you have to look hard.

'Well, take your time. Don't come back until you're ready.'

'Occupational Health are signing me off. I'll be back next Monday.'

Connor's eyes, a quick flick of surprise.

He stood up. I thought how small he made our kitchen look. No dwarf was Connor. The traditional-looking cop. Six foot four. He picked up his hat from the table. Underneath it, the table was clean, thank God. No tomato sauce. Nothing.

The hardest thing was getting in the car again and driving. At first I thought I couldn't do it. My knees shaking, my hand juddering on the gear stick. But Dave beside me, calming me down. It's all right, Jack. You can do it. And I did. After the first hour or so, muscle memory taking over, making it easy. But I would slow down. Especially in a crowded street, especially when overtaking a bus, in the rain, or at the edge of dusk. Creep along at twenty in a thirty-mile zone. My lights on all the time, in the dull winter gloom, whenever it rained, even when they didn't need to be. But I wouldn't drive down the street, the one where it happened. I wouldn't drive down there. Or whenever speed was called for, when we had to put on the siren and the flashing lights. Only once or twice that happened, but Dave took over the driving then. Dave understood.

I pretended at first. Most of the job is mechanical. Form-filling, routine enquiries, answering calls for domestic violence, missing dogs. Dave and I driving around for hours on night duty. The streets look different at night, like the room. Hard glitter of street lights, wet glistening pavements, a straggle of youths always at the corner with their beer cans and cider bottles. The way their eyes flick at you, seeing the uniform. That mix of bravado and fear.

How old are you?

Where did you obtain the drink?

Do your parents know where you are?

What are you doing out at this time of night?

Escorting them home sometimes. Mostly just giving admonishments, moving them on. Nothing too heavy. Unless they're mouthy and aggressive, or up to no good. And these days there's girls, plenty of them. Sometimes they're worse. Lippy. In your face, but vulnerable with it. You can't touch them. You never put your hands on them.

Then later, sitting in the car outside some pub or club, waiting for closing, for the drunks to spill out on the streets, especially if it's a Friday or Saturday night. The brawls you have to prevent, or break up. Abuse in your face, vomit at your feet. Some chancer swinging one at you, but usually missing.

Fucking pigs – you're all the same!

But I managed it. For a while, I managed it. The wooden

14

face, the flat, measured voice. Pushing back the feelings, the thoughts, the pictures, buttoning it all up under the thick serge of the uniform. Thank God for the uniform.

Until that Thursday afternoon. Dave and I were told to go around some bloke's house and tell him and his wife that their son, aged sixteen, had been knocked off his Honda 50. His provisional licence only a month old. Some juggernaut had swung out at its rear taking a corner, knocked the kid clean off his bike. The back wheels had crunched over the kid's head, the crash helmet caved in and flattened like it hadn't been there at all. The driver had carried on, not noticing, not realizing that there was this mix of blood and gore and metal squashed on the road behind him that used to be some kid's head.

It was that time of day too, dusk coming down like a curtain, shapes blurring, the blue mist. About four in the afternoon, a couple of weeks before Christmas. The kid was on his way home from college.

I couldn't do it. I couldn't go to the house and tell them what had happened to their son. A young life snuffed out in an instant. Their lives, that poor fucking driver's life too when he finds out, changed forever. And Dave and I standing on the doorstep like bloody stuffed dummies, keeping it all in. The stiff expressionless faces, the monotone voice. *Excuse me, sir (or madam). May we step in for a moment . . .*

The fear in their eyes, the shock. The wife might start screaming hysterically, or faint. Usually it's the wife, if it happens. But more usually, nothing. Just the total numb, dumb shock of it. The dead glaze in their eyes. One of us will go into the kitchen, bring out hot sweet tea, and all the while that thick fug of pain building in the room, making it difficult to breathe.

'I can't go, Dave. I can't do it. You'll have to get someone else.'

My voice shot through with a flash of energy, a fierceness that I hadn't felt for weeks. Not since ... He knew I meant it. He didn't push it.

That's when Connor sent for me. The next day, in his office.

'Six weeks off initially, and then we'll look at it again. I'll write "stress" on the sick note. That OK?'

The doctor hands me the printed prescription for Prozac.

'That should make things easier. But it'll take two or three weeks to kick in. Don't expect instant results. And we'll start you on counselling as soon as possible.'

I drive home. It's late afternoon, only days to go to Christmas. The windows in the shops are crammed with tinsel and fairy lights, red and gold decorations. There's a tree in the market square. Donated by the people of Oslo, along with hundreds of other similar trees in similar market squares all over England. It's done up very tastefully – they all are these days. Gone are the gaudy baubles and mess of coloured lights. Just tiny pricks of white light, a multitude of tiny stars scattered through the dark universe of its branches.

Thank God for Sam. She's done it all this year. Bought the presents, wrapped them, sent out the cards. There's a turkey in the freezer, and she made a cake the other day. The real thing – loaded with rum and fruit.

'Is it worth it?' I said, tactlessly really. She'd flinched, looked hurt, and I'd tried to cover up.

'I only meant ... the girls – they're too young for rich cake, aren't they? And it's just the two of us this year.'

A quick flick of her eyes. Fear?

'But, Jack, my parents are coming. We talked about it, remember. My parents are coming for Christmas Day then in the evening we're going to Sarah's for drinks ...'

My turn then. Fear.

'I'm not sure I'm up to it, Sam. I can't be – you know – the life and soul of the party.'

Sam slid her hand over the work surface towards mine. It was powdery and white with icing sugar.

'Nobody expects that. Not the life and soul. Everyone understands.'

A pause. Then: 'Have you thought ... I mean ... perhaps you should consider counselling.'

Two days before Connor.

Perhaps you should consider counselling.

That's what everyone is into these days, it seems. Counselling, or being counselled. Bereavement counselling, relationship counselling, stress counselling, drink- and drug-dependency counselling. Counselling for every occasion. At every turn in the road, a counsellor's there hovering in the wings, ready to put you right. How did we all manage in the past? In the war, for instance? My great-uncle was in the Grenadiers. France. The Normandy landings. How did he manage, coming home, getting off the boat? No counsellor's arms to fall into then. Nobody asking how he felt about the shell blasts around his earholes, seeing mates dying. He'd got wounded. A splinter of shrapnel in his eye. Lived with a glass one for the rest of his life. He just got on with it, like they all did. Buttoned it all up under his uniform. Like I'm doing.

'I'll be OK,' I mumbled, retrieving my hand from under Sam's white, powdery one.

But that was before Connor. With Connor I had little choice.

They arranged it quickly; they're good like that, the force. Ready and waiting to help you stitch your life together again, help you live with the cracks. Let's face it, being a cop can be stressful. All the abuse, the pure hate. *Fucking pigs, you're all the same.* Then when there's an incident, there's PTS to fall back on. Everyone's on that bandwagon these days. Early retirement deals for those wanting out.

Not for me, though. No post-traumatic-stress deals for me. Killing Laura wasn't part of the job.

New Year. New shrink. First appointment, January 9th.

Had to get through Christmas first. We'd compromised in the end. Had Sam's parents over for Christmas dinner but left them to go on to Sarah's – Sam's younger sister's – on their own. The girls were put to bed early. They were whining and fractious by five o'clock, fighting and screaming at each other over some toy they both wanted, when all around them a sea of torn wrapping paper, a sea of presents, expensive, discarded. I got irritable, thinking 'spoiled brats' and maybe I raised my voice at them, shouted, just once. Enough though for Sam to shoot me one of her looks, to whip them up and carry them still screaming upstairs, run the bath, get them into pyjamas.

They came back down afterwards for a while, calm and sweet-smelling now, their faces flushed with the heat from the bath. Sam cuddled Jessica on her lap and watched some re-run of *Only Fools and Horses* on the telly whilst Bethan curled up to me on the sofa and I read 'Sleeping Beauty' to her from the new book her Granny had given her. Her eyelids drooped, she sucked her thumb, sleepy, a baby again at the age of six, falling asleep before the story was finished. I carried her upstairs, laid her down on her bed crowded with teddies. Something came over me then, looking down on her. She moaned slightly, and her eyes flickered open, half awake, half asleep, then closed again.

Memory falls like sudden shadows. I saw Laura again in Bethan's face. But this child, *my* child, will wake in the morning.

3

So that's how I came to be here. To see you.

I was expecting somebody different, I must admit. Female, middle-aged, slightly frowsy. A WI type, tweedy and safe. Or bohemian. Great dangly earrings and hair screwed up on her head, hand-knitted jumpers. You were neither of these. You were male for a start. Mid-fifties maybe, and ordinary. A solid, honest face. Quiet clothes – black trousers, Hush Puppy shoes. A pale blue shirt under a dark green V-necked jumper.

Nondescript. You could've been an ex-copper.

You usually met your 'clients' at the outpatients' clinic at the hospital, mental-health section. But I wasn't your regular mental case. I didn't want to see you there, too much stigma. So we arranged a meeting at your house. Surprisingly, it wasn't too far from where I lived. I could walk there at a push. And I did, that first time. Half an hour, it took.

There'd been a frost that morning. It meant clear skies, a hard, cold sunshine. Just the weather for banishing germs, clearing the Christmas cobwebs. The Prozac was starting to kick in now, and what with the sunshine and the exercise, those endorphins, I felt quite a lift. I took a shortcut through the park and felt myself noticing things, the shapes the trees make against the skyline, squirrels picking at nuts on the ground, a kid wobbling on a small bicycle in front of his mother. The bike, a Christmas present no doubt, shiny and new. The mother shouting out, 'Slow down, not too fast.'

I even caught myself humming a small tune under my breath, something the girls have been singing around the house for weeks, and wondered what I was doing here. Walking across the park on a lovely day like this, on my way to see a shrink, when I felt like this. As good as this. I should be at work. Filling out forms, reports on petty theft, anti-social behaviour, stolen cars.

You live in one of those large Victorian town houses. Well maintained. A bay window with wooden venetians. A solid wood, blue-glossed front door with a brass knocker.

You shake my hand.

'Good morning, Jack. You don't mind if I call you Jack, do you? I'm Tom Swift.'

A firm handshake. A hint of a Scots accent underneath a polished urban voice, no doubt from living a long time south of the border.

You show me into your consultation room at the back of the house. It's decorated in soft bland shades. Cream walls, a biscuit Berber-type carpet. There's a landscape picture on the wall, the real thing. The paint applied in thick rough strokes.

We talk the usual rubbish at first. Small talk. How good it is to get Christmas out of the way, the weather, my journey here. Drawing boundaries, keeping it safe.

And then you ask me why I'm here.

'Haven't you got it in your notes?' There's an edge to my voice.

Yes, you say. But you want to hear it from me. You want it in my words.

So I start to tell you about the early morning wakings, the feeling of lead in my stomach, the repetitive thoughts. I skirt over the flashbacks, hardly touching them. A smile sits on your mouth. You're waiting, I know that.

'Tell me more about the flashbacks,' you say.

Our second session. I'm getting used to this room. Its bland walls. The view of the branches of a tree outside the window. You sitting opposite me. You cross your legs, fold your hands across your chest. Not many men sit like that. And yet it doesn't make you less of one. You've placed a small clock on the table between us, angled it so we can both see its face. It's the time that makes it safe. Anything can happen in this room, but when the clock says the hour's up, it stops.

I don't want to talk about the accident. I tell you instead about waking in the darkness. The feeling that something is crouched in the room, watching. The smell that catches at the back of my throat, acrid and sharp.

'Like gas,' I say.

'Gas? Do you think you have a gas leak?'

'No, it's not like that. It's more like a memory. It comes and goes.'

You watch me, waiting. I think, *Shall I tell him, shall I say it now?*

'And there's something else,' I say. Carefully, testing the water. 'I've seen her.'

'Seen who?'

'Do you believe in ghosts, Mr Swift?'

It was about three on a Sunday. We'd had a late dinner that day, a proper Sunday dinner – roast lamb with mint sauce and all the trimmings. Sam's parents were here. They only live five miles away – they come over several times a week. I suppose I used to get jealous. I resented the amount of time they spent in our house. But since the girls have come along it doesn't bother me anymore. Gill was helping Sam with the washing up. I could hear their squealing laughter over some joke or other. Mick was dozing off in front of the telly, his head nodding down on his chest like that Churchill dog. Bethan was colouring with her new set of felts, stretched out on the carpet. Jess had fallen asleep on the sofa. Sam came in from the kitchen carrying coffee cups and saw her there, her face flushed, her mouth half open, trickling saliva onto the red velour.

'Take her up, Jack,' Sam said. 'She'll sleep better up there.'

I carried Jess upstairs. Her body was slack and heavy in my arms. She turned her face into my chest, nuzzling into the wool of my jumper. I worried she was going to wake but she didn't. I put her down on her small white bed. The room was cold. I covered her up with her duvet, drew her curtains and went out.

I went into our room. Sam's and mine. The light in the room was dim. It was a dull day, overcast, at the time barely

23

a week after Christmas. Already at half-past three dusk threatening to fall. I didn't put the light on. I was looking for my watch. I hadn't bothered to put it on that morning, but now I missed it. I found it on the dresser over by the window. I was fastening it on to my wrist. That's when I looked out of the window into the blue winter gloom and saw them.

'Who?' you ask.

'Laura and her dad. Standing together over the road, staring over at the house.'

'Laura?'

'The girl who died in the accident. She was standing there with her father. I recognized him from the coroner's court.'

You don't flinch, you don't bat an eyelid. I admire you for that. A whole wide space opens up between us in the room, a space wide enough for anything to fall into it. Anything at all. Even a dead girl's ghost.

'You're saying you saw Laura's ghost?' you ask, quietly. It isn't a judgement. Just this wide breathing space between us into which anything could fall.

'Yes,' I say.

She saw me. Not him, he didn't. But she'd looked up for a moment and saw my face at the window and a small smile had played over hers. She looked fine; she looked OK. No sign of bruising, no blood curling down from her hairline. Just a young girl in a blue school uniform looking up at me at the window. I was so relieved that she looked OK.

You could say, 'Fading light can play tricks on the eyes.'

But you don't, and that space between us softens and deepens and our words drift into it like feathers, like snow.

I believe you, you say.

The child held my gaze for a while, then looked over towards the man, her father. He didn't look back at her; he kept staring across the road towards the house. I ducked back behind the curtain but I couldn't look away. There was an emptiness in his face, something shuttered away, as if his soul had shrunk back into a recess far behind his eyes. It seemed to me that out of the two of them, she – the girl, Laura – was the most real, the colours of her skin, her hair, her clothes, vivid and bright. He was like an old photograph, faded, dull with age. But she was in Technicolor.

I don't know how long I stood there watching them. That other time had overtaken me, all my senses opening and flowering in the moment. It could have been forever. Or only seconds. But as I watched them the blue gloom settled like grief on his hair, his shoulders, his overcoat, his edges bleeding into the deepening dusk. Then suddenly she was gone. She disappeared in an instant, in a blink of an eye. Then he seemed to shiver, as if suddenly feeling the cold, and he turned and walked away.

'You were a long time.'

Sam and her mum had finished the washing up. They were sitting together on the sofa, feet up, watching the *EastEnders* omnibus. Mick twitching in his chair, slowly coming to, the *Sunday Express* spread out over his chest.

'What was wrong – did she wake?'
'Yes,' I lied. 'I read her a story. She went back to sleep.'
Sam staring at me, eyes wide with concern.
'My God, what's up, Jack?'

4

Write it all down, you say. Keep a journal and every day write down what you're thinking, feeling. Write about the repetitive thoughts, the flashbacks, the bad dreams. That's why I started writing this. When the words are out there, in black and white, they'll lose their power, you say.

So I write about Laura. I write about the accident. When I read it back, it's like it belongs to a film or a book. It's a story that I once played a part in. A major part. But if it's like a story I can turn the page, can't I? Maybe not now, but some day.

But it's funny, because writing about Laura makes me start to remember other things. Things that have nothing to do with her. Things that seem as if they've been waiting, hidden in shadows, and are now pushing their way through to the light. Small things, stupid things. The way some strange woman's coat swings as she walks down the street, the way some other woman's hair flicks away from her face as she turns her head. Sam painting her toenails. The careful way she pushes the brush around the quick of her nails. Why that? I don't know.

And the smell of gas. The hiss of the jets when Sam turns

27

on the hob the moment before it lights. I can't bear that. I have to walk away.

Once a week I walk across the park to see you, to keep our appointment. The words in my journal are growing and stretching. I sometimes read you bits and we talk about them, and how my week's been. How I've been sleeping, what I dream about, what I feel when I wake. Those hard wakings, staring into the suffocating dark.

'Tell me about your parents,' you say.

You're watching me, my reactions. The way a copper watches. Watch their eyes, the dilation in the pupils. Whether they blink or not.

You were bound to say it in the end. Your kind always do. It's part of the job. *Tell me about your parents. Tell me about your mother.* To your credit, it took you several sessions to get around to it. You held back as long as you could.

'Tell me about your mother, Jack.'

'She died.'

'How old were you at the time?'

Your eyes watching me, like a copper.

'Not sure. Seven or eight, I think.'

'How did she die, Jack?'

Gentle. Like someone talking to a child.

Like something pushing its way to the light. Something that's been there all the time.

'She killed herself,' I say.

*

It's amazing how easy it is, to deny reality, to pretend things didn't happen. It's like that little recycle bin on the computer screen. Click the mouse for delete. It's that easy. But it doesn't really go. It's just tucked away, out of sight.

Like that first time I saw Laura. I knew it happened, but I tried to tell myself that it hadn't. I went downstairs and sat in the empty chair. Sam and her mother watching me, sitting together on the sofa.

'What's up, Jack?'

'Nothing, I'm fine.'

Should I tell them? Should I say, I've seen a ghost. I've seen Laura watching the house. You know – *Laura*, the girl who died. What will they do? Laugh, think I'm joking. Make a mental note to tell my doctor about it later. Consider having me sectioned.

'Maybe you need a lie-down too, darling.'

'No, I'm fine.'

Sam's mother looked uncomfortable. She doesn't know how to handle me. Men of over six foot, policemen, men aged thirty-four with families to support, are not supposed to be off work, suffering from depression, going to see shrinks. It's not right. It shouldn't happen.

'And how are you feeling these days, Jack? Do you think you'll be going back to work soon?'

She was trying too hard to sound concerned. Mick was still pretending to be asleep, newspaper spread out over his chest. But his body tensed, waiting for my answer.

Sam twitching.

'Jack can't go back until he's ready, Mum.'

Gill still waiting for my answer, a tight smile on her face.

'When do you think that'll be? They won't pay you sick pay for ever, will they?'

Silence. A space waiting for my answer to fill it. They were waiting for me to say, Hey it's OK. I was only joking. Just pretending to get flashbacks, bad dreams, suicidal thoughts. A spot of malingering, really. Just wanted to kick over the traces, be a couch potato, idle, useless, a waste of space. For a moment their jaws would drop, and then their faces soften with relief. Anything preferable to this thing that comes out of nowhere. It might be catching.

'No, they won't,' I told her flatly.

Sam twitching again. She really wanted to agree with her mother, to say, 'Jack, pull yourself together. Get back to normal. Get back to work.' But she can't switch allegiance yet.

'So when *do* you think you'll be going back?'

The brittle smile still fixed on her mouth. Eyes still watching mine. Put them under pressure, make them sweat. We used to do that in the interviews. Good cop, bad cop. I was good at 'bad'. She's got balls, I thought. I'll give her that.

I looked at her. I met her eyes.

'I don't know, Gill. I wish I did. But I don't. I don't even know if I'll ever go back.'

There. I've said it now. Mick jerked awake. They stared at me, speechless.

'You're right, Sam. I *am* tired. I think I'll go and have that lie-down after all.'

As I went out and closed the door it was like I was closing

it on an open wound. They're all part of it. They're breathing it in and breathing it out.

'Tell me about your mother,' you say.

'I hardly remember her. Although stuff's been coming back. I'm not sure they're memories. Maybe I'm imagining . . .'

'What's been coming back, Jack?'

She was beautiful. At least it seemed to me that as a kid I always thought she was. I can't remember her face clearly. I've seen photos of her, of course. But they were usually slightly blurred, as if I wasn't supposed to remember.

Instead of her whole face I remember bits of it. Her mouth smiling. Her eyes like green pools I could swim in. Her hair was dark and shoulder length. It would fall before her face and she'd flick it backwards as she moved her head. Or sweep it upwards with her palm on her forehead. She was beautiful, but sad.

I remember the sadness. Her face turned from me, staring out of the window. The way her shoulders hunched and fell again as she sighed. She sighed as if she had the whole world weighed down within her, and was trying to release it, each sigh letting out a little bit of the world at a time. Her sadness filled me with dread. I followed her around the house like a shadow, as if I knew I shouldn't let her out of my sight.

But of course I did. Sometimes I had to.

'Where were you when she died?' you ask.

'At school,' I say. 'I walked home from school without her

that day. Sometimes she'd come and meet me, but sometimes she didn't. She worked some days. It didn't bother me. I was used to it.'

'Tell me about it, Jack. Tell me what happened that day.'

It's spring time. Late April, or maybe early May. I know that because there are small trees planted at regular intervals down the road and they're covered in pink blossom. Scurries of it drift around our feet. Like pink snow. Or candyfloss. The sun's warm on my face. I'm wearing my school blazer. It's green. I've taken off my cap and shoved it into my blazer pocket. I'm walking with Stevie Burroughs and we're arguing about some rubbish. Who supports which team. I'm West Ham and Stevie says they're crap. I shove him and he shoves me back. But it doesn't mean anything. It's what boys do.

We reach the road that leads to my estate.

'See ya,' Stevie calls, and crosses the road to his house. I turn right, then left. Then right again? Our house is red brick with a blue-painted front door. My mother painted it herself, stretching up in blue jeans and a T-shirt, then dipping down to load her brush. The sun glinting in her hair, red lights sparking in its dark mass.

I walk around to the back door. I have a key on a string around my neck. When my mum works I get home first, that's why I've got it. I put the key in to unlock the door but instead I lock it. It wasn't locked to begin with, you see. I remember standing stock-still for a moment, the key paused in the lock. I'm afraid to unlock it again and go in. That's when I know something is wrong.

*

'What did you know, Jack?'

Your voice is quiet and far away. But I'm not here with you. Not here in this room, looking at the muted colours of the oil painting on the wall, the fern dipping fine leaves towards the windowsill, the small pine bookcase, its neat rows of books. I'm back there in that house. I'm a schoolboy in a green blazer, a peaked cap jutting from its pocket. I like sausage and chips and rice pudding. I like art but hate music. I'm good at PE but useless at maths. My heart is pounding.

The lock clicks and the door's unlocked again. I open it slowly. The smell of gas hits me, like acid scorching on the back of my throat. I leave the door swinging open and rush to the window and open that too. That's what my mum taught me. If you smell gas then open the windows. Then turn off the gas.

She's lying on the floor, her head propped up on the bottom shelf of the open oven. I can hear the hiss of gas, like snakes. I turn off all the knobs on the cooker. There's a sudden silence. I know what it means. That's when that other time kicks in, the slowed down, non-linear time. My limbs feel papery, weightless, my body as fragile as glass. I've stepped outside myself; I'm watching it all from somewhere up near the ceiling. I see this woman lying awkwardly on the kitchen floor. She's wearing blue jeans and has bare feet. Her dark green blouse is rucked up, showing the pale tan of her stomach. One leg is angled oddly backwards, under the weight of her body. Her head is sliding slowly from its support on the shelf of the oven, sliding slowly onto the lap of the boy who kneels beside her on the floor. He's stroking her dark hair away from her face and crying.

'Mum, wake up. *Please* wake up.'

Bubble of saliva. Eyes stirring slightly. Faint moan.

The sound of the boy crying. Underneath this sound, a sudden hush. Like the sudden hush when the gas stopped hissing. A cold rush of air passing the boy as he kneels. She's gone.

'What are you feeling, Jack?'

I'm slowly coming to. I can hear the traffic outside. Beyond the window the sky is grey and overcast. The clock on the table is ticking. Ten minutes till the end of the session.

I feel very young and very sad. But there's a lightness spreading inside me, spreading from my belly up into my chest.

5

For days afterwards I feel as weak as a kitten. Like something is seeping out through my pores. Draining me but at the same time leaving room inside for something else to fill up from within. I watch Sam doing stuff – the smooth curve of her back at the sink. The way she stoops to pick up Jessica. I want to touch her, to come up behind her and enclose her in my arms, to bury my mouth into her neck, to tell her I love her. But I don't. I don't know why.

Sometimes I catch her looking at me. Concern sitting on her lips. Or judgement. *What's up, Jack?* crouched behind her breath. I pretend not to notice, so the words won't be said. Jessica sits on my lap at bedtime, warm and sweet from her bath. I read her a story and she strokes my face thoughtfully with her small light hand, and I feel it in her eyes, in the frail touch of her hand on my face.

What's up, Daddy? What's up?

Dave calls by the house. He's in uniform, still on duty. I'm in the living room watching *Balamory* with Jessica slack and still on my lap, all her senses breathing it in. I hear the front doorbell chime and Sam goes to answer it. A man's deep voice and Sam laughing.

'Come in, Dave. Jack's at home.'

Where else would I be?

I slide Jessica off my lap and leave her propped against the arm of the sofa. She hardly notices.

Sam's filling the kettle.

'Wotcher.'

'How's it going? Good to see you, mate.'

Dave gets up from the chair at the kitchen table. Our bodies clash together. He claps my back. Dave feels solid and real in his uniform. Like he belongs to the world. The outside world that's moving onwards. Not backwards like mine is.

For a few moments we talk shop. What's Connor up to these days? What's new? Dave moans about the mounting paperwork.

'I didn't join the force to push bits of bloody paper around. The job's not the same anymore.'

No, nothing's the same anymore. We both know that. We need a button that we can pause and hold. Like the control on the remote for the DVD. Which bit of time will I pause or still; which bit will I rerun?

Sam pours out coffee, puts the mugs on the table in front of us.

'I'll leave you two alone,' she says.

She catches Dave's smile on her way out. He spoons sugar into his cup, stirs it slowly, looks at me.

'Sam phoned me at home the other night.'

'Yeah? I didn't know that.'

'She's worried about you, man. She's worried you might

not come back to the force. Something you said the other day . . .'

'I said I *might* not go back. I didn't say for definite.'

'Jack, it's not for me to tell you how to run your life, but you've got responsibilities. A wife and kids. What you gonna live on, man?'

'I know that, but I can't help what I feel. Things have changed.'

'This isn't all because of the accident, is it? Because you know it wasn't your fault. The kid ran right out in front of you. I should know, I was there. It wasn't your fault.'

'I know that,' I say quietly.

'How's the counselling going?'

'Fine.'

'You sure about that? Only Sam thinks it's making you worse.'

Something snaps. I push my coffee cup away. Stand up.

'I don't know, Dave. Maybe you'd better just ask Sam how I'm doing in future, mate. She seems to know better than anyone else.'

I leave the kitchen and go upstairs. I lie on the bed and shut my eyes. I hear them talking together in low voices but I can't hear what they say. Ten minutes or so later, the front door opens and closes. Then Dave's car drives away.

Anger can be all sorts of colours. Mine is grey, a pale grey like a bleached winter sky. I lie next to Sam in bed that night. Neither of us speaks. My pores are sealing shut, the space within me closing again, squeezing tight.

*

'What were you jealous about?' you ask.

· 'I wasn't.'

'Are you sure?'

'No one likes being told how to run their life. No one's *me*. No one feels what I feel except myself.'

'It's painful having feelings, isn't it,' you say. 'Makes life complicated. Better to keep it all buttoned up and hidden away.'

Buttoned up and hidden under the uniform.

Only I don't wear the uniform anymore, do I?

Dave and I have been best mates since we were police cadets together at Hendon. Twelve years ago now, or more. We were young, still wet behind the ears really. Dave had ideals. I remember some training session. Maybe on the first day, or soon after, we were asked a question by the trainer, a sergeant in his fifties – an easy ride for him really, see him out until his retirement, training up us young cadets. But he was good at his job, took it seriously.

'So why do you want to join the force?' he'd asked, and made us go round one at a time and share our answers. He never judged us, he never said, 'That's a daft reason,' or anything like that. He listened and nodded and took it seriously. Except when it was meant as a joke. Like when one girl – flat-chested and mousy – said she's joining because she fancies men in uniform. She'd laughed at herself and we'd all laughed with her, including Sergeant Greenway, because it was meant to be a joke. Only she wasn't joking.

It was like he didn't mind what reasons we gave. Nothing

was right or wrong. But he wanted us to know what they were, to know what we were expecting. A reality check.

I hadn't spoken to Dave before that session. Had hardly known he was there. When his turn came he said he wanted to be a policeman so he could make a difference. He said his dad was a policeman, a good one, and in his eyes his dad was a hero and he wanted to be one too.

He was sitting at the back of the room and we all started turning our heads to catch a look at him. He had a pale, narrow face, acne still red on his cheeks, steady, brown eyes, dark hair floppy over his forehead. I was impressed by what he said. We all were. By his honesty, going out on a limb like that. We could have sniggered at him, but no one did. Mr Greenway made confirming noises in his throat before moving on.

When it came to my turn I said I wanted to be a policeman because it was important that society had rules and they were enforced. And I liked the idea of the uniform.

'Why?' he'd said.

That surprised me – I hadn't expected confrontation, he hadn't confronted anyone else. I felt myself blush and stuttered something like, 'It looks good, it makes you look important,' and then thought what an idiot, what a plonker I sounded. But Greenway just nodded, said, 'I see,' and moved on.

It was illuminating, that session.

I hadn't always wanted to be a policeman. When I was younger, in my teens, I'd been into photography. Did it at 'A' level, then went to Harrow College to do an HND in photography and media studies. In the final year we had a series of visits from working photographers to give us career advice, that sort of thing, and each one of them had said it wasn't an easy option. You had to struggle, compromise, live on tinned beans for years, before you made it in the industry and could do something creative and fulfilling. Many wouldn't. Many would end up in the High Street doing weddings and portraits of fat babies or dogs. We can't all be David Baileys. You need the breaks, the determination to never say die.

But I couldn't do that. I couldn't get off the starting block. I said 'die' right at the beginning. Even before the exams I was sending away for other career choices. Join the navy, the police force, become a firefighter. All uniform stuff. I'd never really thought about *why*. Why this thing about uniform, until that session at Hendon.

'Maybe you need to feel you belong,' you say.

When I first met Sam it was Dave who fancied her most. She was sharing a flat back then with two other girls. They'd been burgled. Usual stuff missing – the telly, the video, the CD player. Whatever cash they could lay their hands on. Sam had come home from work early and found the flat turned over, the stuff gone, and had called the police. We'd taken the call.

She was very relieved to see us. She made us coffee and I sat down opposite her in the dishevelled living room and took an inventory of the missing items. She turned her knees sideways to me. She was wearing sheer stockings and a little red skirt that rode up her thighs. She had a pale blue top on that showed off her tits. Nice tits, I thought. Dave was poking around. He came back, stretched tall in front of her, puffed out his chest.

'Bathroom window swinging open, miss. Did you open it?'

'I don't think so. But I must admit, we don't always check it's closed, I suppose.'

'Must close all your windows, miss, before vacating the premises. Lock them if you can. Particularly in a bathroom like that, ground floor, back of the property.'

'We will in future, officer. It was silly . . .'

'Key normally left in the kitchen door, miss?'

'Sometimes – it's the spare key. But the door's always locked when we're out. I checked it myself this morning . . .'

'And when you came home, miss?'

'Well no. Not then. It was swinging open. Gave me such a shock.'

'One of them climbed in the bathroom window, the smallest one. Let in the other one – they often work in pairs – through the kitchen door. They carried the stuff out through the kitchen, bold as brass. Probably selling it as we speak. Normally, it's drug addicts behind small burglaries like this. They need the cash to fund their habit.'

'Oh dear,' she said. Two spots of crimson had sprung in her cheeks. She looked a bit shocked for a while, then she looked straight at me, flashed me a smile.

'We have been a bit silly, haven't we? Do you think you'll find them at all, officer?'

*

Back in the car, driving away.

'What a sweetheart! What a gorgeous girl!' Dave said.

'Yeah, she's a looker, all right.'

'You lucky bugger!'

'Waddya mean?'

'She fancied the pants off you! Didn't you notice?'

'Don't be daft,' I'd said.

She was lucky. It rarely ever happens. These low-lifes were pulled over in their van for speeding a couple of days later. They had no tax or insurance and there was this stuff in the back of the van. A telly and a video. The other stuff had gone. It matched her description and we called around to tell her she could come by the station and identify it. It was a Saturday morning and she was at home. She answered the door with a towel wrapped around her head. There was another girl with her in the flat. A skinny girl with fair hair. But Sam outshone her miles. She'd looked really pleased – the telly was a present from her parents, almost new.

'What'll happen to them, do you think?' she said.

'If we can stick the burglary on them, maybe a couple of months. Depends if it's a first offence or not, miss,' Dave said. She looked relieved that it wasn't going to be longer. A soft touch, I remember thinking.

'By the way, we're having a party here next Saturday. If you're off duty, you're both welcome to come.'

'She means you,' Dave said to me in the car, driving away. 'She wants you to come.'

'She invited us both,' I told him.

'Well, then, lucky for her I can't make it. Parents' twenty-fifth wedding anniversary. I can't miss it. You going, then? To her party, I mean?'

'Might do. Nothing much else to do.'

'Lucky bugger,' Dave said. 'Lucky bloody bugger.'

He was right, I guess. It was me she was interested in. She let me know it soon enough. She was dressed to kill when I arrived. The little black dress, pearl choker thing around her neck, high-heeled shoes that made her legs go on for ever. I knew nobody there, of course. The girls were mainly secretaries, office workers – that sort of thing. The blokes accountants, junior bank managers, executive types. A couple of Hooray Henrys. No policemen. But I didn't feel out of place. She attached herself to me like a limpet from the start. By the end of the evening, after a few beers and whisky chasers and having decided to catch a taxi home that night and leave the car, we were snogging in a corner. She pressed her tits right up close to me and I knew she was gagging for it. But either way, it was all right because I knew she was special. I knew I was prepared to do the long haul. She was sweet and warm and funny and had a way of moving her head and swinging back her dark hair that made my heart flip. That reminded me of something.

I was the last to leave that night. Dawn had already broken, one of those winter dawns that make you catch your breath. I'd sobered up by then and it seemed silly to leave the car and get a taxi home but I did anyway. I couldn't take the risk, being a policeman, and anyway it gave me an excuse to go back the next day and see her again.

The next day I slept till past twelve o'clock. When I got

up I had a shave and cleaned my teeth and put on a black sweater and jeans and phoned her and asked if she'd like to go for a walk that afternoon, if she had time, and she'd said, yes she would, of course she would, she'd be delighted. We drove out to Cassiobury Park and walked around holding hands like two love-struck teenagers. People were out with their dogs and pushing little kids along on trikes and the air was clean and fresh and frosty in our lungs, a proper January day, and it was like the world was brand new and it belonged to us.

When we got back to her flat it was empty. Her flatmates were out. She wasn't expecting them back for hours, and I gave it to her right there on her sofa. And although it wasn't the most comfortable of places to be doing it and I got a cramp in my leg, it was lovely, she was loving it. And afterwards I wanted to carry on lying there inside her for ages, shrinking inside her, instead of feeling I had to pull out quick and button up like you usually do with a stranger. But I couldn't because of the condom, because of worrying about it coming off. So I got off her and went to the loo to flush it away and when I came back she had tidied herself up and was just sitting there, perched on the edge of the sofa, smiling. She seemed to glow, as if she had a light on inside her. Happy like a kid at Christmas. That's how it started.

I couldn't keep my hands off her after that. And for a while things between Dave and me went a bit sour. I couldn't talk to him about her and he couldn't ask, because we both of us knew that he wished it was him fucking her instead of me. But eventually it passed. He knew it was serious and that was that.

Dave got himself a girlfriend soon after. Nicola, Nicky, something like that. She was a nice enough girl but it didn't last. They weren't suited. She was a bit of a party girl, and Dave's not like that. Dave's happy sitting at home most evenings reading a book, watching the rugby on the telly. But for a while we'd go out as a foursome. It was all right, it was fun, but sometimes I'd catch him looking wistfully at her, at Sam, even with Nicola by his side. Sam would be talking, or more likely, listening to Nicola talking, and he'd be sitting there, his whole face like a sigh. Then he'd snap himself out of it, crack a joke. He'd think I hadn't noticed but I did. I always did.

'Tell me, Jack,' you say one day. 'Why did you never tell Sam about your mother?'

Outside your window, a mid-February day. The first glimmerings of spring. The sky a white glaze of light. In the tree outside the window, its branches almost brushing the pane, a bird was singing its heart out. A thrush, something like that.

'I didn't know myself really. Not the details, not how it happened. I told her what I'd been told, that my mother died suddenly, a heart attack or something, and I was sent away to my aunt and uncle in Plymouth. I suppose I knew deep down that wasn't really true but it was easier to believe it was. It was never really talked about.'

'A conspiracy of silence,' you say. 'Isn't it time you broke it, Jack?'

6

I still remember little of what happened after my mother died. Directly after, that is. Somebody must have phoned the ambulance I suppose, or the police. Maybe it was me. Maybe I was more self-possessed, even then, at the age of seven or eight, than I give myself credit for. More likely it was someone else though. I seem to remember a neighbour, an old man who lived next door. Even now I can see, or *sense*, his shuffling down our garden path, with a bag full of apples from the trees in his garden, or returning the balls I sent over the garden fence. I can't remember his name, but I can feel it inside me, feel the shape of it, tugging at the shades of my memory. I think it began with a 'B'.

Anyway, maybe I'd gone flying around there that day, that afternoon, sobbing and incoherent and the old man, Mister *B*, had gone around to our house to see what had frightened me and found her and phoned the police, the ambulance. I don't know. But when I came to myself again, when I can remember things clearly again, I was safely ensconced down my aunt and uncle's house in Plymouth. I had my own room, a small room with sloping eaves that overlooked their back garden. The plaster on the ceiling had slightly damp patches in the corners and the wallpaper had yellow stripes. I was happy there in that room. I would sit for hours at a desk in the corner building Airfix models of planes, sometimes taking them downstairs, the array of thin grey plastic pieces and small tubes of glue, and working on them with my uncle at the kitchen table.

Aunt Susan was my mother's sister. Her only sister. Uncle Keith was in the merchant navy. He'd be away at sea for weeks on end and then it was just my aunt and myself, shut up together in that little house, safe from the storms that blustered outside. Maybe I pretended that I was with my mother again, just the two of us against the world. I don't know. They were kind to me. They didn't have children of their own. So there was no one else to rub up against, to get in the way. It worked, anyway; I was happy. I went to the local school and got teased a bit for the way I talked until I learnt to talk the same way, to fit in. I did well at school, not too well, not so I was a swot or anything, but well enough. I was good at sport, and I always had friends. But when I look back now, it was like a dream, I was living a dream, and when I got older, into my mid-teens, something began to break a bit, the storms began to break into the house. I was a handful for a while. Drank too much, smoked some puff, ran about with the wrong crowd. Nothing too heavy, nothing that got me a record, or anything like that. But I was a bit of a wanker, I caused them some grief from time to time. I wrote off my uncle's car once and swung at him when he told me off. They didn't deserve that. And then when I passed my 'A' levels and had to choose where to go and study I chose London. Like I wanted to go as far away as possible. They didn't try and talk me out of it. They seemed relieved in a way. Like they had done their duty, and now it was time to let me go.

I went back to see them, of course. Holiday times, Christmas. That sort of thing. But then I got caught up in the life of being a student. Parties, drinking, girls. I got into a new crowd, left the old crowd in Plymouth behind to continue merrily on their way in lives that were going nowhere. My aunt and uncle moved into a little bungalow – one of those purpose-built retirement-home things and there was scarcely room for them and their cat, let alone me. The visits tailed off. Now it's just the cards on birthdays and at Christmas, a couple of phone calls a year. When Bethan was born we took her down to visit – had to sleep in sleeping bags on the floor as they had no room. When Jessica came along we just sent them photographs. I think they'd like to see us more often but it's difficult. Plymouth's a long way away. They've got no money – just scrape by on a pension now and my uncle's got health problems. He has these pills he has to take every day. Diabetes, something wrong with his ticker. I think they prefer to stay at home now, close to what they know.

I am sitting in your consulting room. I am staring at the weave in the biscuit-coloured carpet. You have brought in some snowdrops from the garden, first of the year. Placed them in a small pale vase, as clear and perfect in shape as a teardrop. It sits before me on a low table. Next to it, the alarm clock, so you can check when my time is up. It ticks on the minutes. But for me time has stood still again. I can hear someone calling out from their garden across the road, the distant buzz of traffic. My legs are heavy and inert; I don't think I could move them even if I tried, and around my heart a thousand whispers from the past press in, crowd me like ghosts.

'What's happening for you right now?' you say.

I don't answer you. But my sadness breathes out into the room.

What's up, Jack?

'Do you think maybe you need to go and visit them again? Maybe there's unfinished business there,' you say, softly.

You could be talking to a child. And I feel I am one. I am all ages rolled into one. I'm newborn. I'm just learning to walk. I'm the age I was when my mother died. I'm an angry mixed-up teenager, a selfish young man. I'm almost halfway through my life and I'm lost. I'm even an old man waiting to die, swallowing pills every day and listening to the ticking of his heart.

I saw her again. Laura. It was several days after that session. Sam was out shopping. Jessica was sleeping as only small children can sleep, with the long shadows of a late February afternoon stroking her face in her small bed upstairs. I went up to check on her. Her knees were scrunched up, her bare feet poking out from the bottom of the blanket. I covered them up.

I went downstairs. Brought my coffee in from the kitchen and carried on with the ironing. One of Bethan's school pinafores. I took my time, pressed the iron slowly around the seams, around the edges. I like ironing; it stops me thinking. But then I felt it. This desire tugging on me like a rope. This desire to glance up from the ironing, to glance out of the window, across the street. I tried to resist it. But it kept tugging on my senses. So I looked up, and I saw them again.

Who did you see?

Laura and her father. Like the last time. Standing across the road, staring towards the house, staring into the bay window towards me. But it was different; *she* was different this time. She wasn't wearing her school uniform. She was wearing jeans, and a pink quilted anorak, a fur-trimmed hood up over her hair. She looked smaller, younger, like she was more like a little girl than a child on the edge of her teens. And he looked different too. He looked – not lost – but more like someone who'd been through a storm, was in a storm, his face loosened by it all. I was different too. I slammed the iron back down onto its metal plate and I ran for the door. I was angry, really angry this time. I thought, What right has he got to stand there outside my house, staring, intimidating me like that. What right! I wasn't angry with her, only with him. So I belted through the front door but he saw me coming and turned and started to run for it and as I ran towards him across the road the child – Laura – she melted away like snow. I caught up with him. I grabbed him by the coat and swung him round and he came at me, his fists flailing, and caught me a blow above the eye, a good un. I saw his face. It shocked me. I'd never seen so much loathing directed at me before. Not even from the thugs who hate the uniform.

'You fucking bastard. You killed my little girl,' I heard him say. But the present was reeling away from me. I crouched over, holding my head, and he turned and walked away and I let him.

A swelling came up just above my right eyebrow. Sam didn't notice straight away. I didn't make a song and dance about it. Later in the kitchen clearing up after dinner. The girls were already in bed. They go early on weekdays.

'What's happened to you?' Sam says.

My fingers go up automatically, feel the lump above my eye. It's hot and painful.

'This, you mean? It's nothing.'

'How did you do it? Looks painful to me. It'll be even worse when the bruise comes out.'

'Bumped into a door.'

She looks puzzled, curious, like she doesn't believe me.

'You bumped into a door. How did you manage that?'

'Didn't look where I was going, I suppose.'

That's what battered women say, I think. I should know, I've heard it often enough. Domestic calls, we call them, although there's nothing cosy and domestic about them at all. It's always a door, as if people go around forever bumping into doors, as if people go around blindfolded. Who's ever *really* bumped into a door? And yet they go on saying it, the same trite response and no one believes them. It just came out automatically, the best I could do at the time. Sam doesn't believe me, I can see it in her eyes. But she couldn't say so. Same way I couldn't say to all those sad cases who stand there looking at the floor, trying to hide their bruises, the black eyes, the broken noses, the grazed scalp seeping red through their hairline, the old man bristling behind them, *Don't be daft, I don't believe you.*

'You'd better put a cold compress on it,' Sam says.

Why didn't I tell her the truth? I didn't want to worry her. But later, watching the telly, drinking hot chocolate together before turning the set off and going to bed, 'Do you believe in ghosts, Sam?'

She looks at me, startled. Her mind's ticking over, trying to make sense of this.

'Why on earth are you asking . . . ?'

'No reason. I just wondered.'

Sometimes I wonder if we're not all ghosts. Ghosts of who we could have been. The 'what ifs' again. What if my mother hadn't died, what if my father hadn't left, what if I'd never been born.

'Tell me about your father, Jack.'

I've been waiting for that. I'll hand it to you. You bide your time, you don't believe in rushing things. You've got a nose for timing. That's what makes a good copper. Don't put them under too much pressure in the interview room. All those mealy faced kids arrested for breaking and entry, for drugs, for joy-riding. Soften them up. Lull them into a false sense of security. Then go for the kill.

Tell me about your father, Jack.

You're wearing a blue jumper. Underneath, a cream shirt and light grey tie. Your black trousers have a neat crease running smoothly down the front. Who presses your trousers? Do you do it yourself? I'm staring as usual at the weave in your biscuit-coloured carpet. You've replaced the snowdrops with some crocuses. Deep yellow colour. They're early this year. The weather is mild for the first days of March. There's an edge rising up inside me like a wire.

'I didn't know him,' I tell you.

I didn't. Not the real him. I was four when my parents split. He just walked out one day and never came back. I can't use it – the word 'abandoned'. There's something shocking about it. It's like a secret, something to be ashamed of. It's a blunt blade to the heart. Not a quick death. You die slowly of abandonment but you die.

That's what happened to her. From the day he left. She withered, she caved in. Like her spirit had been sucked out of her, had followed him out the door and down the path. Was some place far away, lost to her now. She was on these pills for depression. Would take them every day, and another pill to make her sleep at night. When she did it, killed herself, it wasn't the gas that did it for her. It can knock you out, make you sick, but it won't kill you. It was the pills. She must have been saving them up. I remembered something else the other day. I remember afterwards, letting her head slide from my lap and running into the bathroom to be sick and seeing all these empty pill boxes scattered in the sink.

I blame him. I always have. Maybe that's why I had a swing at my uncle Keith that day. Because he was standing in for my father, he was trying to be my father, and in the end I couldn't let him. I had to push him away. I'd taken his car without asking. He'd been at the bingo with my aunt and I'd taken his car keys from the hook inside the pantry and gone out joy-riding. Some loser I used to know in Plymouth

53

had challenged me to a race and there we were racing down the road and I overshot a bend and ploughed into some lady's garden and rammed the car up against the wall of her house. I was lucky to crawl out of that one. Later, when they had got over the shock, my uncle had a go at me for taking the car without consent, for driving like an idiot. I swore at him and swung at him. I caught him on the jaw and he ducked the next blow and stepped behind me and locked my arms. He was a strong man, my uncle, a navy bloke. But he never hit me. Not once.

I remember yelling and cursing at him.

'Fucking get off me. Let me go. You're not my father. *You're not my fucking father.*'

But he just held me, held on to me, as if we were drowning together. I could hear him sobbing. Or was it me? Then eventually something went quiet and still inside me and he let me go. I walked out of the room. But it was never the same after that.

A branch of the tree outside your window nudges against the glass in the breeze. A bird is back, singing its heart out. That thrush again? I imagine the buds forming on the tree, the thin lip of green like the lid of an eye. It's almost spring. All the signs are there.

'Have you ever thought of trying to find him, Jack? Have you ever thought of finding your father?'

7

I sit in the study at home writing it down. I write in the evening when the girls are in bed. I write in the early hours of the morning when I can't sleep. I have filled lots of pages now. My handwriting scrawls across their white space like stitches in a wound. I'm stitching myself up. I'm stitching my wounds up. I'm not doing it for you anymore. I did in the beginning. I wanted to please you, to do the right thing, to have something to talk about in those long sessions where time hangs like a rock in that room. I'm not bothered about filling the time anymore. I'm not bothered if silence steps into the room. Silence holds a lot. Silence holds more than words.

'What are you doing all that writing for?' Sam asks me. She comes into the study to print out something from the computer. I'm sitting on an easy chair in the corner, my eyes screwed into my writing.

'It's part of my therapy,' I tell her.

She can't argue with that, she can't answer that. She leaves me alone.

When she goes out I take my journal and lock it up in a metal briefcase. I enable the combination lock. I'm getting to know myself through the writing. I don't want anyone else to know me that well. Not even Sam. Maybe not even you.

I have to go to the doctor again. I need another sick note.

'Counselling sessions going OK?' he asks.

'I think so,' I tell him.

'What about the disturbed sleep, the flashbacks? Still getting those?'

'Yes,' I say.

I wonder if I should tell him, I'm seeing ghosts now too, I'm being stalked by the father of the girl I killed. In my counselling sessions I talk about my mother who committed suicide and how much I hate my father, and not about the girl who started all this off. The girl in a blue school uniform, who ran out in a November gloom as I drove home from work one Tuesday evening. I decide not to.

He scribbles me another sick note. The third so far.

'These things take time. Keep attending your counselling sessions. Come and see me in another six weeks.'

Connor phones me at home.

'How are things, Jack?'

'Fine. They're fine.'

'I understand you've been signed off for another six weeks.'

'Yes.'

'The counselling sessions – do you think they're helping?'

'I think so.'

'So you think you'll be ready to come back to work in six weeks?'

'I don't know. Maybe,' I tell him.

There is a thinness in his voice, a barely concealed contempt. I know that behind his politeness, his attempt at concern, he really wants to say, Look, what's this all about, Jack? You're bringing the police force into disrepute. Making out they're just a mealy-mouthed bunch of sissies, who drop at the first sign of stress, take months off sick for nothing, go and see shrinks. I know that's really what he wants to say, but he can't. It wouldn't be politically correct, would it? Not in this day and age. But Connor's not this day and age. He's from the days of stiff upper lips, when men just got on with it. Men like my great-uncle who came back from the war, back to his work in the docks, having seen mates with their limbs blown off dying in front of his eyes. He wouldn't have had days off work and gone to see shrinks. Neither would Connor.

That night, getting into bed, switching out the bedside light. Sam lying next to me. I can see the outline of her profile, the dark mass of her hair on the pillow. A question forms on her lips, hovers in darkness over our heads. I can feel the weight of it.

'Jack, do you think you'll ever go back to work?'

There. She's said it now. She's waited a long time to say it, but now it's done. The weight over our heads shifts in the darkness, breaks up, scatters down over our faces like feathers.

'Because I don't think you will. I think you'll never go back to work. I think you're done with it. With being a policeman.'

'I don't know, Sam. I don't know.'

'What's going to happen to us? What's going to happen to us and the girls? How are we going to live, Jack?'

I tell you about this at our next session. You're the only one who doesn't make me feel guilty. Who doesn't make me feel that this thing I'm going through is unnecessary, that I'm a malingerer, a phoney.

'Change is scary. It's terrifying to many people. But sometimes necessary,' you say.

A few days later I have a dream. I dream that I'm potholing. Christ knows why – I've never been potholing in my life. I'm trying to climb back up to the ground. I'm stuck in a tunnel, in the bowels of the earth. Damp sinewy walls engulf me. I can't get my breath. Behind me hands clutch at my legs trying to pull me back down, voices plead with me to come back, to stay, it's easier this way. One of them is Sam's.

My aunt's voice on the phone is faint with surprise.

'You're coming to see us, Jack? With Sam and the girls?'

'No, just me on my own.'

'What about your work?'

'I've got some time off.'

'Oh, I see.'

She doesn't see at all, but she doesn't know what to say. I picture her standing there in her little hallway beyond the front door, her face collapsed and pale, trying to make sense of it. Why I should want to come and see them on my own, when I haven't been for years.

'If it's too much trouble, if it'll be easier, I could book into somewhere, a guest house near by.'

'No, that'll be OK, Jack. You'll have to use the sofa bed in the living room, but if you don't mind that . . .'

'No, that'll be fine. I thought I'd drive down on Monday, stay until the weekend. Will that be OK?'

'Well, I'll have to ask your uncle. He hasn't been too well, the heart trouble still. The doctor's put him on these new pills . . . seem to be helping . . . but I'm sure he'll want to see you. It'll be lovely to see you again. It's been a long time, hasn't it?'

She could have said it's been too long, but she didn't. She left that out. Too many things have been left out. So many opportunities wasted. So many years.

It's a long journey. Five hours at least, six if the traffic is bad. It shouldn't be. Not on a weekday. Not out of season. I think about catching the train, but I want to be independent, enclosed in my own world. Not sitting on a train, open to everyone's gaze.

'Are you sure you're ready for it? It's a long way,' Sam says.

'I think so,' I tell her.

But the truth is, I don't know. For over three months I've been sitting around the house mostly, or going for walks, or coming here to see you. I've done the school run occasionally, or gone to the supermarket for the weekly shop. But nothing else. Nothing like this. Driving from Watford to Plymouth on my own then back again. But I was feeling an odd excitement about it, a small flaring of a sense of being alive again.

'I'll be all right,' I tell Sam. 'I'll take my time. Stop and have a bite to eat, coffee, that sort of thing.'

On the morning I leave, Sam stands outside on the driveway to see me off. She's wearing a white belted cardigan that's seen better days. She clutches Jessica's small hand. Bethan is at school. Jessica's face is screwed into the sunshine, trying to smile but almost crying instead. I back the car carefully out into the road.

'Bye, then. Don't forget to phone when you arrive,' Sam calls out, waving.

As I drive away I have a feeling that when I come back things won't be the same again. Why do I think that?

I don't start to relax until I get on to the M5, and past Bristol, beyond the reach of the interminable traffic, the juggernauts on their runs from London. Through the Somerset levels and then the sign for Glastonbury, and I feel something in the air now. Those old Arthurian legends perhaps leaving their mark. Then Bridgwater and that great Wicker Man gazing towards the motorway. He's been caught in the act of striding, his arms swinging, one leg pushing out, but at the same time he's rooted, part of the earth. He looks like he's been there for ever. I imagine the winds over these plains lapping his head and the rains drenching him and then in summer the sun sucking out the moisture, sucking the wicker bone-dry. Now beyond him, the landscape changes, becoming hillier and less open. Place names resonate with me, like a language returning.

There's a tension between my car and the place I'm

moving towards, as if I'm being pulled forward. Like the button on the Hoover that suddenly whips up the snaked lead. I pass road signs for Cullompton, Exeter, Torquay. I take the turn off the motorway, left onto the A380 to Torquay, then left again to drop down through acres of conifers and heath to Teignmouth.

Why the detour? I'm not sure. Suddenly I feel I'm moving too fast, being sucked back into the past, becoming that boy again living in that little house by the sea with my aunt and uncle and the silences, all the things we couldn't say and never would. I want to stall it, to hold it off.

In the summer, when the weather was good, we used to come here on Sundays for a day out. We would park the car at the point, then walk on around the lip of the river to the river beach, past the beach huts, past the stacks of lobster pots, past the small boats pulled up on the beach, the rowing boats and small motor launches, past the wooden jetty where the ferry boat to Shaldon anchors up for trippers in the summer, to the Ship, where the sea at high tide laps against the sea wall. My uncle would buy himself a pint, and my aunt a dry Martini and lemonade and me a Coke and we'd sit at the sea end of the pub, looking out through blown-glass windows, where the glass seemed pooled into swirls in the panes as fluid as the sea. If we were lucky we'd see a big cargo ship, from Russia or Spain, or somewhere else, nose its way into the small harbour, the pilot boat leading it in. My uncle would tell me the names of the parts of the ship, the meaning of the red and green lights, and sometimes we'd see a fishing boat coming in, a squall of gulls screaming behind it.

Or at other times we'd go round to the Den, and have a game on the pitch and putt, or they'd watch me on the go-karts. Or we'd walk down to the beach, to the red gritty sand that ran in a long strip along the promenade. My uncle would kick a ball with me, or if it was hot enough we'd go for a swim, gasping through the cold waves, to the deeper water beyond, our heads bobbing together in the open sea. Belonging together in the wide blue water, so that anyone watching would think that we were any old father and son enjoying a day at the seaside together. Only we weren't.

I retrace our steps. Parking my car at the Point car park and walking around the headland to the river beach. I stop at the Ship and have a pint, sitting alone by the glass window that used to bubble before my eyes but seems clearer now, the view beyond sharper and less distorted. Although that could be just time playing its tricks. There are no ships in the harbour today, and the pub's almost empty. Just a few men with vacant faces and time on their hands. I finish my pint and walk around to the Den, but I don't stay long. It's a cold weekday towards the end of March. No children playing; they'll be in school. Just a few old people down on the red sand walking dogs. Or some brave souls sitting on benches, scarved up against the wind, gazing out to sea like they're waiting for some ship to come into view. To slide before their eyes and fill up the endless sea, the vacant horizon.

I don't stay long. Dark clouds are gathering; there's a smell of rain in the air.

Aunt Susan comes to the back door with flour on her hands. She stands there, her arms held out stiffly at her sides. She moves towards me as if she means to hug me but the flour on her hands gives her a reason not to.

'Jack,' she says. Her voice hangs with surprise. I step towards her and kiss her dry, papery cheek. The kitchen smells of warm beef and onions.

'Lovely to see you again, Aunt Susan.'

'And you, Jack. Did you have a good journey?'

'Fine. I stopped at Teignmouth for a little while. Had a walk around.'

'Did you? That was nice. Your uncle's just popped out for some milk. Sit down. I'll put the kettle on. Just let me get this pie into the oven. I've been rolling out pastry. Bit of a mess, I'm afraid.'

'You take your time, no hurry.'

I watch my aunt trim off the pastry lid on the pie dish, slide it into the oven. She clears up the snips of pastry and rolls them into a ball, cleans up the floured work surface, washes her hands, puts on the kettle. She asks me about Sam and the girls and I tell her they're fine, everyone's fine. But I want to say, I'm not, I've been off work. I killed a girl, it was an accident, but then this depression started and I keep thinking about Mum, what happened. And the girl's father is stalking me and I'm scared about all this stuff, *all this change*, more scared than I've ever been before. But I can't. I can't say any of it. Maybe later, maybe never. So I sit there and we talk about the weather, and how good it'll be to see the spring arrive. My aunt is spooning instant coffee into white cups, scattering some digestive biscuits onto a plate.

'Help yourself, Jack.'

She sits opposite me, folds her hands in front of her chest, and I think how old they look now she's washed away the flour, the blue veins stretched under crêpe skin like bumpy elastic.

'How is he?' I ask. 'How's Uncle Keith?'

'Oh, he's fine, he's fine. Can't do too much, though. Gets out of breath. The angina, you know. They've got him down on the waiting list for a bypass now. Three or four months' time, the hospital says.'

'That's the best thing for him, isn't it? That'll help?'

'Oh yes, everyone's having them these days. It'll give him a new lease of life, the doctor says.'

A new lease of life. I think, I wish it were that easy. I wouldn't care. I'd let them carve my chest open, tweak around with my heart, reroute the arteries and veins, make me feel new again. If it were that easy.

My aunt is watching me. Her mouth is forming a small 'o' of puzzlement, an unvoiced question. Behind her glasses her eyes are cool grey, the colour of the March sea.

'Everything's OK, then, Jack? Nothing's wrong?' she says.

But the kitchen door is opening and Uncle Keith is coming in, his body bulky in an overcoat, a newspaper tucked under his arm, a carton of milk swinging in his hand. He's wiping his shoes on the doormat, bringing in a bluster of wind and wetness, fresh air that sweeps away the need for an answer.

'You're here, Jack! Good to see you, lad.'

I stagger to my feet and fall against his chest, against his wet overcoat. He smells of salt air and soap and something's missing – the smell of tobacco – he's given up smoking now. He steps back and looks at me.

'Been a long time, lad. Too long.'

There's a glint of moisture in his eyes. But it could be the rain.

'Take that wet overcoat off, Keith. You'll catch your death of cold,' my aunt says.

After my aunt's steak pie, which makes me feel like a small boy again, tucking into the thick pastry crust, warm meaty odours filling my senses, I watch the football with my uncle. We don't talk much, we never did, but I breathe him in, sitting in his armchair close by, and he breathes me in, and I can feel his contentment oozing into the room. But there are spaces between us that I know will have to be filled.

Why are you here, Jack?

How are you really?

What's happened?

Later that evening, after my aunt's ham sandwiches and scones and jam, I go out for a walk. The rain has stopped and the wind has died to a whimper. I walk the back streets where I played my boyhood out and those angry teen years, and it's strange because my body knows those streets like they're a part of me, mapped like tributaries under my skin. I walk for half an hour or more, turning this way and that, with the instinct of a hunter. I walk past the village primary school where I discovered my talent for art and football, where I first drew blood when I hit Christopher Smith on the nose. I walk past the Methodist chapel that I attended every Sunday morning with my aunt and uncle. I walk past the bookies where my uncle would take me on Saturday to place bets on the dogs, and the British Legion where he first taught me darts and initiated me into the pleasures of a pint. I walk past the house of the girl I once fancied and past the rebuilt wall of the house that I caved in the day I got drunk in my uncle's car. I walk to the street where we used to live, stand and gawk like a tourist outside the terraced house where I slept for years in the room with sloping eaves. The sash windows are still intact, well maintained and newly painted, but the green wooden front door has been replaced with one of the white uPVC ones. I wonder who lives there now. Does a boy still sleep in that room, build Airfix kits on a desk in the corner? But no, probably not. Do boys still do those things?

I carry on to the bottom of the road, past the rows of terraces with their small squared front gardens, their dustbins and wrought-iron gates, pots of dried-up shrubs waiting for warmer weather, to the Tudor Crown. In the public bar, a few men are playing darts or billiards; the others, huddled at the bar, grunt at the barmaid and gaze into their pints.

A familiar face. Or not quite familiar. Like something layered on something else. In this case, flesh layered on the cheeks, around the jowls where it hadn't been before, eyes puffy, hairline receding, but it was him all the same. Tony Duffy. Recognition is a funny thing. I catch his eyes just for a moment. Then he looks away. Startled, a quick intake of breath. He's seen a familiar face as well. Familiar, yet not quite.

I go to the bar and order a drink. The barmaid serves me with distance in her eyes. A young girl, hardly twenty. Thin, poker-faced, sour before her time. She wants to be somewhere else. Not here, in the public bar of the Tudor Crown serving pints to punters. Tony Duffy a few feet further down, hunched on his stool, waiting for something to happen. I happen. He looks up at me again, then again. Each time letting his eyes visit my face a second or two longer.

'Jack Philips? Is it you, mate?'

The voice familiar too, yet not quite.

I put down my pint and grin at him.

'Yeah, it's me. How yer doing, mate?'

He walks around to where I'm standing, and I can see he doesn't know what to do. Give me a hug, a slap on the back, shake my hand. He shakes my hand.

'Hey, you're a blast from the past, then. Good to see yer, mate. How long's it been, then? Fifteen years?'

Sixteen, actually. Or more like eighteen, really, because in those last two years we hardly saw each other anymore. But sixteen years since I last saw him at all. That was the time I moved away to London, to art school. Cut my ties with the past. All my direction was forward then, to the future, no looking back. Like a horse with blinkers on. Not like now. But what's it matter? Fifteen years, sixteen, even more. Something happens in your life, some transition, and a new life flowers beneath your feet and that's the one you're caught up in, the one you're living, and the past falls away. But now it's like the past has caught up with the present; they're meshed together. I can't keep them apart anymore.

We sit at a table in the corner and catch up with each other, filling in the gaps. Tony tells me he joined the navy at eighteen, but rarely went to sea. He trained as a cook, stayed mostly in Plymouth at the naval base, dishing out meals to officers in the mess. He met a girl and a baby was soon on the way and he'd married young, at twenty, to 'do the right thing'. But it hadn't lasted. Five years down the line, they'd broken up.

'I guess it was my fault. I never acted as if I was married – too young, I guess. Played the field, I did. She got sick of it in the end. Who can blame her.'

But he still sees the kid. Jason, just turned fourteen.

'He lives with his mum and stepdad about five miles away. She married again, but he's all right. He treats the kid OK. He's a great kid. I take him to football on Saturdays. He loves the game. Chip off the old block!'

He buys me a pint, and then I buy him one back, and we fill in the gaps. Funny, though. As we're sitting there, old mates, catching up, I'm thinking this isn't Tony Duffy. Not the one I knew. The skinny kid with spots, whose house I used to go round every day when I was fifteen, sixteen, to play U2 records and smoke pot. Who I got off my head with, boozing and smoking puff on Saturday nights. Anything we could lay our hands on, which in those days wasn't much. Cheap bottles of cider mostly. He was with me that night I wrote off my uncle's car, smashing into the brick wall of that old lady's house. We had crawled out unscathed, just a black eye or two between us, just shaken up, but the car was a total wreck. After that, after I'd swung at my uncle and cursed him, and he'd hung on to me like we were drowning, something changed. A new life flowering under my feet, I suppose. Tony had left school and joined the dole queue for a while, before deciding what to do next, and I'd stayed on and got my head down with 'A' levels and my sights fixed on

the future, to London, to art school, to getting out. I'd seen
him around a few times, hanging about in town with his new
crowd of misfits on the dole, stoned in the middle of the day,
his pupils spilling out of his eyes. But it wasn't the same. I
was moving on. I was leaving him behind.

That was Tony Duffy then. This one, who's been a cook
in the navy, who married and divorced and has a kid he
loves called Jason, who's almost the same age as his dad was
when we were mates, he's another one. Like he's layered on
the old one, the past catching up with the present again.

The time's getting on. He wants me to go back with him,
back to his mum and dad's house where he's living now.
'They'll be bowled over, seeing you again,' he says. But I can't
do this anymore.

'No, I need to get back, mate. The old folks will be
worried where I am. I told them I was only going out for a
walk.'

Back then when we were kids, we never thought about
parents worrying where we were, worrying what we were up
to. Funny how you change.

We shake hands again.

'It's been great seeing you again, mate. Keep in touch. You
know where I am.'

His eyes are gleaming at me moistly and I think, He's
really touched, seeing me; it means something to him still,
after all these years. But I just want to get out, to walk the
pavements again, the sky over my head, fresh air in my lungs.

8

For the next three days winds buffet the town, bringing rain, lots of it, in from the sea. My world shrinks to the size of my aunt's bungalow. I'm cosseted by it, by the small spaces, by my aunt's baking and my uncle's quietness, by the wind lashing rain on the windowpanes. It's like when I was a kid swinging up in the eaves in that old house. I wake up to bacon and eggs and coffee brewing on the stove, walk to the corner to fetch a paper and bury myself in it when I get back, sometimes reading snippets aloud to my uncle from the sports pages. Just before lunchtime, we catch a breathing space in the squalls of rain to walk down to the British Legion. I have a pint and he has an orange juice; as well as smoking, he's given up drinking these days.

'Not good for the old ticker,' he says.

In the afternoon, full with my aunt's home cooking, we doze in front of old films on the telly. My uncle with his hands folded under his paunch, leaning back on the recliner, soft meaty snorings from his nose. I think, I want to stay like this forever. It would be easy in a way, and difficult in another. The moment wraps me like a blanket, insulating me.

From what? you'd say. But I wouldn't answer.

Sam phones. When I hear her voice the comfort blanket slips away. There are barbs with strings attached in my flesh, tugging me back home.

'Jessica's got a chest infection. It's spreading like wildfire around her nursery. Lots of kids are down with it.'

'How is she?'

'She's on antibiotics. She's feeling sorry for herself, poor lamb. Lies on the sofa all day with a blanket, sucking her thumb like a baby. She's been asking after you. She's missing you.'

'I miss her too, I miss you all.'

A pause. Then: 'When are you coming back, then, Jack?'

We watch a documentary about the Aids crisis in Africa, children with eyes as dark and blank as a well stare out of the screen. For them it's all past, all trauma, no future. So much suffering, I think. My aunt sits knitting by the fire. The wool is pale blue. A scarf, the sleeve of a jumper? It drops from the needles like a flag. The documentary ends and it's the ten o'clock news. More trouble in Palestine. A twelve-year-old boy was killed by Israeli gunfire. His father clutches the boy to his chest, covers the boy's body with his own. His face is riven with grief. I think of Laura. My aunt pierces her ball of wool with her needles, lays it down on the coffee table.

'Anyone like a hot chocolate?' she says.

Now's the time. A space has opened up in the room waiting for me to fall into it.

'I'm going home tomorrow,' I say.

My uncle is watching me closely.

'You sure, Jack?'

'Jessica's not well. Nothing serious. But I should get back.'

'Well, it's been good to see you, lad.'

I can almost hear your voice in my head. *Say it, Jack. Now's a good time.*

'The reason why I came – one of the reasons – was to say I was sorry.'

'What on earth for, Jack?'

My uncle's eyes haven't left my face. I turn and look at him directly. Time opens out in his eyes. Anything can fill it.

'For giving you a hard time, when I was a kid. For not being more grateful. That time when I wrote off your car, remember.'

'Jack, that's all forgotten – you were just a kid.'

'. . . and for saying you weren't my dad. Because you were. You *are*.'

'Teenagers say these things. I knew you didn't mean it, lad.'

His eyes are shining with moisture, and I know this time it's not the rain.

'I know. But I shouldn't have. But I was angry see. I was angry about Mum.'

They flinch, as if the words have a sting in them. I pause. *Go for it, Jack*, I think to myself. *It's now or never.*

'We never talked about it – about how she died.'

'We wanted to protect you, Jack. We thought it best not to bring it up again.'

My aunt is sobbing quietly. She has picked up the soft blue flag of wool and is pressing it to her face, wiping away her tears.

We didn't have the hot chocolate. My uncle poured us all a brandy and we sat there till late that night, and we talked. About my mother. For the first time ever, really. My aunt told me stories about her from when they were kids together. My mother was the youngest and my aunt always looked out for her. Her kid sister. Their father, my grandfather, died from lung cancer when my mother was nine. She was his favourite. For some time after she wouldn't eat much, was wasting away. My aunt cut her food into small pieces and fed it to her, morsel by morsel, from small dishes at the kitchen table, coaxing it between her sister's lips like you do with a baby, and bit by bit she'd got better, and put the weight back on.

'In those days you didn't talk about things. Bad things. You just got on with it. We didn't want to upset her, bringing it up again. But sometimes I wonder if that wasn't partly to blame for the way she was when your dad left. Because she'd never got over losing *her* dad, all that grief stuck inside of her coming up again . . .'

'You did your best,' I said. 'You did what you thought was best at the time.'

'I know,' my aunt said softly. She's gazing wistfully into the space between us, looking back into her past. She's seeing my mother again, a girl of nine who has to have her food cut up for her and pushed gently between her lips.

'Trouble is, your best is never quite good enough,' she said.

I sleep like a baby that night, after I eventually get to bed. No waking in the dark, no troubling dreams. When I wake the sounds in the room are different, and then I realize it's because it's quiet. The wind's died down; it's no longer throwing rain at the window. There's a thin light filtering through the curtain, a watery sunshine.

'Good day for driving back,' my uncle says when I fold up the sofa bed, put away the bedclothes and join them in the kitchen. 'Weather's changed.'

I decide to leave after lunch. My aunt says she'll make something light so I don't fall asleep at the wheel. Soup and sandwiches, or something. Whilst she's getting it ready I go to the club with my uncle, one last time. We sit there, me with a shandy because I'm driving later, him with an orange juice, picking through the papers that have been left on the seat. I feel self-conscious, almost shy. Something's different. It takes some getting used to.

'Jack, there's something I've been meaning to say, before you go . . .'

There's something in his voice that makes me sit up, makes me take notice.

'About your dad. I think I might know where he is, where you could find him. If you ever wanted to, that is . . .'

Something shuts tight in my chest.

'You're my dad,' I say.

He clears his throat. He stares down at the table. He can't look at me.

'There's something I never told you. Your dad, he came round a couple of times when you were a lad, wanted to see you. We sent him packing. We thought it was best for you to not see him. But maybe it wasn't, maybe we were selfish, wanted to keep you to ourselves an' all.'

My uncle slides a folded piece of paper across the chrome table towards me.

'Anyway, I've written it down here. The address he gave me at the time. Who knows, he might still be there. Or someone there might know where he is.'

I gaze at the square of paper, slowly pick it up and open it. My uncle's handwriting, jerky and uneven. The name *Edward Philips* and a Bristol address. I stare at the name, trying to fit a face to it. An oval face maybe, dark hair, an infectious laugh. Familiar, yet not quite.

'He came round to see me?' I say, tamely.

'Yeah, a couple of times. First time you were at school. You were about eight. It wasn't long after – you know – your mother died. Second time, about a year later. I don't remember where you were then. Out playing, perhaps. But we never even let him in. We never told you.'

I fold the paper up and stick it in my wallet, behind the picture of Sam and the kids.

'Will you try to get in touch?'

'I dunno. Don't really see the point, after all these years . . .'

'I'm sorry, son,' my uncle says.

There are tears in his eyes. Maybe mine too. I bury my face in my pint.

When I turn right into our road, there's a car waiting to turn left. As I pass it I recognize Dave sitting behind the wheel. I put up my hand to wave to him but he isn't looking, he doesn't see me. He's out of uniform, wearing a shirt and jacket. Sam's in the living room when I get in, watching *Balamory* with Jessica. Jess scrambles off her mother's knee and runs to me, shrieking with delight. I pick her up.

'How you doing, sweetheart? Feeling better?'

I swing down, balancing Jessica in my arms, and kiss Sam on the cheek.

'Where's Bethan?' I ask.

'At Megan's house. Good journey?' Sam says.

There's something different about her. An edge to her voice. She's had her hair trimmed shorter, she's wearing earrings.

Jessica is struggling to get down. She wants to run upstairs and fetch the new doll her granny gave her the other day. I release her and she rushes from the room.

'Yeah, fine. She's feeling better, then?'

'The antibiotics have kicked in now. She'll be back at nursery on Monday.'

'Was that Dave I saw driving out of our road?'

Sam turns a pale face towards me.

'Yes. I phoned him and asked him to come. I was worried about something.'

Jessica is back, pushing her doll into my arms. It has a smooth squashy face like a real baby, long lashes that open and close, piercing blue eyes. She tells me the doll's name is Peggy, like her friend at nursery.

'What were you worried about?'

'That man ... he was standing outside Bethan's school when I went to pick her up yesterday.'

'What man?' I say, but my heart is racing.

'That girl's father – the one in the accident – I remembered what he looked like from that day at the inquest.'

Later that evening, after I've had tea with the girls, and helped bath them, and put them to bed, and read Jessica her bedtime story whilst Sam read to Bethan, who still likes being read to even though she's six and can read a lot on her own, I drive around to Dave's.

He's not surprised to see me on the doorstep.

'Come in, Jack. You got back OK, then?'

'Yeah, fine, thanks.'

I follow him into his living room. Everything is immaculate and in its place, like it can only be if you live alone and have no kids. Dave fetches a couple of beers from the fridge and pours me one.

'So Sam's told you about that bloke? Seeing him outside Bethan's school?'

'I've seen him before. Twice. Standing outside the house staring at it.'

Why don't I mention who I saw with him? Why don't I mention Laura?

Dave stares back at me in astonishment.

'Have you told Sam?'

'No, I didn't want to worry her.'

But that wasn't all. I didn't want to give her a chance to think me crazy. How could I tell her one bit of the story, and not the other?

You saw who, Jack? You saw Laura with her father? But Laura's dead, Jack. Are you telling me you saw a ghost?

'Maybe you should have,' Dave says. 'This could be serious.'

9

LISA

'I've seen her. She's still around.'

She gives me a quick smile.

'That's normal,' she says. 'A lot of people have that experience. It's part of the grieving process.'

I want to hit her. *The grieving process.* She wouldn't use expressions like that if it were happening to her. When you're in it, it's just a way of seeing the world. It's real.

'Tell me about it,' she says. But I don't want to now. I've said enough. I want to keep it to myself. I don't want to spoil it.

'Do you and Derek talk to each other about Laura?' she asks.

I tell her, no. But I'm grateful for the silence. It's like a huge soft ball into which I can fall.

I don't remember what day of the week it was, that first time I saw you. It doesn't matter. My life used to be measured in days when you were alive. On Mondays you had PE and I'd get your gym bag ready for school. I always washed your uniform and PE kit on Saturday, ironed it all on Sunday evenings. I loved those rituals. Pressing the iron around your white collar, imagining it sitting neatly around your neck the next day at school. Wednesdays you had Guides and Thursdays was swimming club. I'd pick you up from school and take you straight there. When you were younger they had high hopes for you, remember. You were the best in the under-twelves section. We paid for you to have extra lessons and I was told a lot would depend on what would happen when you hit puberty, whether you'd be tall, what your muscle strength would be. But you're small, slight of build like me. Your dad was disappointed for a while. But me, I didn't mind. I loved to sit and watch you from the tiers. Watch your small head in its white rubber cap moving through the water. I would take a book along to read but my eyes would keep getting tugged back to you, to your head bobbing up and down.

My life was measured around you into days. Now it just spills out like ragged ends.

Tuesday. November the seventh. That was the day the world ended.

I worked till half five at the garage on Tuesdays. You'd go round to Chloe's after school, then catch the bus home. I was in the garage trying to reassure a customer about his car and you were lying dying on the road in the rain and I didn't know.

'You can't blame yourself,' she says. 'You've got to let them go sometimes. You've got to give them some independence.'

I don't want to hear that. I want her to judge me, to say yes, I was guilty. I should have picked you up that day, or at least have been home so you would have come straight back after school, so you wouldn't have been getting off a bus at five o'clock in the afternoon, in November when five o'clock is late, when it's almost dusk, and running because of the rain. If I hadn't been working, I tell myself, you would still be here. And my life would still be measured up into days, meshed like stitches together. Instead of this loose thing with ragged ends that has no shape.

'Feeling guilty is all part of the grieving process,' she says. And I want to hit her then as well. To beat her face with its pretending kind smile into a pulp, I really do. I didn't know I had it in me.

She is wearing a light green jumper I haven't seen her in before. She has had her hair restyled. Slightly shorter, a lighter shade of brown. Why do I notice these things? Why do I care?

'How do you see yourself moving on?' she asks.

Moving on. She makes it sound like a journey. I tell her that and she smiles that quick smile again and says, 'Aren't we all on a journey of sorts?' And I snap at her, quite sharp then, irritated by the platitudes, by the smile she puts on that hides the truth, that she's really got her eye on the time and wants to get home to her husband and kids (*her* kids). I say, 'Yeah, well if it's a journey then whatever I've been travelling on has crashed.' She doesn't smile then. Just looks at me. Silence. I can hear the ticking of the clock on the table before us. I can hear my heart beat. Although what good it does, beating, I don't know. My veins have silted up. I'm a zombie, like in those corny horror films where the dead rise up and start walking about, clamouring at doors and windows, terrorizing the living.

I think, sometimes, my grief frightens her. It fills this

small room like a fog. She wants to rush away, breathe fresh air, run home to her children and hug them hard and feel their life seeping into her, filling her again.

The first time I saw you I was in the house alone. I was sitting at the kitchen table with a slice of toast lying on a plate in front of me and I was picking at its crust, picking it into crumbs and pushing it around the plate like a baby does when it's first learning to feed itself. Like you used to with those Farley's finger rusks I gave you when you were tiny. Sitting in your high chair, pursing your mouth into small circles of surprise at the texture the rusk made on your fingertips. Everything surprised you then.

And then I became aware that you were there, that you were standing in the kitchen behind me. Something moved through me, a small thrill. At first I was afraid to turn and look at you. And when I did I moved my head slowly, keeping my shoulders rigid, catching you at the corner of my eyes, like looking at a bird, wanting to see it closely but afraid in case a sudden movement might startle it away. You were standing by the door. You were wearing your school uniform and your school bag was swinging on your shoulder. One of your socks was limp and trailing down towards your ankle, and I wanted to say something so you would stoop and pull it up and I had to stop myself, because my voice dropping into that space between us would have been too real, would have startled you into going. Anyway, it didn't matter because you looked wonderful, you looked perfect. Your school blazer was clean and smooth as if I'd just had it dry-cleaned and the white collar of your blouse sat neat and pressed around your neck. You were smiling at me. Your smile lit up the kitchen as if the sun had come out and the cold January morning had suddenly turned to spring.

I felt happy again. Completely, absolutely – joy blasting the silt from my veins, filling my heart. Some people say they're afraid of ghosts. If it was a ghost I saw, then I pray every day for its return. I want to be haunted by it. But it doesn't work like that, it seems. Laura decides.

The doctor gave me their number. I'd gone in to renew the prescription. They'd only give me about two weeks' worth at the time. Maybe in case I decided to do myself in. A woman doctor, it was. I always think they're the best. Got more time, know how to listen, tell things straight. Men. They're afraid of emotion. They're afraid of women's emotions in particular. What good is that in a doctor? Anyway, I went in there and she turned and looked at me straight in the eyes and said, 'How are you *really*, Mrs Jenkins?' and after that I couldn't help myself. The floodgates opened. I must have got through half a box of tissues. I kept apologizing, I felt such a fool. But Dr Armstrong just sat there and looked at me with this look of – oh, I don't know. Not pity, not like you give a dog. Not fear either. But like she felt what I was feeling and wouldn't run from it. I remember she put her hand on my arm and said softly, 'I'm so, so sorry.' And because there were two of us feeling the pain it became easier to let it go and eventually I dried up.

'I'll give you two more weeks' prescription, Mrs Jenkins, but I would like you to ring this number.'

It was the number for the bereavement counsellors. I took

it, and the prescription, and went sniffing my way out, keeping my head down because people would know I'd been crying my face was so blotched and red and because I felt guilty because I'd kept them waiting, taken up more than my ten minutes' worth. It was funny; in there you'd think I was a serious case, breaking down like that. A likely contender for the nuthouse. But when I came out I felt lighter somehow. It was early January then, a couple of weeks after Christmas, and a freezing-cold day but there was a patch of blue in the sky and the sun was out and for a moment, in the sun, it felt almost warm and I began to look forward to lunch – to having a poached egg and a slice of wholemeal and some nice mushrooms perhaps. And maybe I'd catch the afternoon play on the radio. And yet only minutes ago I'd been breaking my heart in front of Dr Armstrong and now I was looking forward to a bit of lunch.

Emotions. I don't trust them. They're fickle, they are.

Not like love, I hear you say in my head.

Not like love.

Although love can die too.

Sheila works with me for the RSPCA. We're involved with fundraising, which normally means we just stand outside Tesco's for a couple of hours on a Saturday morning with collection boxes while people shuffle past us with trolley-loads of food and bickering kids, ignoring us. Although there's always a few that don't. Mostly old ladies, who shuffle coins out of their purses with bony fingers and push them through the slots into the boxes and mutter things like how terrible it is how people treat their pets these days and what good work we're doing, such a good cause. I gave it up for a couple of months, couldn't face it, couldn't face anything, and then I thought why should the animals suffer just because I was. And maybe I was starting to feel a bit better, more normal, like that day when I visited the doctor, looking forward to a poached egg for lunch and a play on the radio. More and more moments like that. And possibly it was the pills working that was doing it, or even just the way the doctor looked at me that morning, her hand lightly touching my arm, or even the counselling – although I don't like to admit to that.

(But mostly it was you. Seeing you in that kitchen that morning. The way you smiled. Mostly it was that.)

After we've done our stint outside Tesco's, or just inside the foyer if it's wet, we like to go inside for coffee in the cafe. Sheila is in her late forties, and if I could have chosen my mother, had a different one to the one I've got, it would be Sheila, although she'd have been a child bride to be my mother – there's not that much between us really. Eleven or twelve years, that's all. It's more to do with a quality she has. Sheila is plump with greying hair she doesn't seem to care about and she wears those awful velour tracksuits that women of a certain age buy from Marks and Spencer's, but she's nice. She's been widowed for three years. I asked her once if she'd ever thought of marrying again, or at least finding herself a boyfriend, if you can still call them that at Sheila's age, and she just shrugged her shoulders and said that when you really loved someone you always carry them with you anyway and she could never quite see the point in second best.

'Don't you get lonely?' I asked. And she just looked at me and smiled softly and said, 'Of course. Doesn't everyone sometimes?' as if loneliness is just a fact of life, like having a certain eye colour or being short. Something to be lived with.

Sheila knows about the grieving process, but she'd never call it that. It's real to her; she lives it. I tell her about you, about seeing you that morning in the kitchen, ready for school and smiling. We're sitting by the plate-glass window in the cafe. Outside, an angry mother is dragging a wailing toddler by the arm.

'She wants to tell you she's OK, she wants to tell you she's happy now,' Sheila says.

We sit there for a while, saying nothing. I feel a warm buzz of pleasure in my chest. Being with Sheila, the winter sun warming us a little through the window. The taste of coffee in my mouth. Sheila is eating a chocolate muffin with her cappuccino. She breaks it into quarters first, tucks each piece firmly into her mouth. Then she picks up her handbag and fishes out her purse and she's looking in the wallet section for something. She gets it out, and pushes it towards me across the table. It's a card, with someone's name and phone number on it.

'I don't know what you think of this sort of thing, Lisa. We've never talked about it before,' she says, 'but he's a medium. I've been to see him a few times, not long after I lost John. I found it very helpful at the time.'

*

86

'Did you ever really talk to each other?' the counsellor asks.

We're talking about Derek. We're talking about your dad. I don't like to talk to her much about you. I keep you to myself mostly.

She's about my age, I suppose. Mid- to late thirties. A bit plump. Her skirt stretches tight across her thighs sitting down. She wears a blouse buttoned up to her throat. A small gold crucifix around her neck. She's all right, really. I'm a bit hard on her at times. The anger coming out, I suppose. The third stage of the grieving process, after denial and bargaining. Only in my case I'd missed the bargaining stage. There was nothing to bargain about. It was so sudden. You were alive when I left for work and dead when I came home. No point in saying, 'Oh, God, let her live and I'll never do anything wrong again. I'll sell up and give all my wealth to the poor.' No point.

'I think so,' I say, carefully. 'In the early days we did.'

But am I lying to myself? Wasn't what I admired about Derek was that he was the strong silent type? Only maybe silence isn't so strong after all.

'Is there some way you could talk to him?' she says. 'To share your feelings about Laura together?'

'I don't know,' I tell her. 'The trouble is, I don't think I love him anymore.'

I told Sheila that. Sitting in Tesco's cafeteria one Saturday morning. I told her she was wrong to say that love never really dies because I used to love Derek once and now I didn't think I loved him anymore.

'Perhaps you never did,' she said, looking at me steadily over the rim of her coffee cup.

'Oh, but I did,' I protested. 'I was obsessed about him for months when I first started going with him. I'd think about him all the time.'

'That's not love,' she said, quietly.

We met at work. I was twenty-two and he was fifteen years older. I admired his dark eyes and his strong jaw and the way he always got on with the job, not stopping for cups of tea and a gossip all the time like the other mechanics, but working for hours, bent over the bonnets of cars, the muscles of his legs taut against the dark cloth of his overalls, his back sinewy. He never said much to me; he didn't flirt or anything like that. Not like the others. But when he handed me the dockets for the jobs from his oil-stained fingers, it was like an electric current passed between us. Then one Friday afternoon as I was packing up to go home he came into the office and asked if I'd fancy going for a drink and my heart raced with excitement and I said, 'Yes, yes, that would be nice.'

He'd got scrubbed up a bit. He had nice clean jeans on under his overalls and a pale green check shirt and he must have gone into the toilet and scrubbed his nails hard because when I sat next to him in his dark green Volvo I thought how clean his nails looked for a mechanic, the cuticles only slightly cracked and only the slightest hairline of black under the quick. It must mean something to him, I thought, taking me out for a drink.

We went to the Three Horseshoes. They'd done it up in

there, art-deco style. Cadiz shell table-lamps and big Chester-
fields and bookcases with old books in them. You can pretend
you're in a posh living room rather than a pub. He bought
me a wine spritzer, and then another, and then because we
hadn't eaten and the wine was in danger of going to my head
we decided to have something from the snack menu and I
had scampi and chips in a basket and he had a double
cheeseburger and chips and I noticed how carefully he ate it,
nibbling small pieces from the edge like a girl, careful not to
get crumbs down the front of his shirt.

I don't remember what we talked about. Work, family,
that sort of thing. But I remember he said that he collected
memorabilia from the war. I asked him what he had in his
collection and he said two gas masks, some copies of the *Daily
Mail*, a ration book, a German helmet and his dad's war
medals. His parents were dead, he said. His dad died when
he was a kid and his mother of cancer this year last. He'd
inherited the house; he was an only child like me. I remember
thinking he'd be good marriage material; he was well set up.
Terrible, I know, thinking that on a first date. But I did.

After that we were an item. Derek moved to another garage
where the pay was better and he was more like management,
but I stayed put. So I didn't see him at work every day but I
would spend every weekend at his house. It was a semi, 1930s
style. The decor was a little dated, I thought, his mother's
presence still there in the G-plan furniture, patterned wallpaper and floral carpets, and dried flowers in vases. There was
a framed picture in black and white on the wall of his parents
on their wedding day and I looked at it closely because I love

looking at other people's old photographs. It gives me a bit of a thrill, you know, like when you walk past these terraced houses when it's dark, with their bay windows that face out on to the street and someone's not bothered to draw their curtains yet and you catch a glimpse into their lives. See them sitting there watching telly wearing their slippers, or stroking a cat or eating off a tray, and you know you're not supposed to look but you do, you can't help it. Maybe I'm a closet voyeur or something. That's what I feel when I look at people's old photographs. Like I'm sneaking a glance into their private lives, seeing things I'm not meant to see.

She looked young, his mother did. Eighteen, nineteen. He looked a little older. He was wearing his soldier's uniform; she was dressed in a cream suit, small pillbox hat perched on her permed hair. They were both squinting a bit, like the sun was in their eyes. They looked surprised.

'That was just before he got demobbed, at the end of the war,' Derek told me.

They were austere days, I suppose, just after the war. Mend and do. I suppose that's why she's not dressed like a bride. But more like a young girl out for the day, dressed up for the occasion.

Derek proposed to me three months later. I had cooked him his favourite, shepherd's pie, and we were sitting eating it at the Formica table in his mother's kitchen. I still thought of it as that. *His mother's kitchen.*

'How do you feel about moving in here permanently?' he said. 'Another Mrs Jenkins?'

I said yes. I was thrilled to bits. But I insisted the house went up for sale.

'We need a place of our own,' I told him. 'We need to start afresh.'

Funny, that was probably the only thing I ever insisted on. It was important to me then.

How much do we ever start afresh? I think now. Is that ever really possible? And how can I ever start over again now, now that Laura is gone? And what happens when we run out of fresh starts, what happens then?

'What happens then?' I say.

I look straight at her, challenging her, waiting for the fear in her eyes.

'I don't know, Lisa,' she says. She's telling the truth now, no platitudes. I admire her for that.

10

I used to think, when something terrible happens, like when your child dies, you're bound to know it. As if the umbilical cord is still there, invisible, and an electrical current, something like that, will be sent up it and into your body, like getting a shock. I got a shock once off a plug just by touching it with a damp hand. It was like a wall jumping up against me, throwing me to the floor. I used to think it would be like that.

It wasn't. When Laura died I was in the office answering the phone, booking appointments for MOTs and services. Just the usual thing. I remember just before five – that's when the police said it happened – someone had come in complaining about his car not being ready yet, and I'd been explaining patiently to him that the part for his Saab was taking longer to come than we'd originally anticipated, but it should be there in the morning and if it were the car would be ready by lunchtime. I was being tactful and diplomatic and calming him down; I'm good at that. No shock, no premonition of disaster, no end of the world. Funny how your world can end and you don't even know it. I didn't say, 'Sorry, sir, but my daughter has just died. She's been knocked down by a car and is lying dead on the road in the rain and I'll never see her again.' I just carried on talking to him, being polite, being helpful. I told him I would leave a note for Joanne who works on Wednesdays to chase it, make sure it had been dispatched, and he went off quite pleasantly and I looked at my watch and thought, Less than half an hour to go. I wonder if Laura is home yet? Derek normally brings back a takeaway Chinese on a Tuesday and then it's put my feet up time to *Coronation Street* and *EastEnders*.

It was ten past six when I got home. I'd left work just after half-past five and it's barely three miles, but the traffic was bad. The police were already waiting outside the house, sitting there in the car. I don't know how they trace people that quickly. Of course she had her name on her, on her schoolbooks in her bag, in her wallet thing with her bus pass. They'd have known what school she was at by the uniform. Maybe they keep records of the children on the Internet. I don't know.

They got out of their car when they saw me and said, 'Mrs Jenkins?'

I said, 'Yes.'

Then they said they had something to tell me and was my husband at home yet. I said no, but he'd be home in a short while and they'd better come in.

They looked so big in my small front room. I told them to sit down and they took off their hats and sat there twiddling them in their hands and looking uncomfortable, but it wasn't for long – seconds really, because before they could start talking the Volvo drew up and out he got. Derek came in and I introduced him to the PCs – I remember he shook their hands, like they were guests or something – and then they told us what had happened. But of course I knew all along. In my blood, I knew. I could feel the silt building up then.

I remember Derek was still holding the takeaway bag on his lap. The sweet-and-sour sauce carton must have fallen over and was leaking. There was a thick shiny red stain at the bottom of the bag, seeping onto his jeans. It reminded me of blood.

The doctor came around that first night and gave me a jab to knock me out and it worked. I slept the sleep of the dead. Ironic, really. My daughter dies and I sleep the sleep of the dead. No dreams, nothing. I was lying on the bed with my clothes still on when the doctor came. I'd been lying there for hours. Not sleeping, not even crying. Nothing really. But every so often I would hear this terrible noise like an animal makes in pain and I would realize it was me. Mrs Brookes from next door had come in and she'd made us both sweet tea and tried to get me to have some soup but I wouldn't have it. And then she said I should go and lie down, I was looking pale, I was looking like I might faint. She took me into the bedroom and left Derek sitting at the table, his face all collapsed like the structure that held it together had crumbled, had come to pieces.

Mrs Brookes drew the curtains, and tried to get me to get undressed, but I wouldn't, only my cardigan. I lay on the bed with my blouse and skirt on and she pulled the duvet up over me. Then later she came in and said she needed to get home and she was going to call the doctor. It was an hour before he came. Dr Murphy, it was. He's in his late fifties, and probably looking forward to retirement, and to the day when he won't have to come out at all hours to see women lying on beds and moaning. I heard him say, 'Mrs Jenkins, I'm just going to give you something to help you sleep. Is that all right?' and I must've grunted consent or something because I felt him ease up the sleeve of my blouse and a cold swab on my arm and then the needle went in. Minutes later I fell into this darkness, like a light switching off. But before I went down, I remember thinking, *I hope it was as easy as this for Laura, I hope she didn't suffer.*

He came back in the morning. Mrs Brookes let him in – she'd taken home our keys – and Derek and I were still in bed, lying as we did in separate rooms, as we'd done for years. I heard the door open and I heard low voices in the hall but I didn't want to get up. My body had turned to stone. I wanted to pull the duvet over my head, I wanted to bury myself.

The doctor put me on these strong sleeping pills for the first two weeks, and others for anxiety, but he wouldn't give me them. He gave them to Mrs Brookes and she'd come in twice a day and gave me the anxiety ones in the morning, and the sleeping pills at night; each time I took them they would knock me out. And that's how I spent those first two weeks, alternating between dead and barely alive. Sheila came to see me several times a week, and if I was in bed she'd pull a chair up and sit there quietly knitting. I could hear the clicking of the needles. She didn't say much; she didn't need to. But I knew she was there and it was a comfort to me. She fed me chicken soup, pushing the spoon between my lips, and slices of toast cut up into small squares. I wouldn't have eaten at all, if it hadn't been for her.

It was different for Derek. Everyone has their own way of coping, Angela the counsellor says. After the first few days he said he didn't want to be drugged anymore, he didn't want to walk around like one of the living dead. That's when he took to walking the streets instead. Or hiding away in his workshop at the bottom of the garden for hours.

Sometimes in the middle of the night I get out of bed for a glass of water and look out of the kitchen window and see the lights on at the bottom of the garden. He's still there doing God knows what in the small hours of the night. I don't know what. I never ask.

There was only a handful of us at the funeral. Derek, myself, Sheila. Chloe and her mum, and a teacher to represent the school. But I hadn't wanted anyone else to be there at all. I had wanted to be alone, so I could bury my face in the soil, so I could lie on top of her coffin, feel the earth fall like hard rain on the back of my head.

I hadn't wanted to go to the inquest. But Derek said we had to. We owed it to you to know the truth. And so I went and I saw that policeman up there in the box giving his evidence. He wasn't exceeding the speed limit. Yes, he'd had a pint on the way home but that was all, he said. She'd come at him out of the blue. He hadn't had time to brake. I saw the shock in his eyes, reliving it, and I didn't want to feel sorry for him, but I did.

'Why didn't you have your lights on?' the coroner asked,

a bit sharply, and the policeman looked flustered for a moment, guilty. But I knew it was an accident; there was nothing he could have done.

I saw him again briefly outside. We'd parked our car just down the road at a meter and Derek was fumbling in his pocket for his keys. He came out of the building and stood on the steps with his wife, blinking into a slanting winter sun, and just for a moment I thought I'd caught his gaze; I thought he looked over at me. I could see this blur in his eyes, like he wasn't really there. I wanted to walk up to him and say, I know it wasn't your fault, I know it was an accident. But I couldn't. It would have been disloyal to you.

All the way home Derek was going on about how he'd got away with murder, how they'd let him off because he was a policeman. How he should have his licence taken away and never be allowed on the roads again. But I just sat there and remembered the look in his eyes.

He still blames him.

Sometimes I pick up the newspaper and there's a neat hole in one of the inside pages, a square or rectangle or an L-shaped hole where he's taken a pair of scissors to an article and cut it out. Articles about road accidents. People – kids mainly – killed or maimed for life by drunken drivers, by teenagers driving recklessly. Or maybe just plain accidents, like yours.

'What did you cut out of the paper?' I asked, the first time I noticed. He looked surprised at the question.

'Another murdering bastard loose on the roads. A wanker in a lorry, not paying enough attention, took some kid clean off a motorbike on a junction. His head's crushed like an egg.'

I'm thinking, Why does he have to say it like that? As if he enjoys the violence, the gory details. But my face gives nothing away.

'Why did you cut it out?' I asked quietly.

'Someone's got to keep a record of these murders,' he said. But his voice was sending signals to me to keep out, to lay off. I was straying into territory in which I didn't belong.

Every Tuesday and Friday, when the locals arrive, I flick through them anxiously, looking for holes. Usually there'll be one or two. Sometimes there'll be nothing for a couple of weeks, and then a whole spate of them, so the paper will feel like a jigsaw with pieces missing. Sometimes it annoys me, like when I want to read my horoscope and I can't because there's a great gaping hole smack in the middle of it. Not that I care really about the future. It's just a habit. Just a harmless way of passing time. But I've never talked to him about them again, although I wonder what he does with all these clippings, where he keeps them. I sometimes hold the papers up in front of my face and gaze through the holes and think my life's like that. Something with holes in it out of which I stare, my sight narrowed to what I can see directly ahead. The rest screened out.

11

I've carried the card that Sheila gave me around in my handbag for several weeks. Sometimes I take it out and look at it, just to check it's still there, and it's a comfort to me that it is. A talisman. Something to fall back upon.

'Have you tried that number yet?' Sheila asks me, one Saturday in Tesco's. We've had a good morning. Our collection boxes sitting on the table before us feel weighty with coins. The early spring sunshine has put smiles on people's faces; people are always more generous when they're happy.

'No, not yet,' I tell her.

'Well, it's not for everyone,' Sheila says.

But her saying that pushes me towards action.

After tea that evening Derek says he's going to the workshop for an hour or so; he's got an engine in there he's fixing up for a friend. But I know he'll be there for the rest of the evening, he always is. I stack the dishes into the dishwasher and put it on and then I pour myself a glass of wine and bring the phone into the living room where I can sit in an easy chair. I take the card out of my purse and slowly dial the number.

Three rings. Four, five. I'm almost relieved that there's no answer. He must be out. I'm just about to put the phone hurriedly down when I hear a voice on the other end.

'Hello?'

'Er, is Martin there? Martin Clows?'

'Yes, speaking.'

What do I say? My daughter has died and I've heard that you can help me; I want to speak to the dead. How stupid, when I speak to you anyway all the time in my head.

'A friend gave me your number.'

'Yes.'

'She said that you're a medium.'

'Yes.' A pause. The voice on the other end softens. 'Have you lost someone?'

'Yes, I've lost my daughter. My daughter died.'

Two days later, the day before I'm to have my reading (he calls it a reading, as if you're going to write down words for me!) I'm standing at the sink peeling potatoes. Derek will be back soon, wanting his tea. I'm listening to the news on Radio 4. They have found the body of a missing child in a wood and I think, That poor mother, what will it be like for her? Then suddenly I know you want me to look up, to look through the window and down the garden, and I do. I look up and through the window, with that same slow movement of not wanting to startle you, because I know it's you that I'll see. It's still light, although there's a hint of dusk in the blue shadows of the cypress trees that partially hide the workshop from the house. You're standing beyond them, by the workshop door. I know it's you, although I can't see your face clearly, you're too far away. You're not wearing your school uniform this time. You're wearing the blue jeans that you change into when you come home from school and a pink anorak with the hood up, because it's chilly in the garden in March at this time of day. I can't bear that I can't see your face clearly, that I can't see if you're smiling or not. I throw the potato and peeler down into the bowl and run for the back door, over the grass, past the trees, but before I reach the workshop I can see that you're not there anymore. I can see that you've gone.

I park the car just down the road from the house where he lives and sit in it, smoking a cigarette with the engine turned off. I gave up years ago when I was pregnant, when you were on the way, but now I've started again. Silk Cut Extra Mild, a pack of twenty a day. I imagine you frowning, hear your voice in my head. *Mum, they're bad for you. They'll give you cancer.* 'What does it matter now?' I say back to you, but I still feel guilty.

What am I doing here? I could still turn back. I could start the engine, drive away. I could go home. But I don't. I stub out the cigarette, climb out of the car and lock the door, start walking back up the few yards to the house. It's an ordinary enough house. A terrace with a small neat bay and a stripped wooden door. The outside is pebble-dashed and painted white. There's a small front garden with pots of shrubs and daffodils nodding their heads in the weak sunshine. I ring the doorbell and the door opens almost straight away. A man with his hair pulled back in a ponytail, early forties, wearing a black T-shirt and jeans, holds out his hand to me.

'Mrs Jenkins? You found the house all right?'

'Yes, no trouble at all.'

'Do come in,' he says, stepping aside to make room for me.

I step into the hallway, and follow him through a door that leads into an interior room. The room is painted lilac and blue. There are candles everywhere, a low table with packs of cards on it and a crystal ball. What am I doing here? I think to myself. What am I doing?

'Do sit down,' he says, motioning towards a low armchair, and he sits opposite me on the small sofa.

'I take it this is your first time?' he says, then, seeing the confusion on my face – the first time for what, the first time I have lost a daughter? – 'The first time you've come to see a medium, I mean,' he corrects himself, slightly flustered.

I tell him it is. I tell him I'm feeling nervous. I tell him I'm not sure I should be here at all.

'I was brought up a Christian, you see,' I explain. 'C. of E. Sunday school every week. They don't approve of this sort of thing, do they, the Church?'

'No,' he says, calmly, flatly. 'Unfortunately they misunderstand our work.'

We sit there for a moment in silence. It could be like the room where I visit the bereavement counsellor, only here there's more for me to look at. A small Buddha head carved in dark wood on a shelf, a ceramic dragon glossed a fiery red, a picture of a rainbow on the wall. The rainbow arches above a plain of corn, a line of dark-blue hills in the background.

'Mrs Jenkins,' he says at last, 'there's really nothing here to fear, nothing to be nervous of. Would you mind if I light a candle?'

I tell him no. A candle is all right. Candles are, after all, what they have in churches. He lights a tall cream candle and the flame gutters down for a moment into the wax and then springs up again, steady and strong, and all of a sudden, watching it, I feel safe, I feel OK. The nerves are gone.

'Mrs Jenkins, I work in a number of ways. I sometimes use the tarot cards to channel spirit, or the crystal ball, or we could try psychometry.'

'Psy . . . psycho . . . what?'

'It's where I'm given an object that was once owned by the person who has passed on to the other side. It helps me link with the vibrations. But I didn't mention this to you on the phone and I don't expect you have brought anything.'

But I'm reaching into my bag, taking out my small red leather purse and opening it, fishing with my fingers down into its depths amongst the coins. I hook out a small gold cross on its chain and hold it out towards him.

'This was my daughter's. She was wearing it when . . . she had the accident.'

I tip it gently into the palm of his hand. He closes his thick fist around it and draws it towards his chest, as if he knows how precious it is.

'This'll do fine,' he says softly, closing his eyes. Silence again. I hear the very faint hiss of the candle flame eating up wax, the ticking of a clock on the wall. But the silence between us is full of softness, like a bed of feathers into which my thoughts roll free.

I am praying beneath my breath, beneath the level of words, that she will come – that *you* will come – into that room and sit down with us. That you will be wearing your newly washed and ironed uniform, like you were on the first day you came to me in the kitchen. You will be smiling again and happy, and joy will penetrate my heart like a thunderbolt.

'I see a child. She is about twelve or thirteen. She was taken suddenly from this world. An accident, it seems. Yes, a car accident. There has been much sorrow around this passing but the child is happy, she is well in the spirit world. She doesn't want you to grieve so much anymore.'

How much did I tell him, I think, how much did I say on the phone? But he must have picked up on my scepticism; he must feel it in the room, like a wall going up.

'I have a name – beginning with "L". And an anniversary in June. A birthday, perhaps. She says, "Tell her about the cat we used to have, the cat named Sheba. Tell her about Gemma with the long blonde plaits who used to live next door. Tell her I miss the lemon meringue pie."'

I must be crying. I can taste salt tears in the corner of my mouth. It's like she's in this room with us; she is slipping her cool hand into mine.

'Tell her the uniform is clean again. The blood is all washed out. But she says, "She'll know that anyway." She says you'll know what she means.'

'Yes, I know,' I say.

He is looking beyond me, through me. At something at the periphery of his vision, just past my face.

'Yes, I see,' he mutters quietly, under his breath. 'Yes, I'll tell her that.'

He is looking at me more directly now. The energy in the room has fallen; I draw my arms across my chest, feeling cold. He lowers his voice.

'Mrs Jenkins, she says she is worried about her father.

"Tell her," she says, "to look inside the workshop." Do you understand this at all?'

I shake my head. 'No, n-no, I don't understand. That makes no sense at all.'

Liar, I hear you say inside my head. *Remember yesterday, in the garden, the small figure you saw standing by the workshop door. Wearing the pink anorak, its hood up, shadowing her face.*

Silence again. But now a cold jagged silence. I want to rush out, go home. Forget I'd ever been.

He smiles at me, a quick, wan smile. Suddenly he looks tired.

'I think she's left us now, Mrs Jenkins. I don't think I can get anything else.' He unlocks his fingers and holds the small gold cross out to me, slides it back into my hand. I put it away quickly in my purse.

We stand up. He shakes my hand.

'I hoped you found it helpful, Mrs Jenkins. If not now, then later. We can't control what the spirits tell us. We're just a channel; we have to give out what we're given.'

I offer him money but he declines, says what he has is a gift and it's his duty to give it back freely.

He sees me to the door, shakes my hand.

'By the way, who was the man who was standing behind you all the time, his hand resting on your shoulder? Mid-fifties, thick grey hair. Wearing a green pullover, a three-leaved clover embroidered on the left-hand side in gold.'

'That was my father,' I hear myself telling him, as if it's something that happened every day. 'He died when I was sixteen.'

12

When I get home the house is empty. I run upstairs and get into bed, get right down under the duvet with all my clothes on, and pull the duvet up to my ears.

It's not about you. Forgive me, but that time it's not about you.

Who was that standing behind you, he said, *wearing a green V-necked pullover with an embroidered clover leaf in gold?*

He was planning to play golf, out on the greens in all weathers, get lots of exercise, slim down, keep fit, acquire a network of golfing buddies, improve his handicap. In between building a new conservatory on to the house and an aviary at the bottom of the garden to breed canaries in. What I've always wanted to do, breed canaries, he'd said that morning when he announced to us the early retirement plan. The car plant where he had worked for thirty years was making changes in its workforce, trimming it down. The shop stewards were working overtime, winding everyone up. But Dad was OK about it. A blessing in disguise, he'd said that evening, telling my mum and me the news. He'd get a lump sum which he'd put towards paying off the mortgage. A little left over for a holiday for all of us, somewhere in the sun perhaps. Spain, the South of France. And seven years' enhanced company pension. Yes, we'd have to tighten our belts after that. But he was ready for a rest. Ready to get to do all those things he'd always wanted to do but had never had time.

Be careful what you dream for, my grandmother used to say. I hadn't understood her then. We didn't get to have that holiday in the sun. It seemed too extravagant in the end, with no real wage coming in. And Skegness or Scarborough in a caravan had always done for us before. What was the use of changing old ways? And anyway the cost of materials for the conservatory and aviary were more than he had bargained for. He even got a pair of mating birds, from the *Exchange and Mart*. But he only kept them a couple of months. The female laid eggs. I'd seen them there in the small nest, amongst shreds of paper and cotton wool. Tiny and translucent, shimmering with possibility. But none of them hatched and my dad put them back up for sale. 'Why?' I asked him. 'Birds are meant to be free,' he said. 'Not stuck in a cage, like I was for thirty years.' But there was something in his voice that made me think he was missing that cage still, in a way. He was free now, supposedly. But his wings were still clipped.

The golf didn't last long either. My mum had bought him that golfing sweater as an early retirement present, and he'd bought himself a pair of golfing slacks, and loafers, and a light grey jacket for when the weather was less clement, and a new set of clubs. In the first few months he was out there on the greens twice a week, with men from the factory that had also been laid off, or early retired. But then the matches got less regular. Some of the other men he played with got new jobs, some drifted off to hang around the pubs instead. And my dad started to lose interest.

'They're a lot of snobs up at that golf course, anyway. Half of 'em never done a real day's work in their lives.'

When the autumn came in on a north wind the golf went for a Burton, despite the weatherproof jacket my dad had bought for the colder weather. And the sweater stayed folded in the drawer and the jacket in the wardrobe and I'd come home from school and see the new clubs standing in the golf bag by the umbrella stand in the hall, all polished and shiny, and know my dad hadn't been out. Not out playing golf, anyway. By then he'd joined the gaggle of older men, men who'd given up hope of new jobs, down at the pub instead. Two or three hours he'd spend there in the middle of the day, reading the paper or playing a few rounds of snooker. Or just grumbling about the state of the world. How the Thatcher government and the yuppies were making this country go to the dogs, were ruining the lot of the working classes. And then he'd roll home dopey on drinking pints in the middle of the day and go to bed for a snooze and I'd come home from school and find him there snoring and my mother doing extra hours as a care assistant at a nursing home. If he was still in bed when she'd get home at six, laden with groceries for tea, and her face pale and pinched and tired from the long shifts and resentment, because she had to work harder now there was no decent wage coming in, there'd be hell to pay. I'd keep out the way, hide myself in my room with *Crossroads* on my portable black-and-white and homework books open I was pretending to do, and I'd hear her go at him, call him a useless good-for-nothing, a waste of space. And I'd hear him have a go back, tell her to get off his back, tell her she was a nagging castrating bitch. Then sometimes the ugly words would suddenly dry up to a whimper, to a muffled, padded, clogged-up whimper, like a dog in pain, like someone choking on tears and rage. I'd know my dad had hit out at my mum because he'd felt driven to, to silence the pinched hating face stuck up towards his. My mother would limp upstairs, holding her hurt rage inside, and shut herself in her room and my dad would clatter about in the kitchen and I'd know I had another evening of getting my own tea. Opening a can of beans and having them on toast and eating silently across the table from my dad who would bow his head over his plate and speak to me in a small remorseful voice.

But I didn't blame him. I blamed her. Because she couldn't see that he did those things because he was hurting. He wanted to be what he'd always been, for as long as I could remember. My warrior-dad, my hero. But all she could do was rub salt in the wounds.

I blamed her when *it* happened. I blame her still.

Who's the man in his mid-fifties, thick greying hair, standing behind you, his hand firmly on your shoulder?

I lay on the bed and sobbed my heart out that afternoon, Laura, not because of you but because suddenly I remembered what it had really felt like, that June afternoon when I came home from school. It was weeks before I was due to sit my 'O' levels. My hormones were all over the place. I was in love with a sixth-former called Gerry who played drums in a band. I planned to revise for my English exam that evening for two hours, then meet him in the bus shelter in town. If his parents were out he would take me home with him. We'd go up to his room and lie on his thin, creaking bed and kiss each other till our lips were sore to Dire Straits playing on his stereo, below a poster of Madonna in thigh-high boots pouting red lips at us. But I did none of that in the end.

When I came home my mother was home from work and was sitting in the lounge with Mrs Davey from next door. There was a strange feeling in the house. I felt it the minute I came in. Something not quite right. They turned to look at me as I came through the door and my mother's face was all blotchy and red.

'Your dad's had a heart attack,' my mother said. Her voice sounded mechanical, as if she didn't know what she was saying. 'Mrs Davey found him lying on the lawn.'

I knew they'd already been and taken him away, but I walked all over the house, into every room. As if I needed to make sure he wasn't still there. Playing hide and seek, like he used to do when I was little. Out of the bedroom window I could see the Flymo lying on its side on the back lawn.

'Do you think this is wise, Lisa? You're in a very vulnerable state. These people could be seen as exploiting people such as yourself, people who are vulnerable.'

She doesn't approve, Angela, the counsellor. I knew she wouldn't. Maybe that's why I told her.

'But it's helped me. I feel better since I went to see him.'

'In what way has it helped you? How do you feel better?'

'I don't know – more accepting of what's happened, I suppose. Like maybe it has some purpose, only I don't know what it is yet. The things he said were so true; he must have been getting this knowledge from her.'

She is looking at me with a smug smile playing at the corners of her mouth. She doesn't want to believe it's helped me. She doesn't want to believe in anything other than her psychology books, her training in the bereavement process. The six stages. Where am I at now?

'Lisa, how do you see yourself progressing with counselling? Do you feel you still need to make this commitment?'

How do you see yourself moving on? she means. How do I?

'I think I'll be all right now. I think I'm past the worst.'

She looks relieved. She'll shake her head, see me to the door, think that's another client she's supported through the grieving process.

'You've done really well, Lisa. Really well, considering you've been seeing me for only three months. Please feel free to come back and see me if things start getting difficult again. If you feel yourself getting stuck.'

She makes it sound like grief is a kind of glue. It had coated my limbs with its fine adhesion, stopped me moving forward. But now when the allotted hour is up, as I shake her hand, as I find myself saying, 'Thank you for all your support,' as I walk down the path and through the gate into the street, into my own future again, my limbs unglue themselves, the clockwork of my life is set into forward motion again, and I'm feeling a strange surging of excitement.

It's like something's waiting to happen. Some adventure. I'm weaving a small thread in the pattern, and Laura's still there, weaving the pattern with me. I don't want to go home. Not yet. I can't face it. I think of that house with its empty rooms, its silences, like it's a train that's stopped at a railway station and can't move on again. I've got off the train; I've got tired of waiting.

I drive into town and walk around for a bit, trying to hang on to this feeling of excitement, terrified that if I go back home it'll fade into the magnolia walls, into the silence and I'll feel stuck again. The fine sediment of glue creeping back and coating my limbs. I go into stores and buy clothes on my debit card, charged to the joint account I have with Derek, thinking, Why not? I've never done this before, been this frivolous. Why not just this once, when I'm feeling like a new person, doing new things? I buy a couple of tops with plunging necklines, bright colours I've rarely worn before. A skirt in a soft material that clings to my shape, sling-back shoes with heels in summer pastels. I try them on in the cubicle and swing around, seeing reflected in the mirror this new person, this person who's moving on with her life.

I still don't want to go home. With my purchases in their smart carrier bags swinging from my arm I wander down side streets, find a cafe with stripped-pine floors and café lattes on the menu, little tarts of goats' cheese and sun-dried tomatoes, spinach-and-ricotta quiches, sitting temptingly in the glass counter. I sit at a table with a red-and-white-checked tablecloth, stir my café latte and think, There are decisions to be made. Big ones. And I know I'll have to make them sooner or later. And I don't feel scared. After Laura, there is nothing left to be scared of losing.

'Excuse me, dear, do you mind if I join you?'

A lady in her mid-fifties. She has got up from another

table and walked over to mine. She's wearing a green coat, is carrying bags of shopping. I want to say, Yes, I do really, why can't you stay where you were? But I nod instead and she sits down. She shuffles her bags onto the floor, under the table. She looks at me. Her face is ordinary, she could be anyone, any middle-aged lady passing hours of her day, shopping, having coffee, trying to strike up conversation with a stranger, so she can go home to her empty house and feel she's done something with her day. I find myself wondering if she has grown children, grandchildren, a husband she can talk to who comes home every evening for his tea.

'My dear, I hope you don't mind me speaking to you, but I felt I had to. The girl who was with you when you came in. The girl in the blue school uniform. She's gone now, but she was there beside you when you first came in. You know who she is, don't you?'

My heart starts racing. I stare back at her, horrified.

'Your life is going to change soon, my dear. It'll be difficult, but it'll be for the best. You're very psychic, my dear. But you know that, don't you?'

'I don't know what you mean,' I mumble, groping for my bag, putting my jacket back on. Her turn now to stare at me, horrified.

'I'm sorry, dear. I didn't mean to upset you.'

'You don't know what you're saying. You shouldn't say these things, you've no right.'

I scatter some change onto the table.

'I'm sorry, dear, yes, perhaps I was mistaken . . .'

I rush outside into the street.

13

It was unusual for it to happen so suddenly like that, out of
the blue. No prior warnings, no pains in his chest or up his
arms. And my dad who'd been fit all his life, had rarely had
a day off sick. And still quite young, only fifty-six. I didn't sit
my English exam. I didn't take any 'O' levels. I could have
gone back in the autumn and taken them but I didn't. There
seemed no point. I sat around the house and watched endless
television that numbed my mind and ate chocolate and grew
fat. Gerry kept coming around the house to see me and he'd
sit there on the sofa with me, talking about stuff I couldn't
bear to think about. Who in our group at school had passed
their exams and who'd failed. Who was going out with who.
What gig his band were planning next. I'd grunt and just
stare at him, not wanting to know. Not caring. My world
had shrunk to the sofa and the television and a box of
chocolates. So he'd got bored and drifted away and no doubt
went and got himself a proper girlfriend, one who had a life.

Eventually, after waiting for me to grow out of it and
getting worried that I wasn't, my mother took me to the
doctor's and he put me on a course of antidepressants then
sent me to the local hospital to sit in a room with a group of

blank-faced despairing teenagers who all thought there was no point in living, just like me. Maybe their apathy was what set me on the road to recovery, because I got so sick of them going on, moaning and moaning, that I'd get really angry with them sometimes, and the anger was a good thing. It was like a switch switching me on again. Ungluing me. I started going out with a bloke called Pete who dressed from head to toe in black and wore black eyeliner and was into all things gothic. But eventually I got sick of him; he was always talking about death and dying, about a thousand and one ways to kill yourself. So I told him one day he was a waste of space and if dying was all he was interested in then why didn't he just go ahead and do it, nobody would care. Then I left the group and stopped taking the antidepressants and went out and got myself a place at the local college to learn office skills. From the outside, to the new friends I was making at college, to my mother, I began to look normal again. I smiled at jokes and laughed at sitcoms on the telly, and started to care about what I looked like again. I'd go out with my new friends to a disco or a party once in a while. But on the inside there was this frozen place. This hard knotted scar that felt ice cold, that nobody else knew was there.

My mother got on with her life. She stopped working at the nursing home and started working for Sainsbury's, on the tills to begin with, but then within months she was promoted to supervisor. I watched her changing, small things at first that no one else would really have noticed except me. Exchanging the plain skirts and jumpers she'd always worn to the nursing home for tighter black skirts and blouses with low necklines. Growing her hair longer and having highlights put in it. Buying high-heeled shoes and new earrings and bright vivid lipsticks she'd paint carefully on her mouth before going to work every day. Then little more than a year from my dad being found lying dead, face down on the grass, she joined a social club for the unattached and took up jive classes, and even, to my disgust, clubbing on Saturday nights. I would sit at home alone, watching late-night films, and she'd swing through the front door humming small catches of tunes and smiling to herself at some silly memory from her evening out.

And then of course she started dating again. A woman of forty-six, dating. Lovesick and preoccupied and waiting for the phone to ring. Bringing them home even, the odd time. These leery men who spoke too loudly and tried too hard to be nice to me, but I wasn't having it. I wasn't giving an inch.

'Why can't you at least be polite?' my mother would complain.

'Why should I?' I'd say, but she had the upper hand, didn't she. It was her house; she could do as she liked. And then she went and married one of them, she married Graham from Sales, and I moved out. I was nineteen then. I moved down to London, to Harrow, and got a job in accounts with a small computer firm. I rented a flat with some girls from work. Then I moved out to Watford where the rent was a little cheaper, changed my job to the one in the garage, and a few years later I met Derek and that was that. The rest is history, they say.

Did I ever tell you any of this stuff, Laura? Did you ever know? My unfinished business, they call it. Are things ever really finished? I don't think so. I think we carry all the bad stuff like frozen embryos inside us, sealed into our cells. And if something should happen, later down the line, if something should break the seal and the thing should thaw and start to grow, God help us. That's what I think. God help us.

No, I don't think you ever knew; it wouldn't have showed. On the surface everything was what it should be. And she doted on you, her only grandchild, why wouldn't she? But deep inside, I never forgave her. For not understanding more, for those words, spoken in anger in the kitchen while I pretended to be doing homework in my room upstairs. *You're just a drunken good-for-nothing, that's what you are.* For my dad's absence when I came home that day. A coronary arrest, the doctor said. But people die of broken hearts, don't they. People do.

'I'm leaving him.'

Sheila puts her coffee cup down on the table. She looks at me. There's no judgement in her face. Just a space waiting for understanding.

'Are you sure that's what you want to do?'

'Yes.'

'You don't love him anymore?'

But we both know it's not just that. It's worse than just love stopping. It's like love never really being there to begin with. It's like waking up to the fact that I've been living with a stranger, sleeping with him, having a child with him, burying that child with this stranger, this person I don't really know at all.

Sheila lives in a neat new-build semi in a cul-de-sac. There are probably thousands and thousands of houses that all look similar to Sheila's, but for me today, now, there's no other place like it; it's the only place I want to be. Sheila has these cream Shaker-style units, and above them, small square pale-blue tiles, the colour of the sky, and the kitchen walls are cream too. There's this light coming through the kitchen window, the kind of light that only belongs to April, a soft clean light that makes everything look new and fresh, so that I can't see the smudges and the fingerprints, the marks on the walls where the plaster has been touched up. And Sheila's face looks softer too, younger, her ashy hair framing her head against the light like a halo. I walk to the sink and place my empty cup on the draining board and through the window I can see that the forsythia is pricked with blossoming buds, like tiny stars of gold, and I think, Yes, yes, it is possible to begin again. It's always possible. Even after the hardest winter the leaves and the flowers have the courage, the daring to put out their colour, their new life.

'Have you told him how you feel yet?' Sheila is saying. I turn to look at her.

'Not yet. No. But I will.'

But I didn't have to in the end.

'Mrs Jenkins?'

The policeman at the door is youngish. Thirty-two, thirty-three. But they say all policemen look younger when you get older yourself. Although I can't be that much older – four or five years? But no matter how young they look there's still something about the uniform that makes you feel you're on shaky ground, that you need to watch what you say. Like the way you felt when you were a kid waiting outside the headmaster's office.

'Yes?'

'Is your husband in, Mrs Jenkins?'

Maybe I should have asked to see his badge, his ID. He could have been anyone; he could have borrowed the uniform, stolen it. But I didn't.

'No, I'm afraid he isn't.'

He looked surprised. Seven o'clock. Isn't that the time most men are home with their wives? Finishing their tea, settling down to watch something on the TV.

'Do you know where he is, Mrs Jenkins?'

Why do I feel I have seen him before? Something stirring, ripples under the water.

'No, I don't.'

More surprise. I feel like an idiot saying it, I feel like a fool.

'Any idea what time he'll be back?'

'No, I'm sorry I don't know that either, officer. My husband and I . . . you see, we're not very close.'

Why did I say that? Why did he need to know that? What business was it of his, anyway? Maybe I needed to say the words out loud so I would hear them. *My husband and I aren't very close.* For that, read we don't talk anymore. There is no thread that links his life with mine, in spite of the fact he is supposed to live in this house, that sometimes he still takes his meals here, sometimes still sleeps here. (In separate rooms, always in separate rooms.) In spite of the fact that for thirteen years we shared a child's life together, and five months ago we buried her. In spite of that, officer, we are strangers.

He stands there, like he doesn't quite know what to do. Like he hadn't anticipated this, Derek not being in. He shifts his weight from foot to foot.

'Has he done something wrong?'

Funny, someone puts on a uniform and everyone starts feeling guilty. It's like a weapon, that uniform.

He hesitates again, he glances away to his car, then back again, and I think there's something wrong here. There's something not quite what it should be.

'Would you mind if I came in for a few moments, Mrs Jenkins? We've had a few complaints about your husband's behaviour. I'd like to discuss them with you privately.'

I let him in. Again, it's the uniform. He could be a rapist, a serial killer, but wearing that uniform, he'd get away with it, wouldn't he.

He follows me into the house and through into the kitchen and I offer him a cup of tea and as I'm filling the kettle I think it's like he's giving me the upper hand; he's a guest and I'm playing host. He's sat down at the kitchen table and he's removed his hat and put it down on the table and smoothed his hair. He is getting ready to speak, getting ready to say something, clearing his throat.

'I'm very sorry about your daughter, Mrs Jenkins.'

I was pouring the hot water into the teapot when he said that and a tremor started in my hand and for a second I had to stop pouring and grip the handle of the kettle harder to control it, so as not to spill it. How did he know about you,

Laura? How did he know *that*? I carry on pouring, but I don't have the upper hand now; he does.

'Is my daughter's ... accident anything to do with why you're here, officer?'

I replace the lid of the teapot and set out the cups.

'I'm not sure, Mrs Jenkins. It might be.'

I stand with my back to him looking out of the kitchen window. I can see the workshop down at the bottom of the garden.

Look in the workshop, you're saying. Your voice in my head is like my thoughts made clearer. Like my thoughts made so clear I can see them. Dark shadows traced under water.

'Milk and sugar?'

'Yes, please. One sugar.'

I can hear the clock ticking and I think, No matter what we are doing the clock is ticking. Even though time has stopped for us, even though it may have stopped for good, the clock is ticking. Moving us on. Moving the world nearer.

Nearer? you say, in my head again. *Nearer?*

I stir the teapot and pour out the tea. My best china cups. I place the cups on the kitchen table and sit down opposite him. He looks at me, then looks away. He seems uneasy. Why does a man in a uniform need to be uneasy, I think.

'This must be a very difficult time for you,' he says.

'What's my husband done, officer? Has he done something wrong?'

He's putting me on edge now. He's making me feel defensive. Isn't that the word she'd use, Angela the counsellor? Defensive.

He sips his tea, winces at the heat.

'I'm not here to arrest your husband, Mrs Jenkins. I just want to talk to him. There's a reason to be concerned about his behaviour.'

I wait. He looks at the clock on the wall. He picks up his cup again, blows it gently, sips it, clatters the cup down in the saucer.

'Have you heard of Jack Philips, Mrs Jenkins?'

I sometimes have this funny feeling that all the people who are going to be important to me in my life, all their names, are written down on scraps of paper and put into a hat and before I was born I picked the names out of the hat and decided what role each will play. This one will be my mother. This one, the man I'll marry. This one, *Laura*, will be my daughter. Is that where I'd heard the name before? I'd seen it on a scrap of paper? This one, *Jack Philips*, will be the man who'll kill my daughter – even though I know it was an accident. *A policeman on his way home from duty was driving the grey BMW* . . . I have suddenly remembered where I have seen this policeman before. He'd been there at the inquest, sitting next to that Jack Philips.

'No, I'm afraid not.'

I want him to work for it. I won't make it easy.

Jack Philips. His name had been called when he took the stand. I hadn't wanted to listen. Hadn't wanted to see him as a person with a name.

'Jack Philips was the driver in your daughter's accident, Mrs Jenkins.'

He lowers his voice, pauses. I can feel him watching me,

waiting for a reaction. He gets none. I'm staring down at the toast crumbs on the table, examining whorls in the wood. I want to pick at them with my nail, as if they're scabs.

'Why are you here, officer? What's my husband's behaviour got to do with him?'

'There is reason to believe that your husband might be stalking his family, Mrs Jenkins.'

'Stalking?'

'He's been seen several times standing outside Mr Philips' house. Then a few days ago, his wife was sure she saw him outside her daughter's school.'

'There must be some mistake. My husband is quite an ordinary-looking man. There must be lots of men who look like him . . .'

'They're both quite sure it was your husband, Mrs Jenkins.'

'Are you this man's friend, officer? Is that why you're here?'

He twitches, his hand momentarily goes to his shirt collar.

'I hardly think that's relevant, Mrs Jenkins.'

'The police haven't sent you, have they? You're here on your own accord.'

'The family are concerned, that's all, Mrs Jenkins. They're concerned about what he might do next.'

Remembrance falls like a clear drop of rain. He was there at the coroner's court. He took the stand, gave a testimony about Jack Philips' driving. *In my opinion the accident couldn't have been avoided. He was driving with due care and attention . . .*

'What do you want me to do about it?'

Anger, that's what I'm feeling. He's given back the power; I've the upper hand again.

'I was hoping you could talk to him, make him see sense.'

'You're not here officially, are you? You're here because you're that man's friend. You thought you'd warn Derek off.'

They know how the uniform works, how it makes people feel.

He puts down his cup and stands up, picks up his hat.

'Thanks for the tea, Mrs Jenkins. Very kind of you. I didn't intend to distress you. Perhaps I'll call back when your husband is here . . .'

'Well if you do, I hope you do it officially. My husband's committed no crime . . .'

He left. I heard the car door open and slam, I heard the car drive away. I sat there for a while at the kitchen table doing nothing. I finished my tea. I stood up and placed the empty cups in the sink. I ran the hot water into the bowl and washed them, along with a few plates left over from breakfast, and while I was washing them I looked up and over towards the workshop. It was getting dark now. The garden was full of shadows, full of suggestions of shapes crouched behind trees and behind shrubs. Funny how the dark brings so much uncertainty. Things seen in the daytime just are what they are. In the dark, anything is possible.

Go and look, I hear you say. *Look in there*. I take Derek's workshop key from the nail where it's hanging over the kitchen door and walk slowly through the garden. The workshop is locked. It always is. I fumble the key into the lock. It finds its place and turns. I push the door open with a creak, go in.

What am I expecting to see? I don't know. At first I see nothing, nothing extraordinary. Derek's tools hanging up on their racks, the workbench brushed clean and tidy. The vice is fixed to the edge of the worktable, its jaws open and empty. Then I turn around. On the back wall of the workshop, plastered from floor to ceiling, an array of newsprint. Photographs and text, newspaper articles either torn with ragged edges, or cut out carefully into geometric shapes and thumb-tacked to the wall. I walk over and begin to read them.

A mother and her toddler were ploughed into by a hit-and-run driver while walking home from nursery school. The toddler, aged two and a half, died outright from multiple injuries. The distraught mother, Mrs Sarah Bradshaw who lives in Bushey, said the car seemed to come out of nowhere; they had no warning. Police are calling for witnesses.

Stephen Foster, 18, a student from South Oxhey, received severe spinal injuries after being knocked down by a van on a zebra crossing. It is thought he may never walk again. The driver, Darren White, 30, was found guilty of reckless driving and received a suspended sentence . . .

I read on and on. A whole family crushed to death in a car when an unsecured load slipped off the back of a lorry. A teenage girl killed when her drunken boyfriend lost control on a bend. An old lady run down while crossing the road. A motorcyclist grievously injured when a reckless van driver cut him up on a roundabout. And there at the centre, Laura. Three snippets taken from three local papers. In one, there's even a photograph. Laura in her school uniform, smiling.

A 13-year-old girl was fatally injured in a collision with a grey BMW while crossing the road. The driver, a policeman on his way home from duty, said at the inquest he didn't have time to stop . . .

I didn't think we had a monopoly on suffering. But when you're in it, cocooned by it, when it extends to the far edges of your known universe, there's no room for anyone else's grief, only your own. But the world is full of it, choked by it. Accidents and bad, bad stuff happen to people every day. Children with their lives blighted or ended, families destroyed. Every day. And this wall, just the smallest tip of the iceberg. Behind it, all the newspaper stories that Derek did not see, did not cut out. The endless lives destroyed, shunt up like silent witnesses, cram this small space with ghosts . . .

I hear a noise behind me, feel somebody standing there, and I think it's you. I think I can smell the particular scent of your skin, your hair and I turn, but it's not you I see.

'What are you doing here?' Derek says.

His voice is as cool as the ocean, his face as still and empty as snow.

Nothing happens. No violence. Derek has never raised a hand against me, so why should he now? I have found him out, discovered, if you like, his secret. But what after all is his crime? To build a shrine to our daughter, that's all. To build a shrine to her, and to all those other sons and daughters, who died so needlessly. Is that so bad? But I've opened a window on something now, and I can't close it.

What had I wanted when I married him? A father figure,

I suppose. He was fifteen years older. He was settled, with a home of his own. He was a man of means. He would take care of me, and in return, then, what had he wanted? Someone who wouldn't ask too many questions, who would accept him the way he was, even if the way he was turned out to be something unknown to me like this.

Like a man who walks the streets for hours, never saying where he's going or what he's doing. Who stalks people, who cuts articles on road accidents out of papers and builds a secret shrine out of them. If he's capable of this, what else is he capable of? What other windows will I need to open to see him the way he really is? And when all those windows are open, where will love be? Where is it now? Where was it ever?

Angela, the counsellor, asked me some weeks back, 'Do you love Derek, or just need him?'

'Aren't they the same?' I answered.

He looks at me. There in his workshop, before the wall of newsprint, before all that pain. But his look reveals nothing. He's pulling the blinds down again, his mouth shutting tight on words, his pupils shrinking back.

'I want you to go, Derek. I want you to leave. We'll put the house on the market, go our separate ways. But I want you to go. Tonight.'

'Have it your own way,' he says.

The sort of thing a child would say. And I thought he was the adult, the parent, the one who would take care of me. Who would take the place of you, Dad, who'd fill the absence you left. He turns sharply and walks out, walks down the garden towards the house. I watch him go. I watch the stiffness of his shoulders, the jerky movement of his legs. I watch him like someone watching something that's common-place, and being unmoved by it. No shock, no sorrow. Like watching the postman walk down the path, like watching a neighbour pass by.

I slowly begin to take down the newsprint from the wall, easing out the stiff thumb tacks with the edge of a putty knife. I take down each one and place them carefully in a pile on the worktable. When I have finished I pick up the pile and put them away in the drawer at the front of the workbench.

But I leave the ones of you, Laura. I leave those.

For days I just sit at home in the empty house. It's easy sometimes just to pass time, to let it slip through you leaving nothing changed. I want it to be like that, an empty vacant space, nothing filling it. I walk from room to room, I pick up a book or magazine, then lay it down again. I put on the television or radio for a short while but the sound of human voices, life humming into my head, is too real to bear for long. I make myself cups of tea, open cans of soup for lunch, make toast, but leave the food, what little there is of it, half eaten. I want to feel thin and vacuous, so that time can slip through me more easily.

He packed his two bags with clothes but took nothing else. I stood at the door when he left and watched him load the bags into the car.

'What do you want to do about money?' he said.

I shrugged, not being able to think about it. Money had too much to do with the real world, the everyday world, a world that had meaning in it, where my daughter hadn't died.

'I don't know. I'll get a job.'

'I'm willing to pay the bills for a few months, send you housekeeping. Then we'll see.'

'Thanks,' I said. He didn't have to do that, he didn't have to be that reasonable. 'I'll get in touch with estate agents. Put the house up for sale.'

'If you're sure,' he said. But I don't think he wanted me to change my mind. He looked almost relieved. It made it easier for him this way, he didn't have to pretend. He could build another shrine somewhere else now, not worry about me finding it out. He could go on doing what he's doing, stalking that man, that Jack Philips, trailing perhaps after every man who looked like him, planning God knows what.

What was he planning? I wanted to ask him, but I couldn't. Perhaps I was afraid of what he might say.

'If you need to get in touch you can reach me at work,' he said, and I said OK and he left.

In that empty house, wandering from room to room, with nothing to do but think, remember, picking up photographs in their frames, one of you smiling in your uniform, Derek and me on our wedding day, it is like my life has stopped again. The first time was when you died. The seventh of November, at five o'clock. But this time I'm glad of it.

I take the photo albums out from the box under the stairs and spend hours flicking through them. Your baby photos. You lying on a rug smiling up at the camera, tottering around my legs. Your first day at school, proud in your new school uniform, clutching your satchel as if it were a gift. And earlier photos. Me, maybe ten or eleven, standing between my parents on the prom at Skegness. My dad squinting in the sun. Who took the photo – did he stop and ask a stranger? *Would you mind taking a photo of my family?* – the shadows not yet looming over his head. Others when I'm younger, clutching at my mother's skirts, holding her hand. She's smiling down at me, and I think, Was it really like that? Were we ever as happy as that?

I talk to you a lot, in those empty days in that empty house. I talk to you all the time. Sitting on the sofa amongst that sea of photographs, standing before the kitchen window looking out at the garden. Colour is breaking out everywhere now, all the flowers coming into bloom and I think, Spring's a bad time to die, the worst time really. The world too loud and too bright. But a good time to be reborn.

And then after days of this, days of this empty house and the empty time on my hands and the space opening up in my head and in my heart, opening it up wide so that it feels as big as a church with only you in it, the memories of you, I collect all the photographs together, the albums full of those years of you, and the framed photographs, and I put them all into a large box and slide it under the stairs, under old coats and shoes. And then I phone the estate agents, Bradleys. I tell a man with a pleasant affable voice that I want to put my house on the market. He says he'll call around the next day at ten and give me a valuation and take some photos, if that is convenient, and I say yes, yes it is. And then I call Sheila.

'He's left, Sheila,' I say, calmly, matter-of-factly, as if I'm talking about the weather. 'We've split up.'

'Are you all right?' she asks, sounding concerned. A rush of questions on her lips she is holding back.

'I'm fine,' I say, because I am, really I am.

'I'll come around to see you tonight. Will you be in?'

I will be; it'll be good to see her, I say.

The next phone call is the hardest to make. As my fingers dial the number I can hear my blood beating in my ears. When she answers, when my mother answers, her voice sounds distant and tired, not like I remember it at all. Older and sadder, the anger squeezed out of her.

'Yes?'

'It's me, Mum. It's Lisa.'

A sharp intake of breath, then, 'Lisa! Lisa, is that really you?'

Then I tell my mother about you, about you dying, because she doesn't know, because I hadn't even told her. How could I have been that cruel? I expected anger, but I got none. We both sob together on the phone, and I say, 'I'm sorry, I'm so sorry,' and she says she is too. As I listen to the sounds of my mother's sobbing, press them to my ear, the room about me suddenly isn't empty anymore. It's full of ghosts. Yours, and my dad's too, and my stepdad's. Pressing close to me, wanting to comfort me, their breath on my cheek, their hands like the touch of falling leaves on my shoulders.

14

JACK

'I didn't see him, he wasn't in.'

I nudge the door up gently with my foot. I don't want Sam to overhear.

'I saw *her*, though. I saw his wife.'

'And?'

I remember her. That day outside the court. Smallish, mousy-haired, would pass easily in a crowd. She glanced up at me, then I looked quickly away. What did I see in her eyes, besides the pain?

'I told her about the stalking.'

'Christ, Dave!'

'I thought maybe it was better. She could talk to him, warn him off. If she knows, he'd think twice about doing it again. And anyway, she got on to me. She knew it wasn't a police matter.'

'Christ! She'll report you.'

'No, I don't think so. I had a feeling about her. Anyway, she doesn't know who I am.'

'It won't take them long to figure that out, will it? They know who I am.'

'Don't worry. I think it'll be all right.'

'We'll see. If he hangs around here again, I'll make it official next time. I'll file a report.'

'Sam OK? And the girls?'

'Yeah, they're fine. Thanks, Dave. Thanks anyway, mate. You didn't have to do that. You took a risk, you did.'

Sam's opened the kitchen door. She raises an eyebrow at me, mouths, *Who's that?*

I hang up.

'Dave,' I tell her. 'He just phoned up for a chat. Asked about you and the girls.'

Several weeks pass, and I'm beginning to think maybe he did the right thing, maybe it worked. I don't see him again. Mr Jenkins. If he doesn't come back, I wonder, will that also mean that I won't see her again, I won't see Laura. Then I realize that I want to. I want to see her again. I want to see her smooth unmarked skin, her smile.

'I'm not going back. I've made up my mind.'

Our usual Tuesday appointment. How comfortable this room feels to me. Over three months I've been coming here now, week in and week out. Except that week when I went down to Plymouth. You're going to Crete for a fortnight's holiday, and I feel slightly panicky that I won't be coming next week, or the week after. What will I do instead?

'Maybe it's too early to make definite decisions, Jack.'

'No, it won't change. I've made up my mind. I won't be going back.'

Back to putting on the uniform, to buttoning it up. To driving around in a car at night, while other people leading decent lives are sleeping in their beds. The kids hanging about on street corners, shooting up in alleys. Heroin, crack, whatever. Wasted. Or the drunks piling out of pubs and nightclubs. One look at the uniform and they threaten violence. Or try it, lunging at the uniform, lunging at what it stands for. Pure hate in their faces.

Fucking pigs. You're all the same.

And we are, I guess we are. The patronizing way we speak. *Come on, sonny. Come on, sunshine. What's this all about?* And then we lock some poor bastard up for the night, to sober up, to cool off. And in the morning we let them out, to go back to their miserable lives, to go and do it all again some other night. Or maybe it's the magistrates' court. Drunk and disorderly, possession of drugs, assaulting a police officer. A fine, or community service, a month inside maybe. But whatever, we're papering the cracks, sticking on a plaster, making ourselves feel better. Not them. For them it's no different. Just part of the cycle. Nothing's changed.

I tell you about that kid, what was his name? – Wayne something or other. It's always some Wayne, or Shane, some sad old cowboy name like that. Some dreaming single mother in a council flat, shut up with only the telly for company. He was young – sixteen, maybe seventeen – no more. I hadn't been in the force long – maybe a year. I would have just finished my probationary year. I hadn't brought him in, somebody else did, but I was on duty that night. He'd been found sitting on some street corner, no fixed abode, off his head on something, and brought in for the night. We had a sergeant in those days, Sergeant Jones. A tough kernel. In his fifties, been in the job too long. He'd barked questions at this kid and this kid was incoherent. Couldn't get beyond his name, his age. Couldn't give us an address. And when the sergeant started yelling a bit, losing it, his patience worn thin, the kid's face started twitching, little relays of fear flickering through his muscles, and his eyes were everywhere in the room but on the sergeant's face. They'd found some cannabis in his pockets – not much – half an ounce, but in those days it was enough. So he was put on a charge and chucked in the cells for the night. We'd done the usual things, taken off his belt, emptied his pockets. Every half an hour someone went down to check on him. I went down a few times. He was lying still on the bed, his face white as a sheet; he seemed to be sleeping. But in the morning he was dead. At the inquest they said it was his heart. His heart had given out. All the crack he'd had in his system that night. We didn't know that. But we should've. The doctor should have been called. I remember someone said to Jones that night that the kid was too quiet, too pale. They'd gone into the cell to listen to his breathing and it was so shallow they could hardly hear it. But Jones had said, 'Don't be daft, we're not here to be nursemaids; leave him to sleep it off.'

Nobody said anything against Jones at the inquest. Loyalty is what matters in this job. You close ranks, you protect yourselves. It's how you survive. We were only doing our duty. No one was found to blame.

'Do you blame yourself?' you say. Quietly.

'No, not really. Or at least, only so much as we're all to blame. We're all culpable, in a way, aren't we? A conspiracy of silence. Isn't that what you'd call it? Passing the buck, not taking responsibility. That kid – only seventeen – he shouldn't have been in there in the first place. That wasn't the right place for him, banged up in a cell, peeked at through a hole every half an hour. Maybe it wasn't just the crack he died of. Maybe it was fear too, maybe it was a broken heart.'

You look at me and for a moment you say nothing. Then.

'That's a very sad story, Jack.'

'Yeah.'

'So you don't want to be part of the silence anymore?'

'No.'

'Have you told Sam about your decision yet?'

I tell her that night. No point in waiting. The girls are in bed. I'm watching, pretending to watch, something on the Discovery channel. Something about the Egyptians, how they built the pyramids. All the imagination, all that hope. Sam is flicking through magazines.

'Fancy a glass of wine?' I ask her.

'That'll be nice.'

I go through to the kitchen and open a bottle of cabernet that's in the cupboard. When I come back into the living room Sam's put down her magazines. I hand her a glass.

'Jack, I've got something to tell you.'

I sit down with my glass of wine. This is not how it's meant to go. It should be the other way around.

'I've decided to get a job. It's time I did. A full-time job, that is. I've been making enquiries and Brenda – you know Brenda, she's got a little girl who goes to Bethan's school, same age. Well, she's got a job at the hospital as a receptionist and there's an opening there in the admissions department. I want to apply for it. The money's not great but it'll be a good start. What do you think?'

'It's up to you. If you want to . . .'

'It'll mean you'll have to look after Jessica. But she's at nursery now five mornings a week, so it'll only be for the afternoons. And pick up Bethan from school – twice a week from after-school club – that goes on till five . . .'

'It'll be all right, I can manage . . .'

I'm thinking all the time, It's like she knows. I haven't told her, but she knows.

'I know you're supposed to be off sick, Jack, but you're a lot better now, aren't you?'

She pauses. She looks at me. She's thinking, How much of this can I risk saying? How much? And then she goes for it.

'We need the money. Because you're not going back to work, are you? When the money runs out, when the sick pay stops in two months' time. It will, won't it? They don't have to pay you for more than six months. You won't go back, will you Jack?'

'No, I won't,' I tell her. How easy it is in the end to tell the truth. All those things that we think are hard to say. They're not in the end. By the time they need to be said, people know. They know anyway.

The trouble with having integrity, it doesn't let you off the hook. It makes life harder, and yet easier too. No shades of grey, not so many choices to get in the way. Having decided I wasn't going back, I had to tell Connor. I couldn't just pretend that I still might. I went into the station to see him. He closed the door, told me to sit down, asked about Sam and the kids, arranged for someone to bring in some coffee.

'So how you feeling these days? Still going to see that counsellor chap?'

'Yeah.'

'How's that going, then?'

How he hates it, talking about this stuff. Grown men, *policemen*, getting in touch with their feelings.

'It's going all right. It's helping.'

'So you'll be coming back soon, then, eh?'

This is my opening; I know what he wants me to say. I'll make it easy.

'I won't be coming back to work, Sergeant Connor.'

A quick flick of surprise, then relief. He couldn't hide it.

'Are you sure, Jack? It's a big decision.'

'I'm sure.'

'What will you do instead? You've a young family to support, after all.'

'Sam's going back to work full time. Eventually, of course, I'll need to look for something else.'

Twelve years I've done in the force. That earns a certain amount of loyalty. Twelve years of pension contributions for a start, nothing to be sniffed at. I'll be able to draw on it when I'm sixty. And they won't stop paying me straight away, the guy from HR explains. I'll get two months' full salary. 'Garden leave', he calls it. I like that. Sounds like I can sit in the garden for two months, taking in the sun and contemplating my navel, I tell him, joking. Yeah, something like that, he says. He's a friendly sort of guy, about forty something. The sort you could go for a drink with.

I remember thinking, You'll be proud of me, when I tell

you what I've done. Sorting things out, telling the truth.
You'll be proud of me when you come back from your
holiday, back from Crete, sitting there in that room of yours
with your tan, and I tell you what I've done. I find myself
wondering who you're with in Crete. Do you have a wife or
a girlfriend? Or are you on your own? How do you spend
your time? Poking around ancient sites, sitting on a beach, or
in a bar? How little I know about you, and how much you
know about me. It doesn't seem right, somehow.

And it's about then that the letter arrives.

My uncle Keith forwards it on. In a short covering letter he
explains how after my visit he'd remembered it, remembered
getting it in the post shortly after my dad had tried to see me,
all those years ago. He'd looked for it for ages, couldn't
remember throwing it away, couldn't remember what he'd
done with it. Only that he hadn't wanted me to see it. And
then, after he'd given up on it, it suddenly turns up, buried
in a drawer amongst other stuff. Out-of-date insurance poli-
cies, household bills. The letter's still in its envelope, but the
envelope has been opened, and for a moment I feel a surge of
anger, thinking, He opened it, my uncle Keith. He opened it
and didn't tell me, and for an instant I'm that kid again with
all that resentment festering slowly inside me. But then I let
it go. It was so long ago; there's been so much water under
the bridge. I'm too tired for resentment now.

The letter is waiting for me on the doorstep when I get
back from dropping Jessica at nursery. I sit down at the
kitchen table. The radio is on but I hardly hear it. The other
time kicks in again. The slow-motion, almost standstill time.

I notice the postmark. Bristol again. The date, twenty-four years ago. All that time, the letter waiting like a time bomb amongst my uncle's papers. Why didn't he find it when they moved? Surely they sifted through things, threw things away? Maybe he did, but couldn't bring himself to throw it away. Stored it again knowing that one day it might explode in his face, come to light. Like now. The past breaking in on the present.

I slip my fingers into the ragged opening of the envelope and slowly draw the letter out, notice the slight tremor of my hands, notice, as I unfold the letter and spread it out on the table, the fine creases in the paper, the slight smudges of ink. It was written with a fountain pen, was written with care. There is an address at the top of the page, and a phone number. The phone number is the same as the one that's scribbled on the piece of paper that my uncle had given me. I should know; I've looked at it often enough, slipping it out of my wallet and studying it, as if it contains a code (a code to unbreak a heart). A date: the tenth of May, twenty-four years ago. My mother died in the month of May. I know it was May because of the cherry blossom. I can see them now, the small trees lining our street as I walk home with Stevie Burroughs that day. The clouds of pink. *Candyfloss trees*, I used to call them, and my mother would laugh. My mother died on another day in May, in another year, three years before my father sat down somewhere in the Bristol area and wrote this letter, carefully, with a fountain pen. Did he know my mother was dead? Surely he did. Did he go to her funeral? I wouldn't know. I wasn't there. No one had taken me. *It would have been too much for you*, my aunt said back in March when we talked about my mother's death for the first time ever. *We thought it was for the best.*

I start to read.

Dear Jack,

I am writing this letter in the hope that your uncle Keith will let you read it. If not now, then one day, perhaps when you are older. You probably do not know that I have tried to see you. Your uncle and aunt didn't let me. They thought it would upset you to see me, that it would remind you of things best forgotten. I was angry at the time. But they're your legal guardians now and I must abide by what they say. They tell me you're doing well at school and you're settled so they must be doing a good job by you, which is more than I did I'm sorry to say.

I was very sorry to hear about your mother. We were very happy once, your mother and I, although you probably can't remember those days. You were very little then. But things went wrong and for that I take the blame. I was in a funny place then in my head, very mixed up. I know I can't expect you to understand – you're just a kid – but maybe one day you will. Maybe one day you'll be able to forgive. Maybe one day you'll want to see me again and maybe one day your aunt and uncle will let you.

That's why I'm writing this letter, son, in the hope of that. Meanwhile, take care of yourself and work hard at school – you've got a good brain, I always knew that you had – and be good to your uncle and aunt. They love you very much. As your mother did, son, and as I do too, in spite of everything.

Your loving Dad

I read it twice. Then I read it again. Then I just sit there for a while staring at my father's handwriting, which is loose and slightly shaky, as if he's sitting there (where?) finding it hard to find the words, to shape them with his hand holding the pen.

I was sorry to hear about your mother. I'm to blame.

I can see her clearly now, in that space inside my head where time slips through like sand through a sieve, bringing back the past, as if it's only been waiting there crouched around a corner, stored in a drawer, waiting to be brought out again. Like this letter. I can see her pale face, the tremor of her eyes under their closed lids. I can see Laura's face too. And just for a minute I seem to sense them both standing behind me, feel the light pressure of their hands on my shoulders. My ears tune in again to the radio. An old Elvis song: 'You were always on my mind'. There are tears on my face. I'm that child of seven coming home from school to the smell of gas and his mother dying on the floor. I'm that boy of twelve, hiding in the attic room in the house in Plymouth, losing myself in Airfix models of planes, dreaming of flying away. And I'm thirty-four. I'm married with two daughters. I killed a child by accident, and my wife and I are slipping away from each other and there's nothing I can do to stop it, no way I know of holding on to the past. My tears slip like warm rain down my face, fall onto the paper, smudging the ink that has waited for me to read the trembling words it has formed for twenty-four years.

15

Sam goes off to the interview in a close-fitting charcoal-grey suit, the skirt quite short, showing off her legs, her hair clipped up. She gets the job; I knew she would. For the first two weeks she comes home wiped out, is edgy with the girls, with me, goes to bed early. And then she gets into her stride. Gets familiar with the routine. She's enjoying it now, enjoying the buzz of being around people all day, the gossip that goes on. I get into the different routine. I drop the kids off in the morning, come home, do the washing, clean the house. Then I pick Jessie up and take her out for an hour or two if the weather's dry. We walk around parks and feed the ducks. I push her on swings and listen to her chortle. We explore half-empty shopping malls where nearly everyone I see is either old or female. Or some misfit youth with tattoos on his head and vacant eyes who can't get a job. The highlight of my week – the weekly visits to this room. Sometimes I sit here for an hour and nothing happens. Sometimes tears spill into my eyes at the slightest thing. The sound of birds in the garden, children playing outside. Am I getting better? I don't know. I take the pills. I come here. I fill up the pages of my journal with words. I write about her sometimes. Laura. Her father hasn't come back to stand outside my house and stare through the windows into my life, to taunt me with his hate. I haven't seen her again, either. I miss her. I wonder where she is, how she is. Is she wearing her blue school uniform, or the pink anorak with the fur-trimmed hood? Is she all right, or is the blood still trickling down from her hair, welling in her chest?

My father's letter is still there, folded between the pages of my journal. No one has seen it but me. Although I've told you about it. I wanted to do that.

'Do you want to see him, Jack?'

'I don't know.'

But there's a piece of ice inside me that is shifting; the creak and crack of its thawing unsettles me.

'You're quiet tonight?'

I'm watching Jessica stab the prongs of her fork into the spaghetti hoops. She slurps them into her mouth, tomato sauce trickling down her chin. I reach for a tissue and wipe it off. My job now.

'Am I? Sorry.'

'Just so there's nothing wrong.'

'No, I'm fine.'

Sam is sitting at the table, sipping coffee. She's still wearing the suit she wears to work. She's kicked her shoes off and is twirling her ankles, to ease the circulation.

'Tired?' I ask.

'Yes. Busy day. Hardly stopped for a minute. You'd think the world and his wife were in hospital. What about you?'

'The usual really. Did the shopping this afternoon with

Jess. Oh yes, and I took her to that new play cafe. What's it called – Billy Bears?'

'Wow! You're good at this, aren't you. We should have done this years ago.'

Did she notice something on my face? Did a shadow pass over?

'I mean role swap, of course,' she adds, flustered a little.

'I know what you mean.'

'What's for dinner? You have remembered I've got yoga tonight, haven't you? I need to leave by seven. You don't mind, do you?'

There's a voice in my head – my voice, or maybe yours – and it's saying, *Why don't you tell her? Tell her about the letter. Tell her now.* But the moment passes. Now's not the right time, of course. Jessica starts squealing because her bowl slips off the table because she's playing silly buggers with her hoops, and now there's all this mess on the floor. Bethan is finished and is asking Sam to help with her spellings and I have to check on the lasagne in the oven. Maybe later, I tell myself, when she gets back.

Dinner's over in a hurry with Sam having her eye on the clock. I take the girls to get them ready for bed whilst Sam gets ready for her yoga class. She pops her head around the bathroom door and blows them a kiss and they blow her soapsuds back. Her face is all lipsticked and powdered and her body looks trim in her pink tracksuit.

'You look good,' I tell her, and she laughs, pink spots springing to her cheeks to match the rest of her.

'Thanks,' she says. 'See yer later, then.'

I get the girls into their pyjamas and they snuggle down on Bethan's bed while I read them 'Sleeping Beauty' for the umpteenth time.

'I'm going to marry a prince when I grow up,' Bethan announces, as I close the book.

'You're my princess, sweetie,' I tell her, dropping a kiss on her already sleepy cheek and carrying Jessica over my shoulder and back to her own bed.

I pour myself a beer and sit down in the lounge. I take the letter from between the pages of my journal and read it again, although I know the words by heart now; I won't forget them. I fold the letter up again and slip it back into the pages of the journal and drain my beer. Then I get up and pour myself something stronger – a malt whisky, a large one, and sit down again. I pick up the phone and dial the number that's also written now in my heart.

I'm not sure why I'm doing this. I'm not ready to speak to him – I don't want to. But I have this urge to see if he's still there. To hear what his voice would sound like, after all these years.

Three rings, four rings, five.

'Hello?'

A woman's voice. For a moment I'm flummoxed.

'Er, sorry to bother you, but I wondered if you could tell me if an Edward Philips is still living there?'

Edward. I've seen it written on my birth certificate. But maybe he calls himself Ted, or Ed, or Eddie. I don't even know.

'Who is this speaking, please?'

Slight suspicion edging her voice. Who is she? His wife, girlfriend?

'Do you know an Edward Philips?'

A pause. She's thinking, how much can I say?

'I might. Who is this?'

'Are you his wife?'

'No, not his wife. I'm his sister.'

'*His sister?*'

'Yes. His sister, Vera.'

'Then I must be your nephew, Aunt Vera.'

'*Jack?* Is that *Jack?*'

There is shock in her voice, and delight, and disbelief, and for her all the years come crowding in again. She knew me as a baby, she says. I'd been to visit when I was little, with my mum and dad. The last time she'd seen me I'd been three and it had been a week after my birthday. I'd come with my parents for a day out and they'd taken me to visit the ship my dad worked on – he was in the merchant navy too, same as Uncle Keith. I'd rushed up and down, my feet stamping all over the decks, and they'd had to take me off and when we got off the ship I'd cried my heart out and pulled on my dad's hand to go back on again.

'Don't you remember?' she says. Not really, I tell her, but I'd always loved ships and maybe that's why, and she sounds pleased.

'Nobody told me my father had a sister. But we never talked about him.'

'No, but they wouldn't. I only met them a couple of times; they didn't really know me. They knew your dad well enough – or at least your uncle Keith did. That's how your parents

147

had met – through your uncle Keith. But when they split up, your uncle turned against him. He blamed him, I suppose.'

'I know.'

'Your dad moved in here with me for a while. He was down on his luck for a couple of years. But he's married again now.'

Maybe she senses something in the silence. Silences are not all the same. Some are empty and easy; others are full of things that are not said.

'He tried to see you, Jack. He tried to see you a few times. Your uncle Keith told him to stay away, said he wasn't good for you.'

'I know.'

'He always loved you, Jack.'

'Where is he now?'

Does she hear the edge in my voice?

'He moved to Canada. To Vancouver.'

I feel myself falling through a great distance. An ocean of water stretching over my head.

'Come and see us,' my aunt Vera is saying. 'Come and meet your cousins.'

'Why haven't you told her?' you say.

Disapproval in your voice. It's a warm day today and you're wearing light-coloured trousers, a pale-blue polo shirt that shows off your tan.

'I'm not sure,' I say. 'Haven't had the opportunity, I suppose.'

'Then you should make it.'

'There's always stuff going on, with the girls and that. And Sam's really busy these days working . . .'

'Red herrings,' you say, stiffly, a little impatient. 'Why don't you want to tell her, Jack?'

Honestly, you could have been a policeman if you hadn't been a counsellor. You're not scared of challenging me, I admire you for that. You'd do all right in the interview room.

'Cut the crap, Jack. Either choose to tell her or choose not to, but be honest with yourself about why you don't want to.'

Truth is, though, I don't know.

'We've grown apart. We're not as close as we used to be.'

'Then how important is it for you to change that? To get close to your wife again?'

You look at me, and I'm struggling with this because I don't know the answer. There's a soft light in your eyes. You don't get that in a policeman's eyes in the interview room. It draws me in. It accepts me. No matter if I talk a lot of crap, no matter if you disapprove, get impatient. It's still OK. I'm still OK.

For several days afterwards I rehearse in my mind what I'd say to Sam, how I'd tell her. When would be the right time? When the kids are tucked up in bed, and she's sat curled into the sofa with a glass of wine, relaxing and watching some rubbish on the telly. *Wife Swap*, or those awful women that tell other women what not to wear.

What would I say? Sam, I've got something to tell you, something important. Would she flick off the telly and turn to me, give me all her attention? Or would there be a slight irritation sitting on her mouth, tensing the muscles around her lips? *He's stopping me from relaxing. Doesn't he understand what a hard day I've had? No, how could he. It's so long since he's worked. Over five months now.*

Or maybe a better time to tell her would be in bed, after we've made love maybe. Only how long has it been since we made love? I can't remember. Maybe the New Year. Or did we do it on Valentine's Day; we had made an effort then to be romantic, sitting down to dinner with candles and a bottle of wine. Maybe then. More than three months ago, because now it's near the end of May and the cherry blossom, the May blossom, is drifting like snow from the trees. It's a world away from a cold night in February. I watch Sam sitting on the sofa. She's taken off her slippers and her slim feet are tucked beneath her, already pale brown from wearing sandals. Her face is transfixed into a soppy smile over something that silly Trinny woman is saying on the telly, and I want to sit beside her and nudge her bare foot onto my lap and stroke it. But I can't.

In the end I have to say something. Because we have to arrange for her mum to look after the kids for a few days. I'm going down to Bristol to see my Aunt Vera, the aunt I've only just discovered I have. But I don't tell Sam the truth. I tell her I'm going to visit an old mate, someone who used to be in the Met but transferred to Portsmouth, married a girl who lived there. All lies. You wouldn't have approved.

'What was his name, then?' Sam asks, looking surprised.

I make one up.

'How come I've never heard of this Rob? How come I never met him, if he was such a good mate of yours?'

'He was at Hendon with me. He stayed with the Met, but we used to meet up for a drink once in a while. Then after a couple of years he transferred. Just before I met you, I think.'

I'm surprised how easy it is to lie, once I start.

'And he phoned you up today, just like that? After all this time?'

'Yeah. His marriage has split up. Just wants to catch up with old mates, I guess. I said I'd go down for a few days. I could do with the break.'

'It's all right for some!' she says, a slight sneer on her mouth. A flash of anger inside me, but I don't show it. Right then I'm glad I haven't told her. I'm glad I have this secret life. An aunt, and cousins in Bristol. A father in Canada. The letter slipped between the pages of my journal. All the words locked in my briefcase, written in my journal, a thick jumbo pad inside a ring-binder, like kids use in school, that she'll never see.

Aunt Vera lives in a council house, on a street that's a mix of other council houses and a few new-build private houses breaking in. An old estate, in the days when they built them solid and comfortable with huge back gardens for kids to be kids in. I walk up the garden path, feeling nervous. The front garden is a mix of lawn and flower beds full of established well-trimmed shrubs, ablaze with colour now. She's a woman who likes her garden, I'm thinking. There's a collection of gnomes in the middle of the lawn, grinning and pushing wheelbarrows or holding garden rakes, and I think, Sam would laugh at those, she'd say they're naff. But I like them, they look like they belong, and then just as I'm about to knock on the door it opens and there's a woman standing there, late fifties, a little overweight, flesh bulging in the gap between a red jumper and jeans, and it's funny, it's like looking in the mirror, really. There's something in her face that reminds me of mine: same chin, same set of the eyes. What does my father look like? Does he look like this too?

'Jack,' she says.

Her voice is breathless. She stands there just staring at me.

'Aunt Vera,' I say, and I step towards her and give her a hug and she hugs me back. And it's funny because it's not like hugging a stranger; it's like hugging someone to whom you belong, who makes you feel instantly at home.

We release each other and she steps back and tears glisten wetly on her cheeks. She wipes them, embarrassed, on the back of her hand.

'Come in, Jack. Come in. They're all in there, waiting to meet you.'

I follow her into the lounge and it's full of things. The windowsills are crammed with ornaments of elves and mementoes from Spain, pictures on the walls of children and dusky maidens, furniture bracketing the walls, most of it antique, out of keeping with the house. And people.

'Jack, this is my husband, Terry. He remembers you when you were a baby, don't you, Terry.'

Terry is slight of build with a face lined and grey from a lifetime of hard work at the docks. He offers me his hand. His eyes crinkle at me from behind thick glasses.

'And this is my son, Paul, and my daughter Jenny. And Jenny's husband, Gareth, and their children, Ashleigh, Marylou and Troy, and this little one, and that one, they're Paul's. Kirsty and Taylor. Paul's separated, but we still have the little 'uns over often, thank God.'

They smile, chorus, 'Hello Jack,' and stand up to shake my hand, smiling, jostling for their turn. The children, dipping their heads shyly, shepherded into a queue, pushed forward to shake hands with this strange man, this Jack, this second cousin they've never met before.

It's lovely to meet you, Jack.

Lovely to meet you.

Lovely to meet you after all this time.

My eyes are pricking now, tears threatening to fall. I never thought it would be like this. All these people belonging to me, knitted into my past. But there's somebody missing, a wide wilderness still stretching between us.

When they're gone, and the table's cleared and the plates stacked away in the dishwasher, Aunt Vera and Terry sit down with sighs of relief.

'Have another, Jack?' Terry says, waving the wine bottle at me.

'No, thanks. I'm fine, thanks.'

'A beer, then? I've some cold cans in the fridge.'

'No, I'm fine, thanks.'

'A coffee?'

'I don't want to be any trouble . . .'

But my aunt's on her feet and in the kitchen without another word. Minutes later she brings in a steaming hot cafetière on a tray, milk jug and sugar bowl, three cups.

'Well,' she says, putting it down on the coffee table, sitting down again. 'Well, fancy that. You here with us all, Jack. After all this time.'

'Yeah.'

'Enjoy it? Meeting my rabble.'

'Yeah, they're great. You've done well.'

'We're all hoping you're going to keep in touch.'

'Try and stop me.'

She laughs, pushes the filter gently down the cafetière jug. She pours out my coffee and passes me the cup.

'Course, I realize for you it's been a bit of a let down. There was someone else who should have been here.'

I want to say, 'No, you're wrong; he was with us all the time. He was here in your face and in the tone of your voice, in your children's faces, even the little ones. He was here, the cold Atlantic Ocean, the snow-covered tracts of Canada, filling this room with us.' But I sip my coffee, say nothing. We're silent now for a few minutes, letting it all wash over us, the excitement of the afternoon, ebbing away, dying down.

'So he's in Vancouver, you say?'

'Yes.'

'Married again?'

'Yes. Rosalind, a lovely girl. They met over here – she's half Canadian – and after they were married they decided to emigrate. Apparently it's easy if you've got a Canadian parent. Gives you automatic dual nationality, or something.'

'New start, new life, eh?' I say softly, and I feel my aunt looking at me, feel the words on the tip of her tongue. *Don't be bitter, Jack, don't be.*

'Any kids?'

'One. A son, Ben. He'll be about twenty now. Still at college. What's he studying, Terry? Architecture, something like that, isn't it?'

'Something like that,' Terry grunts. He's sensed the edge in my voice. He doesn't want to get involved, doesn't really want to be here.

'Does he know about me?'

It's like scratching an itch. It doesn't make it any better, but you have to scratch it. You can't not scratch it. My aunt looks surprised by the question.

'I don't know, Jack. We've never met – only talk on the phone now and then – Canada's a long way away. Keep meaning to go but we never have. But he must know about you; I can't imagine your dad would have kept something like that a secret from him.'

No, I think to myself. But he would have kept some things a secret from his new wife, his new son. He would have kept my mother a secret. How he walked out on her, on me, how she died. He wouldn't have allowed something like that to tarnish his new life, his fresh start. And if he would have kept those things a secret, then why not pretend I don't exist too.

I finish my coffee, put the cup back down on the tray. I glance at my watch. Eight o'clock.

'I should be going. I told the guest house I'd pick up the keys by now.'

'But, Jack, there's no need for that. I assumed you'd be staying, I've changed the sheets on the spare bed, ready for you . . .'

'No, that's very kind. You've been very kind, but I've booked this room, I think it's best . . .'

'Maybe the lad needs to be by himself for a while, Vera. It's been a lot to take in . . .' Terry murmurs, but then gets a look from my aunt.

'I thought maybe you could ring him. Ring your dad in Canada. It's about midday over there – there's a good chance he'll be at home.'

'Have you told him I was coming here?' My voice is sharp. Of course she has; I know she has.

My aunt's voice, a little sheepish, a little embarrassed.

'He'll be over the moon to hear from you, Jack.'

I get to my feet, feel my face reset itself into that hard look I learnt as a copper. No nonsense. Don't mess with me.

'I'm not ready for that. I can't do that yet. You're very kind and it's been lovely meeting you all but it's best I go now.'

Aunt Vera is disappointed, but she knows not to argue with me now. She fetches my jacket, she sees me to the door. Terry shuffles behind us in the hallway. She stretches up and drops a kiss on my cheek. Something leaves a trace of moisture on my face.

'Don't be a stranger, Jack. Keep in touch,' she says, as I turn and walk away.

Later, in the room, lying on the slightly narrow, slightly too hard bed, I don't know why I did it. Came back to this seedy bed and breakfast, when I could have stayed. The room is depressing, hardly big enough to swing a cat in. Dingy magnolia painted over woodchip, a washstand in pastel pink in the corner, mould encroaching on the silicone seal. Why hadn't I stayed? I wince, remembering my aunt's desperate hurt face. *I've changed the sheets, ready for you.*

But I had needed to get away, get some fresh air, draw myself back from it all. It had been lovely, meeting them all, sitting down to that meal with them. But after a few hours it was like they wanted to carve me up and divide me amongst them, claim a bit of me each for themselves. I can't just turn it on like that, the happy family thing. One bit of me is still that kid, on his own in the attic of that old house, losing himself in Airfix kits.

And my aunt's demands, I couldn't cope with those.

Phone him, Jack. He'll be over the moon.

If I wanted to phone anyone, I think, staring up at the ceiling, at the tatty pale blue lampshade, vague traces of cobwebs in its tassels, it would have been you. What would I have said?

I still hate him. I'm not ready to forgive him.

The cold winter of Canada freezing my heart. What would you have said?

That's all right, Jack. You don't have to forgive him.

I slip on my jacket and my trainers, go downstairs and out of the front door on to the street that is dark and wet. Keeping my head down against the rain, I make for the bright lights of a pub on the street corner, a hundred yards away. Two women huddle by the roadside at the corner, their stare boring into me.

'Fancy a good time, luv?'

'No thanks,' I say back, politely, not sarcastic, not taking the piss.

Inside, I'm swallowed up by light, by noise, by bodies

crowded in on me. I have to fight my way to the bar. It's a Saturday night; it's packed. Old faces, young ones, but all of them hard in a way, as if they've been vigilant all their lives, looking over their shoulders. Sailors mainly, men in their twenties and thirties, still in uniform, young bits of things hanging on their arms. Older men too, out of uniform, maybe retired. Sea-beaten faces. Years of changing tides and storms in their eyes.

I wedge myself into a corner of the bar and order a pint. Some woman gets up and leaves her perch on a barstool and I grab it, order another pint, then another, then a couple of whisky chasers. Some bloke tries to talk to me, tries to spill his hurt and hate into my ears. This woman, this bitch, she ruined his life, she took him for a ride. Spent all his money she did, for years, fucked his best friend. The fucking bitch, all women they're all the same. But I freeze him out, and he gets bored, turns to find some other wanker who'll listen to it, hate flowing freely between them.

The light and the noise, the grinning faces and leery ones, are inside my head now, rushing around inside of me, making me sick, and I leave and fall out again into the darkness and the glistening street. The women again, maybe the same ones, maybe different ones. It doesn't matter.

'Fancy a good time, luv? Special price for you.'

'No thanks. Thanks all the same, very kind of you.'

My voice too loud now with the drink, and the words slurred together. The women laugh.

'Just as well, luv. Be a waste of money for you, in your state.'

*

I sleep with my clothes on that night; I don't even bother getting undressed. In the early hours of the morning I wake up wondering where I am. The room presses in on me, its contours unfamiliar. I've left the blind up and a full moon is spilling its cool, green-white light into the room, making shapes take on a ghostly form. I stagger out of bed, wincing with a hangover, splash cold water over my face, swallow two aspirins I dig out of my holdall, pull down the blind to shut out the light, fall eventually into a deep, dreamless sleep.

I was intending to go back home. When did I change my plans? When did I decide to make that diversion?

'So you're going on an odyssey,' you said to me that day when I told you about my intention to visit my Aunt Vera. It was a warm day. The sun made a haze about your face.

I laughed. 'I don't know about that. It's just something I need to do.'

'You need to do?'

'Yeah. Part of finding where I come from.'

'That's what I meant. An odyssey.'

Or maybe I'm kidding myself. Maybe I'd intended it all along. It wasn't that much of a diversion. I got into the car and then got out the road map and looked up the best route. I knew the name of the town. Even though no one had mentioned it to me since the day I left. But why should I not know it? Seven's not that young. By the age of three and a half I read once, maybe in the *Reader's Digest* – it's full of weird facts like that – a child has learned most of the grammatical structures he'll ever know. So why shouldn't I remember the name of the small town where I'd lived most of my life up to the age of seven, nearly eight?

I knew it wasn't far from Bristol. I don't know how I knew that but I did. Once I'd come off the motorway at the right junction it was about forty minutes' drive, that's all. When I drive into the town I have this sensation like déjà vu, like I'd been here before, which of course I had. But of course it would have changed a lot since I was seven, so it was familiar and yet not. I knew what the road was called, in the same way I remembered what the town was called, in the same way I knew it wasn't far from Bristol. Cherry Tree Avenue. So obvious of course. Corny, really. The blossom. The pink cherry blossom lining the road, pink clouds of it all the way down. But that's how they named roads then, in the fifties, in those years after the war when they had grand visions of how the poor should live. Not in slums anymore but in solid brick-built houses with huge gardens where people grew their own vegetables and had room for children to run and play in. They'd probably planted the cherry trees after laying down the tarmac for the new road, staking them out at neat intervals, and what better name than that to give the road. Cherry Tree Avenue. A dream of how life should be lived, amongst the pink blossom, flowering like candyfloss in April and May. I remember it scattered around my shoes as I walked home that afternoon from school, tipping off my hair like pink snow.

I almost find the road all by myself, my body dipping to the left and to the right, remembering like a rat who has run a maze so many times the route's encoded in its brain. Like those Plymouth streets. Yet I'd been only seven, not quite eight, when I'd moved away from here. But a boy who was always out with other boys, in those days when kids were let out to roam, to kick balls on greens, unhassled by weirdos. Was this a myth, that it was safer then? Or was my mother too locked into her own sad head to care? Was I escaping from her sigh, from the closed-in look in her eyes? Yet I remember how I would follow her around the house like a shadow, how I ghosted her, afraid sometimes to let her out of my sight. Can both things be true? What can we trust from our memories? What is safe, indestructible? Is anything?

I have to stop once and ask the way. A lady in her late middle age, carrying shopping bags home from the Spar, who looks as though she has lived here all her life, who looks as though these roads are mapped upon her face.

'Cherry Tree Avenue. Yes, dear. Next on the right, then second on the left into Elm Road then right again, what's that then, Longmeadow that one, then it's the next on the right again. Cherry Tree. That's the one.'

And it is.

I stand outside the house. Number fifteen, and it is like that feeling I had arriving at the town. Like I'd been there before but not quite. Something has changed. A lot has changed. I remember the front garden had been laid to lawn with a big oval-shaped flower bed in the centre out of which tumbled poppies and nasturtiums in the summer time, and there'd been a magnolia tree in the corner that dripped its glorious shell-pink petals all over the grass. She loved that tree. *Japan – that's where they come from; my touch of the Orient.*

But it isn't there anymore. And nor is the lawn, or the flower bed, or the thick privet hedge that used to separate the garden from the pavement and the road. It's all open now, and the lawn replaced by that block paving you pay a fortune for, a small red Renault parked upon it. And the house looks less like a council house, the giveaway overhanging porch at the front door replaced by a closed-in, double-glazed uPVC one, the metal casement windows turned to plastic too. A satellite dish protrudes from the brickwork near the roof. It's gone upmarket, probably sold off to its tenants in the 'proud to be a house-owner' Thatcher years.

I park the car at the kerbside and stand there just staring at the house. For a moment I have an instinct to walk up to the front door and knock on it and say to whoever opens it, 'I used to live here as a boy – would you mind if I had a quick look around?' But then reason gets the better of me. There will probably be no one at home. They'll be out working, to pay for their mortgage, the credit repayments for the block paving, the instalments for the satellite TV. Or if someone's in at this time of day it will probably be a woman, a pensioner perhaps, and she'll think I'm a weirdo, one of those men they warn you about on the telly who worm their way into the homes of defenceless women, wanting to rob them, or worse. So I think better of it, turn to go. And then I see the curtain twitch, a woman's face peer out at me, and I think for a moment – crazy, I know it sounds – I think for a moment it's Mum. She's peering out to see if I'm coming, if I'm on my way home from school. It's late, I should be home by now. Then I see the face at the window is old, is grey-haired, and I think she's aged, she's grown old; I've been so long in coming home and she's been watching, waiting all this time. I'm crying now, as if I'm that small boy finding my mother on the floor in the kitchen that day. I get in the car and drive away, the tears in my eyes blurring my sight, so for a while it seems I'm driving in the rain.

16

Gill is in the house when I get home. She looks surprised to see me, and then I remember I had said I wouldn't be back until tomorrow. Jessica is back from nursery. She's sitting at the kitchen table shoving bits of fish finger into a pool of tomato ketchup on her plate before putting them into her mouth. I bend my face towards her.

'Hello, honey. Been good?'

She leaves a tomatoey kiss on my chin.

'Had a good trip?' Gill says.

She looks at me in this uncertain way. As if she still can't work me out. As if I'm suddenly going to grow two heads, start talking gibberish, foam at the mouth.

'Yes, fine. Girls been OK?'

'No trouble at all. Been visiting an old friend, then, have you?'

'Yes, that's right.'

'Someone you used to know at Hendon?'

But it's harder now to carry on with the lie.

'Yes. That's right.'

I drag the words out. We both notice how hollow they sound.

'You're back early. Sam wasn't expecting you until tomorrow.'

'Yeah, well, change of plans.'

'Oh well, now you're back, I'll get off home, then. You can manage now, can't you?'

'Yes, of course.'

'You won't forget to pick Bethan up from school at three thirty?'

I look at her but say nothing. I want to say, 'Don't worry, I haven't lost my marbles, I haven't gone gaga yet.' But I don't, I hold back. Maybe I don't feel entitled. I've lost the moral high ground. Anyway, she looks slightly flustered, as if she realizes she's overstepped the mark, then hurries away to collect her things and I see her out to the door. She is eager to be away, to get back to her normal husband, one who has worked all his life, who doesn't hang around the house all day having a breakdown, or whatever it is. People like my mother-in-law, people like Gill, they live in the light. In a world of activity and doing. They can't live any other way.

I take Jessie to the park after she's finished with her fish fingers. She scrambles up and down the slide, calling, 'Watch me, Daddy! Look at me, Daddy!' It's a nice afternoon and there's a couple of mothers there sitting on the bench gossiping, one eye on their children as they swing, and I wonder what they think of me. Alone here with my three-year-old when other men, their husbands maybe, are at work all day, driving lorries, working on building sites, managing shops or offices. Keeping crime off the streets, even. Or maybe not in their case. They look like they live in the council houses, with their bleached hair and tight jeans, and then I think, I'm turning into a snob these days. What does a copper's wife look like? What does a copper look like, come to think of it? Does he look like me? Then I think, It's time you got another job, Jacko. But what? What could I do? I've spent twelve years in the force and I don't know what it's done for me, what skills it's given me. Except a nose for something that doesn't smell right, a certain turn of phrase. A rulebook way of seeing the world. But I don't want to be like that anymore. Isn't that what this is all about? Wanting to change.

When Sam gets home at six I've already bathed the kids, given them their tea. They're in the living room watching *Mary Poppins* on DVD and I'm in the kitchen cooking a risotto. Maybe food is the way to a woman's heart, as well as a bloke's, maybe I'm feeling guilty. I dropped off at the supermarket on the way home from picking up Bethan and I bought all the works. Arborio rice, the right stuff for making risotto, and shallots and peppers, oyster mushrooms, parsley, garlic and chives. White wine for the stock. A fillet of cod, and prawns and scallops. Garlic bread, and Parmesan cheese, the real stuff, shaved off from a wedge I bought from the delicatessen, to top it off. I've cleaned and prepared the fish. Set it aside, to go in for a few minutes at the end. The garlic bread is crisping in foil in the oven, and the rest is cooking away a storm in the wok when I hear Sam at the front door.

She stands at the kitchen door and looks at me. I turn down the heat and walk over to her and put my arms around her, kiss her cheek. She doesn't move.

'Where did they come from?' she says. She's staring at the

flowers I've arranged in a vase on the table. White roses. Sam always loved white roses. I can't remember when I'd last bought them for her.

'From the supermarket. I'm cooking you a special tea tonight. Seafood risotto.'

'Feeling guilty, Jack?'

Did I blush, look away, stumble over my words? Yeah, maybe. I wasn't expecting that. The coldness in her voice, that edge.

'Back early, aren't you? Change of plans, then?'

'Let's eat first, Sam. Then when the girls are in bed, we need to talk. There's something I need to tell you.'

'Yes. I expect there is.'

'Sam?'

'You might as well turn that lot off. I'm not hungry. I know where you've been. I know you haven't been with this Rob from Hendon. I know about your aunt in Bristol. I know about the letter, the one from your father. *She* told me. She phoned last night. She thought maybe you'd come straight home. She thought I knew you were going to see her. Why did you lie to me Jack?'

The girls are in bed. The risotto has gone to waste. Sam won't eat any. She isn't hungry, she says. I try but end up just pushing it around with my fork. I can hear Sam upstairs, moving around. Eventually she comes downstairs and stands in the doorway.

'We need to talk.'

'OK, let's talk. Do you want a coffee?'

'I want a trial separation, Jack.'

'Just because of that? Because I told you a little white lie?'

'Not just because of that. Other things too.'

I wasn't expecting that. What's a trial separation, anyway? Either it's a separation or it's not. Like either it's a lie, or it's not? Is life really that black or white?

Perhaps it depends on the motive, you would say.

Perhaps it does. What was mine?

'Lots of things,' Sam says. I see her struggling with her thoughts, struggling with her feelings. The steely look she had on her face is beginning to slip.

'You've changed, Jack,' she says. 'Ever since the accident. I know you've been ill, I know it wasn't your fault. But it's more than that. You're closed off. You've put up a wall. I don't know you anymore.'

'Because I didn't tell you about the letter from my father? About going to see my aunt Vera?'

'Yes, because of that. Because of how that makes me feel, being lied to. Other stuff too. All that writing that you do in the evenings, all those visits to that counsellor. You never tell me about any of that. You never let me in.'

'You've changed too. Since you got that job you're out all the time, making new friends. How do you think that makes *me* feel?'

'I've changed because I had to. Not because I want to.'

The blood's rising now; she's angry; she's almost shouting.

I stare at her and she stares back at me. And then she seems to go limp inside. She sighs.

'I just can't deal with it anymore, Jack. I'm moving out tomorrow with the girls. I'll stay at my mum's for a few weeks. We need a break from each other.'

'What'll happen then? In a few weeks?'

'I don't know. We'll have to see, won't we?'

I sleep on the sofa that night. Although I don't sleep. Not really. Just toss and turn. It's a warm night, an early heat-wave. Even with the living-room windows open, I can't settle. But I must have fallen asleep somewhere around the early hours because Sam coming downstairs and moving around the kitchen, getting the girls' breakfast ready, making coffee, disturbs me.

I stagger into the kitchen.

'How did you sleep?' she asks. But she doesn't need to. She just needs to look at me.

'Like shit,' I say.

'I didn't sleep that well either,' she says.

'I'm sorry,' I say. She pours me a coffee.

'I'm phoning in sick today. I'll ring Mum after breakfast. She can come over maybe and help me pack some of the girls' things. If they need any more, we'll collect them later. I'll need her to give us a lift, anyway. I'll leave the car with you. I can borrow Mum's for work.'

Just for an instant I feel relieved. She's leaving me the car. Then I think, You jerk! Your wife and your kids are leaving you and you're relieved she's leaving you the car.

'How long is this going to be for?' I say. But what I want to say is, Don't go. Please don't go. I'll make it up to you. I'll change. But I can't say it. The words shrivel into dry leaves and die away.

'I don't know,' she says.

Gill arrives whilst I'm out dropping the girls off. When I get back she answers the door. She gives me this look for an instant, like, 'I'm not surprised,' but I won't react to it, I won't give her the satisfaction. I go through to the kitchen and pretend to be busy whilst she goes upstairs to Sam. They come down later with a couple of bulging suitcases and a holdall full of the kids' toys and games and that makes my heart lurch, seeing that, the toys going out of the door. Gill has the sensitivity for once to go ahead to the car on her own, to start loading cases into the boot, and Sam hangs back for a little while. I want to hold her, I want to kiss her, but I don't. Who kisses their wife goodbye when she leaves them?

'What about the kids? What'll you tell them?' I say.

'I'll talk to them tonight. I'll say we're just going to have a break for a while.'

'That's all it's going to be, isn't it, Sam?'

'Maybe,' she says. I can see this is hard for her. I can see this is almost as hard for her as it is for me.

'Phone them whenever you like, Jack. Come to see them too, whenever you want. Just ring, to let us know you're coming. That'll help the girls, seeing you.'

'Of course.'

She steps towards me suddenly, drops me a dry kiss on the cheek.

'Take care, Jack.'

'I love you,' I say, suddenly realizing how strange the

words sound coming from my mouth. I haven't said this for a long time. But she's gone, carrying the last suitcase through the door towards the car. I wonder for a moment if I should carry it for her, but then I think, No I can't do that.

'I'm sorry, Jack,' you say.

I half expect you to say, I told you so. You should have told her. You shouldn't have lied to her. But you don't. You just look at me steadily. I breathe in and out slowly, feeling my chest rise and fall, feeling the quietness in the room enter my breath, so that for a few moments that's what I am. Just my breathing and this quietness in the room. At home I'm a mess. I'm all over the place right now. But here I can pull myself into the centre. Just be.

'How are you feeling now?'

'I just want her to come back. And the kids. I just want everything to be the same again.'

'But it won't be the same, Jack. You're not the same, she's not the same. Maybe you need to let go of the need for certainties,' you say, gently.

I feel like I'm seven years of age again. Things are happening, things are ripping me away from my world. I want to cry but I can't let a man see me do that. Even a man like this.

'I don't know how to.'

The June heatwave arrives with a vengeance. I drag the sunbed out of the shed into the back garden and lie on it every afternoon; the sun's like red coals on my eyelids. I'm gripped by inertia, too hot to think or feel. Indoors, even with all the windows open, even after sunset, the heat is close and heavy. It is hours before I fall asleep at night, and even when I do, I wake three or four times, feeling the heat around me.

I phone every night and talk to the girls.

'Miss you, Daddy,' Jessie says. 'When we coming home?'

'Not sure, honey. Soon, I hope.'

She starts to whimper, and if it wasn't for this unrelenting heat, maybe I'd feel like whimpering too.

'Do you want your wife back?' you say.

'Yes, of course.'

'Then you need to open up to her. You need to start sharing your feelings with her.'

But right now, I don't know what I'm feeling. The heat has turned my flesh molten. I slump in chairs, flick idly through magazines, through the sports page of the *Express* that lands on my doormat every day, channel-hop through daytime TV, the curtains drawn to keep the sun off the screen. I struggle the hundred yards or so down the road to a small shopping precinct to stock up with provisions: bread, milk, coffee and cans of Stella, a bottle of whisky. I never used to drink at home, or hardly ever. But now the drink is what gets me through the evenings, when the silence about the house is at its worst, is unbearable. I'm off the Prozac now; I need something to get me through this. No Bethan pushing her school books into my face. Look at this, Daddy, look what I did today at school. Look at my poem about the sun. Look at my picture of the seaside. Test me on my spellings, Daddy. No Jessica, crawling onto my lap after her bath, dragging a book along with her.

'Read me the princess story, Daddy.'

'Which one, honey?'

'The one where she pricks her finger and sleeps a long time.'

My voice moving over the words in small tides of sound, and Jessie limp against my arm, sucking her thumb, a baby again.

Isn't that what we all want? I think, sitting in the silent house, gazing out through the patio doors into a garden where dusk is gathering like a storm. Whisky in my glass, the amber liquid flashing against the crystal sides, like sun distilled into a glass. To be little again. Taken care of. Decisions made for us.

I take a large gulp. It burns like molten gold down through my chest, spreads fingers of warmth out from my belly. I know why people drink, I think. Because they get back to that state when they were babies. Boundaries merge, they're not separate anymore. It's the separateness that hurts the most.

The garden leave's over. I'm finished now; I'm on my own. I'm not a copper anymore. I don't know what I am.

'I'm willing to go on seeing you on a reduced rate for a few months, Jack, if money's an issue.'

I'm out of work, my wife's left me, of course money's an issue, I think. But it's not your fault. You didn't have to say that. That was good of you.

'I've got a bit of money put away. I can afford to commit at the full rate for a few more months. Anyway, I'm going to start looking for a job now.'

'Do you feel ready for that?'

'Yeah. Get me out of the house. Stop me dwelling on things.'

I guess it's a matter of pride in the end. If you were a friend, if you were my father, for instance, I could put pride aside, I guess. But you're not. You're just a professional doing his job. I'm just a client, like many others. I've never forgotten really where the balance of power falls. Paying you the full rate is just my way of keeping my end up. Making things feel more equal. So I don't get tempted to forget. You're not my dad; you're not even a friend. You're just a bloke doing a job and getting paid for it.

It's a boiling-hot Sunday afternoon. Sam's parents are out when I call to see the girls. I've bought a present for Jessica. One of those dolls that gurgle and cry and only stop when you stick the dummy in its mouth. I think they're spooky but Jess loves them. She had a birthday on Friday. Celebrated it with a party yesterday. Sam had invited me, but I gave it a miss. It would've been full of kids rushing round with smeary mouths from too much cake and ice cream, and mums who would look at me funny, thinking, Why has she left him. What's *he* done? And anyway, I didn't want to see her celebrating her birthday in a place that wasn't at home. Our home.

Jessica snatches the present from me and I get a wet kiss in return. She rips it open. I've remembered to stick the batteries in it before I wrapped it. I flick the *on* switch across, and it starts to cry as soon as she picks it up, its big blue eyes flicking open at her in surprise. Jess rams its dummy in its mouth and it stops. Sam and I laugh.

'She'll make a good mother one day,' Sam jokes.

'Where're your parents?'

'They're having dinner at Sarah's. She's got this new man in her life she wants to introduce.'

'You didn't want to go?'

'No. Not quite up for that.'

'Let's go out,' I say. 'Let's take the kids out somewhere.'

She looks at me oddly and I can hear her thoughts. Should I be doing that, going out with my husband and the kids? Neither of us knows the rules in this separation game.

'OK, then. Only for a couple of hours, though. I need to get back by four.'

I don't ask why. That'll be pushing it.

We pile into the car and drive to this place we know where there's an adventure playground for kids and a small animal zoo and a cafe garden where we can sit and drink coffee and eat cake and watch the children play. It's hot. Sam is wearing a white cotton shift dress. Her legs and arms look tanned.

'You're brown,' I say.

'Mostly out of a bottle. Haven't got much time to lie in the sun these days.'

I feel her eyes on my arms, noticing my tan. She doesn't comment. I wouldn't be able to say it's out of a bottle and she knows it.

'How's the job hunt going?' she says.

'Couple of ideas. Nothing positive yet.'

And then, because I need to say it. Because I really need to say it, 'I miss you, Sam. I miss the girls. I want you back.'

A tightness settles on her mouth.

'We'll see, Jack. We'll see what happens.'

As suddenly as it arrived the heatwave goes. The weather is normal again, more bearable. Occasional summer showers, cool spells of overcast clouds. The guy interviewing me at the job centre doesn't know what to make of me.

'You were in the police force you say for twelve years?'

'Yeah, that's right.'

'Why did you leave?'

'I decided it wasn't for me.'

'So you left voluntarily?'

'Not exactly.'

'What do you mean?'

'I'd been ill. I'd been off work, sick for several months. I didn't feel I could return to the job.'

'Because of medical reasons?'

'Sort of.'

'Do you have a letter from the doctor to that effect?'

'It wasn't exactly the doctor's decision. It was mine.'

'If you can't provide a letter from your doctor then we may have to treat you as leaving your job voluntarily. That could mean you won't get any benefit for six weeks.'

It's no big deal. The benefit I'd be entitled to would be peanuts anyway. I'm beginning to understand why people turn to crime.

'Then I'd better get a job as quickly as possible.'

Touch of sarcasm in my voice. He notices.

'That's why you're here, Mr Philips, I presume. What kind of work would you consider doing?'

'I'm not sure. Maybe something advisory. Something that helps other people.'

'There's a job here for a youth worker. Working on a project to reduce truancy in comprehensives. But it doesn't start till September and it's only temporary. For four months.'

But something about it draws me. It's the other side, isn't it. Helping to prevent kids getting into crime, rather than catching them afterwards. I take the contact details and when I get home phone up for an application form. It arrives the next day. The bit on the form that gets me stuck is the question about how much time I've had off work in the last year. Should I tell the truth or should I lie? I decide to come clean. If I'm starting a different life, I want to start as a different person. I want to live in the open, in the light.

17

I get the job. Six weeks to wait. I decide to spend the time decorating the house. Something in the back of my mind says get it ready, get it prepared. Not for Sam and the kids to come back because I'm beginning to think they won't, that won't happen. This trial separation has gone on for weeks and is beginning to feel like something else.

I buy tins of paint, pale neutral colours to bring more light and space into the house: stone and calico and Maine white. I open all the windows and start stripping paper off the walls. Long skeins of paper layered with paint. Layered with the past.

I go and see the kids on Sundays. Sunday is my day of rest. Gill looks at me funny when she opens the door to me, like I've done something wrong, I shouldn't be here.

'Bethan, Jessica. Daddy's here. Come and talk to Daddy.'

Come and be polite to Daddy. Sit there and smile and talk about what you've been doing in the holidays, the swimming club you've joined, the summer play-scheme where Granny takes you every day whilst Mummy's out working, earning the bread. Show him the lovely pictures you made the other day with Granddad in the kitchen. Be nice to Daddy.

If Sam's in she usually looks distracted, her head full of things that have nothing to do with me anymore. She looks prettier, I think, she looks stunning. She wears clothes I've never seen her in before that show off her long, tanned limbs, and her dark hair has copper low-lights that flash in the sun. There's someone else, I think.

A few days later, it's Sam on the phone. I'm in the middle of painting the kitchen, stroking long runways of Maine white onto the walls with a roller. The radio is turned right up so I hardly hear the phone at first. Some man on *Woman's Hour* on Radio Four is talking about depression. How it hung like a dark cloud over his life for years. He is softly spoken, but I can hear his suffering in his voice; I recognize it.

'Where were you – in the garden?'

'No, I had the radio turned up. I'm decorating the kitchen.'

'Oh. What colour?'

'Maine white. Hint of blue in it.'

'Well, it'll be an improvement on the old yellow.'

But Sam hasn't phoned me to talk about colour schemes.

'I need to talk to you,' she says. 'Can we meet somewhere later?'

We meet that evening in the Woodcutter's Arms. We used to bring the kids here sometimes on a summer's evening. There's a large garden for children to run about in, with swings and a climbing frame at one end, two goats chomping grass tied up to stakes at the other. She turns up looking stunning in a skimpy pink dress. I buy her a gin and tonic and

179

myself a pint. We settle at a table in the garden and watch the kids, other people's kids, play on the climbing frame, push handfuls of grass towards the goats' mouths. Does she remember those evenings, I think, when we used to come here? We were OK then. Happy, even. One moment you can be happy, and the next not. Something can happen that can tear your happiness away, like quicksand shifting under your feet. Nothing is for keeps.

'You said you wanted to talk?'

Sam twiddles the stem of her glass. There's something she wants to say to me but I don't think I want to hear it. I think I may even know what it is.

'It's about what happens next, Jack.'

'By the way, I've got a job,' I tell her. 'I start in September. Working with kids in a youth project.'

I'm stalling, aren't I? I'm putting off the moment. I know what's going to happen next.

'That's good, Jack. I'm pleased for you.'

'Yeah, feels like the right direction.'

The right direction. How do we ever know what that is? We drive home from work one day, taking the usual route, and a kid runs out from behind a bus, and the right direction suddenly becomes the wrong one. A boy comes home from school one day and finds his mother dead, and the right direction may mean he's ripped out of one life and put in another one. Things like that happen to people every day. A life gets ripped apart, gets thrown away. You think you're on one path, and then you're on another. You're lost. You may never find your way again.

Sam is still twiddling with the stem of her glass. She looks down into her gin and tonic, as if she's looking for the right words. I'll make it easy for her. I'll point the way.

'So. What happens next? What do you want, Sam?' I say.

'I want us to sell the house. I want us to make a clean break, Jack.'

You marry someone and then they become a stranger. Your life goes one way, their life goes another.

'Is there someone else?'

'I knew you were going to ask me that.'

'Is there?'

'It's nothing to do with that. It's us. I don't love you anymore. Not the way I used to, anyway.'

So what's the right direction? What happens next? Nothing lasts for ever; nothing's that real. You love, and then you don't.

'How can you say that, Sam? You don't just stop loving someone.'

'I'm sorry, Jack. It's not the same anymore. I can't make it the same anymore. I want to make a fresh start. I want a divorce.'

Later, back in the empty house, sinking half a bottle of Scotch to help me sleep, I suddenly remember she'd never answered the question.

Is there someone else, I'd said.

'I'm sorry, Jack,' you say.

'I'm sorry too. Everyone's sorry. But that doesn't stop it happening, does it?'

*

181

We agree we won't meet during the month of August. You're off on holiday again. Tuscany, this time. You've rented a villa. You're taking the family, you tell me. Your wife, a grown daughter and her husband, two grandchildren. I want to ask, 'Does your wife love you, is she faithful? Does she ever tell you she wants to leave you?' I want to ask, 'What is your daughter like, what are the grandchildren like?' A boy and a girl, you told me. I bet they'll never stand on street corners swigging cider out of a bottle, giving lip to the copper who tries to move them on.

'Maybe when I see you again things will have moved on for you, Jack. You'll have started your new job by then, won't you?'

'Yeah, maybe even sold my house,' I say, and you wince slightly, the irony not lost on you.

'There's a lot going on for you right now,' you say. 'Maybe you feel like you're being abandoned?'

I shrug, say, 'No, not at all.' I wish you a good holiday. But that word, abandoned, it stays with me for some time. It rankles with me.

August heat is like no other heat. It shuts you in. There's nowhere to go to escape it. The nights are the worst. We're not equipped for heat in this country. Don't get enough of it, I suppose, to think about air-conditioning. When it comes, it comes on you suddenly, like a shock. It takes your breath away.

I lie in a bed that's grown too big for me, covered only with a sheet, but even then I'm sweating like a pig. The silence of the house at night with no one in it burns in my ears. When the kids were here, even when they were sleeping, I would know they were there. Like a kind of sixth sense. I get up and go to the window to try and open it even further but it's as far open as it can be.

That's when I notice a light in the house opposite, flickering and moving across an upstairs window, like torchlight. But the house has been empty for months. The owners have gone abroad. There's a 'For Sale' sign in the garden at the front, and now there's one in mine. Two houses waiting for their life to change.

The policeman's nose; I still have it. Should I go and investigate, or more sensibly, phone the police? But then I think, Maybe they've come back from abroad to do something to the house. The electricity supply is disconnected, so they're moving around in there with a torch. Moving around in a house on a hot August night, in a house where life's on hold. Like in this one, I think. I watch the light flickering across the window, moving away. Then it snaps out. The windows of the house are blank and empty, like the eyes of someone who is blind.

I've started having the kids over regularly on Thursday nights and every other weekend. I'm playing the 'single dad' game – hunting around for things to do with them, places to take them. A park, a zoo, those pubs with soft play areas where children can run amok while sad single dads sip a pint of beer and read the paper.

'I've told them we're not going to be living together again,' Sam tells me. 'They were upset at first, but then they seemed to forget about it and went out to play. I think they'll be all right.'

But the first time they come over and stay the night, the first time since the separation, Bethan mopes and won't leave my side. Jessica is all right. She runs in excitement all over the house, exploring it, treating it as if it still belonged to her, as if it is an old friend she's coming home to.

'Daddy, my bedroom looks just the same,' she says excitedly, jumping up onto my lap, putting her arms around my neck, pressing her face against mine.

'Of course it does, honey. Why shouldn't it?'

'But Mummy said we don't live here anymore.'

'No, but it hasn't changed yet. It won't change until after the house is sold and some other little girl comes to live here.'

'But I don't want some other little girl in my room,' Jessica says, wide-eyed at the thought of it.

I catch sight of Bethan's scowling face in the doorway.

'Why can't we come back and live here with you? I don't want anyone else to be our daddy. I want you.' Her face is red with upset. She runs away. I let her go.

But later, when I've given them a bath and tucked them up and read them their favourite princess story, the way I always used to, pretending we're just an ordinary family, a happy family, and gone downstairs and poured myself a drink, a double Scotch, I sit there thinking, Why did she say that, that thing about not wanting another daddy? Why that?

Is there somebody else? I asked, that night in the pub garden. The sun was going down, casting shadows in her eyes. She didn't answer.

For days after I take the girls home the same thoughts turn in my head. Too much time to think, I suppose. That time when I drove home from Plymouth, Dave's car was pulling out of our road. And why had he been so keen that time to go around to the Jenkins, to warn that guy off after Sam thought she had seen him outside Bethan's school? Putting his job on the line really, taking a risk like that. 'Misappropriating the uniform', the police would call it. Then I get to thinking other things. Those nights when Sam was so keen to go out. Yoga class, aerobics, whatever. Putting on makeup carefully in front of the bedroom mirror, taking time over it, painting her mouth a rich pink and smudging it off on tissue. Who bothers to do that when they're just going to an exercise class, when they're probably going to end up red-faced and sweaty? Those nights she came home late, very late, sliding quietly into bed next to me. If I asked about it the next morning she'd say, looking innocent, 'Just went for a drink with the girls after class.' But twelve o'clock sometimes she came back, and I'd swallow it, I'd fall for it. You fucking idiot, I tell myself, you jerk!

When the girls come over again on Sunday I do what I've always told myself I wouldn't do. I start to question them. Not in an obvious way, just slipping in little questions, dropping them into the conversation. 'Who cooks tea at Granny's?' I say, watching them tuck into hamburgers and chips. Does Mummy cook? Meaning, *Does Mummy have time to cook?* Or is she busy getting ready to go out?

'Sometimes Mummy. Sometimes Granny,' Bethan says.

'I bet you miss her when she's out working every day. Still, you have her to yourselves in the evening.'

'Sometimes.'

'Only sometimes?'

'Sometimes she goes out in the evenings too.'

'Oh. Where does she go then?'

Bethan's mouth full of hamburger and chips. Too full to answer. She's closing up. She's getting the gist of this.

'Does she go out with a friend then?'

'I think so.'

'Does this friend ever call at the house to wait for Mummy?'

'No. I don't know. Are there any more chips, Daddy?'

Stop, I think. *Stop this*. Don't play this game.

So I have to find out for myself in the end. Been in the force too long, the detective coming out. Although I never was plainclothes, only uniform.

I decide to go on a Friday night. If she is seeing him, that's the night most likely. At the end of the week, winding down after a week at work. Saturday night she'll more likely want to spend with the kids. I decide to drive around to Dave's late, twelve o'clock, maybe later. If she is seeing him they'll probably be out earlier on, having a meal out, or a drink somewhere in a country pub, or maybe they even do stuff like go to the pictures. The kind of stuff you do when you're courting. Isn't that what we did once?

Of course I'm reckoning on the fact that she stays the night, that it's got that far, otherwise at twelve or later she'd be back at her parents' house, back with the kids. But Sam's not a teenager; she's a woman of thirty-two. She's not going to want to get dressed again afterwards, go out into the dark night, rush back to Mummy's. No, if she's seeing him, she'll still be there at twelve, at two in the morning, at four, even at six. Lying there in bed with him all night. Does she spoon into his back, or he into hers? Does he lie with his arms around her all night? (Like I used to, back in the early years, before the mortgage and the kids came along.) The images crowd into my head, bruising my mind. But I can't stop thinking them.

When Friday night comes it's hard to know what to do with myself. I can't get into the double Scotches like I usually do. I have to keep a clear head. I have to drive for a start then I have to take things in, note what I see, be sure. Early in the evening I go for a walk several times around the block, then I come back and channel-hop, but I can't settle to anything. The phone rings about eight; for a crazy moment I think – It'll be Sam, she's calling to ask me to take her back.

A woman's voice, but not Sam's.

'Hello? Is there a Jack Philips living there?'

'Yes, speaking.'

She hangs up; I wasn't expecting that. I hold the phone to my ear for a few moments, the meaning of the thin continuous bleep catching up with me. A flash of anger. Who was it? How dare she hang up? I dial 1471 but get that irritating taped voice saying the caller withheld their number. Then I think, Maybe it was my dad's wife over in Canada, checking me out. Trying to make contact, then losing her nerve. Maybe. A longing for a drink, for the blurring of edges, overtakes me again. But I resist it. Must keep a clear head.

I get out my briefcase from the study and open it and lift out the journal. It's fat with words, with my scrawl trailing backwards and forwards over the paper.

Write your thoughts down, you used to say. *Whatever comes into your head, the obsessional thoughts, the flashbacks, write them down. It's easier when they're out there, pinned down on paper. The terror of them goes.*

I end up writing for a couple of hours. Strangely, I don't find myself writing about Sam or Dave, any of this stuff. I write about my father, wondering what he's like. Does he have a beard, or is he clean-shaven? Is he bald now, or does he still have his own hair? He had thick dark hair back then, when I was little. It fell loosely over his forehead, got in his eyes. What colour were his eyes: were they dark blue like mine? I can't remember. Where does he live – in the suburbs, or out in some vast empty place that Canada has so much of? By a lake maybe, or up in the mountains, where the view catches his breath every time he sits on the terrace, no matter how many times he's seen it. Is his house one of those ranch-style clapboard houses? Did he build it himself? – so many do who emigrate to Canada – on a piece of land bought for a song. What is he doing right now? I wonder. Sitting watching some huge flat-screen TV, with his wife curled up next to him on the sofa. His son, my half-brother Ben, out cruising with his mates, or at a drive-in movie snogging with a girl in the car. Or is that the States, drive-in movies? This cold wind again, blowing around my heart. What is he really like, this man, my father? I scan through the pages I've just written, and realize it's full of questions, questions without answers. And no matter how hard I try to pretend it isn't there, there's this invisible cord stretching across wilderness spaces, stretching across an ocean, tugging me towards him.

*

I fall asleep for an hour in the chair. When I awake it's one o'clock. A good time to go. I grab a thin jacket from the hall and go out of the front door, closing it quietly, so as not to disturb my sleeping neighbours. I get into the car and start it, sit for a minute, letting the engine idle. That's when I see it again. The torchlight in the house opposite, flickering this time against the downstairs window. Then it cuts out, it's dark again, and I wonder if I imagined it. Maybe it was some weird reflection from a street light, or from my headlights coming on. I drive slowly down the road, and make my way through empty sleeping streets, avoiding the ones where I know drunks will still be stepping out from nightclubs, the odd brawl breaking out. My job once, to go to scenes like that, arresting some bloke out of his head on God knows what, marching him into the back of the van, head down, arms held high behind his back, throwing him into the cell for the night to sleep it off, before we decide whether or not to prosecute. My job once, but no more. So much has changed. So much I'm having to remake, to start over.

Even in the dark I instantly know it's Sam's; it's her mother's little blue Clio. But I park some distance up the road and walk back, stoop and examine the number plate. There's no mistake. Some men would have felt instant rage, but instead I feel cold, ice cold, snaking from my belly up into my chest. What to do next?

If I leave it now, go calmly, quietly back to my car, drive home, sleep or try to sleep till the morning, and then phone her, confront her with what I know, she'll accuse me at first of paranoia. She'll get defensive, say I've been creeping around spying on her, and even if she owns up to it in the end, it'll be in a grudging way, and I'll be the one who ends up being made to feel guilty, in the wrong. But if I confront the pair of them now, drag them from their bed, there will be no doubt where the guilt lies. The time of night will say it all.

I walk up to the front door and lodge my thumb over the doorbell and let it ring. I hear it ringing in the silence behind the door. Shrill, insistent, like the siren of a police car – something you can't ignore. I lift off my aching thumb, give it a break for a few seconds, then back again. *Come on, you bastard, open the door.*

Footsteps clattering hurriedly down the stairs. Then it opens. Dave. He's wrapped a towelling dressing gown around himself. His jaw drops in total shock.

'J-Jack, what the hell, mate. W-what you doing here!'

I don't know what I'm going to do until I do it. I have nothing planned. I land him with a smack on the side of the head and he reels backwards into the hallway. Then I'm in after him, my hand around his throat, pinning him up against the wall.

'You bastard! You fucking bastard! How long has this been going on? How long?'

'Leave him alone! Leave him, Jack!'

Sam's on the stairs. Wearing a dressing gown – not hers – too big for her. It's falling open at the front and I can see her breasts, naked and pale. She screams, runs at me, puts her arms around my chest and tries to yank me backwards.

'Let him go, Jack! *Let him go!*'

He's choking now. I come to slowly, release my hand from his throat. Red marks from my fingers on his neck. He

leans into the wall behind him and does nothing. Just stares at me, rubbing his fingers against his neck, to ease the soreness. I can hear her sobbing now.

'You bastard, Jack. You bloody bastard!'

I go, slamming the door behind me. I get into the car and drive. Nowhere, anywhere. Down empty streets with sleeping houses, rows and rows of terraces, roads turning left and right, a maze of terraced streets. Then turning into streets of semis, then roads of quiet sedate detached houses, crouched behind tall hedges, beyond gravel drives. I'm not even sure where I am. I drive until the blood's not beating in my ears anymore. Then I stop the car, turn off the engine. Pressure building in my chest. The noise I find myself making frightens me. I didn't even know I could cry like that.

It's three in the morning when I get home. I pour myself a double Scotch and sit in the back garden and drink it. The heat is still heavy in the air. It's not a night for sleeping. The Scotch is doing its job. Fingers of warmth spreading out from my belly, blurring the edges. Then another. Then I stumble my way to the bathroom, rattle through the cabinet looking for the pills the doctor had given me back in the winter when I had trouble sleeping. I haven't finished them. They should still be here. They are. I take two and swallow them down with another gulp of whisky, stagger upstairs to the bedroom, strip off my clothes and lay naked on top of the bed. Within minutes darkness closes in on me.

Sleeping pills take you to another place. Whisky does as well. The two of them together – you have no choice. You're out there beyond the shore, sinking into a dark ocean, beyond the reach of light or sound. When the light comes to claim you again, when the outside world, the morning, reaches down into the depths and drags you back up again, it's no joke.

At first I think it's the alarm clock, and just lie there, ignoring it, trying to swim back into that darkness, to feel it close again over my head. But I'll have to move, I'll have to wake up enough to turn it off. Then it dawns on me it can't be the alarm. I hadn't set it; why would I have done that? It's the front-door bell. Ringing and ringing. It's Sam. She wants to plead with me to forgive her. She wants me to take her back. So I start swimming back up towards the surface, opening my eyes on light streaming in towards the window. I move to get up. Needles darting into my head. I pull on some jogging bottoms and a T-shirt that have been left on the floor, stagger to the bathroom, splatter cold water over my face. In the cabinet, a bottle of paracetamol. I take two and wash them down with water from the tap. The ringing is going in rhythms. Two rings, then a ten-second break. Then two rings again. She wants to come back. I hurry downstairs.

Of all the people it could have been – Sam or her mother come to fetch some more of the kid's things – Dave even, full of shame and contrition – one of Sam's friends not knowing she's moved out – I wasn't expecting her. Laura's mother. I recognize her at once. Although she looks different than she did outside the coroner's court that day. How long ago that all seems now. Her face is no longer downcast; there's more colour in it. Her hair's cut shorter, in a more trendy style. She's wearing jeans and a pink top.

'Mr Philips?'

'Yes.'

'I'm sorry – it must be a shock, me coming round like this out of the blue. But I need to talk to you.'

18

LISA

For weeks I long to see her again. But she doesn't come. If she did, would she be wearing her blue school uniform? The blazer fresh and clean, no blood on it. Her white school blouse with its pressed collar sitting neatly against her pale neck. Or younger, in her pink anorak with the fur-trimmed hood, her blue jeans, standing at the bottom of the garden near the workshop door, her face in shadows. Sometimes I imagine I hear her singing to herself outside in the garden, and I glance up and look through the window, and think for a moment that I see her sitting there on the grass, in the pale lavender cotton frock that once was her favourite. A little girl of five or six, her hair, almost blonde then, glistening in the spring sunshine. She's singing catches of songs she learnt at school and threading daisies into chains. But when I blink and look again she's gone; she isn't real.

Sometimes I'm out shopping and I think I see her. Walking up ahead of me in the street. It could be a child of almost any age. A child of three, tottering along, her small hand slipped into the hand of a stranger. A child of six or seven, with thin limbs and a pretty frock. An older child of nine or ten in jeans. Older still, a child that's almost not a child, a teenager, in a royal-blue blazer and skirt. It doesn't matter; she is timeless now, my Laura. She is caught like a leaf in a whirlpool, going round and round in my heart. Sometimes I race to catch up with her and getting close almost say her name out loud. But then a slight turn of her head, a different aura about her, the way she moves her shoulders or her limbs. And I realize it's not her, it's not Laura. My heart aches to see her again. But weeks pass. She does not come.

'Mrs Jenkins?'

They look young. Too young to be buying a house, to be tying their lives up to mortgages.

'Yes. You must be Mr and Mrs Richards. Come in.'

I should have asked the estate agent to come around and do this. I'm no good at selling a house, at selling anything really. How do I do it? This is the house where I've lived for fifteen years. Where I raised my child. Look, this is the bedroom, where she was conceived. This is the living room where the police constables sat that day and twitched uncomfortably, and told me my daughter was dead. So now I'm selling the house, I'm letting go of my life, you see, letting it break away from me piece by piece. What will be left of me when it's all gone?

Still, I don't think I do a bad job. I'm not overenthusiastic, but they seem to like what they see. The wife is really pleased about the kitchen. She likes the beech-effect units that Derek fitted himself two years ago, the terracotta tiles. She loves the views from the window down the garden.

'Is the summer-house staying?' she asks.

'Yes, it is. My husband used it as a workshop, but he doesn't live here anymore. We've split up.'

'Oh, I'm sorry,' she says, looking embarrassed.

'Of course there are other houses we'd like to see before we make up our minds,' they say, shaking my hand on the doorstep when they leave. 'But we like it very much.'

But I don't hear from them again. They must like one of the other houses better, or maybe they've decided to go for something smaller. A three-bedroomed semi is a lot for a young couple to buy these days. I've been lucky, I suppose. It was handed to me on a plate, along with Derek. Twenty-two years of age, and a three-bedroomed semi dropped into my lap, with no mortgage to pay. Bought with the proceeds from his mother's house.

'I suppose you'd like me to carry you over the threshold,' he said. I said, yes, of course. And he did. But almost reluctantly; there was no joy in it. He'd swung me up like it was an effort and almost bumped my head on the jamb going through. I should have known then it wasn't going to work.

For the first few months Derek did nothing but DIY on the house. He'd come home from the garage and put on his painting overalls and get down to it, stripping off paper, plastering up cracks, painting. He worked his way through every room. For months and months, the house did nothing but reek of white spirit and paint. Then he started on the kitchen. Putting in new units and retiling the floor. That's when the terracotta tiles went down. The beech units are more recent. The first ones were pine, to make it look cottagey. That was all the rage back then. One bit of me used to think I was so lucky, having a man who was so practical, who could turn his hand to anything. The other bit used to wish he'd ease off, come and give me a cuddle on the sofa, sweep me off early to bed. If I wanted to be near him I had to change into overalls and give him a hand, and I did for a while. But it got boring, night after night, especially after a long day at work. I was working full time before Laura came.

I should have seen the red lights even then. But I didn't. I just thought I must be ungrateful, moaning because my husband worked too hard. When you think what some women have to put up with, it seemed selfish, complaining about that.

'About what?' Angela the counsellor had said. 'Because your husband didn't pay you any attention? Didn't show you affection?'

She made me laugh, putting it like that. Put like that, maybe it wasn't such a bad thing, feeling hard done by. Maybe I had a right.

'Was your sex life ever satisfactory?' she asked.

They're always asking personal stuff like that. Making you feel embarrassed, watching you squirm. Then if you do they make a mental note that you're neurotic, you've got hang-ups about sex.

'I used to think it was, but then I had nothing to measure it against,' I said. 'I've had a few boyfriends before him, of course, but I'd never gone all the way with any of them.'

She raised her eyebrows a bit then, as if it was hard to believe. Being a virgin, a rare thing these days. Those days too. It wasn't as if I'd never had the opportunity. I'd had lots of those. Saving myself, I suppose. I wasn't interested in 'fly-by-nights'; I wanted something that would last.

Was my sex life ever satisfactory?

It was a bit predictable, I suppose. We did it quite a lot in the early years, but then after Laura came, once a week, on a Friday or Saturday night, that sort of thing. Derek had these little routines. He would brush his teeth and gargle, he would put on his pyjama bottoms but not his top. He would turn off the light then turn to me and say, 'Not too tired tonight?' That was it. Not very passionate, I suppose.

I make myself laugh. Here am I, thirty-seven and I'm thinking of passion for the first time in my life.

'What kind of work are you looking for?' he asks.

He has a baby face and a nice smile. Twenty-two, twenty-three. No more than that.

'I don't know. I've been a receptionist in a garage part time for years, but maybe it's time to do something different.'

'I know what you mean,' he says. 'I sometimes think of going back to college to do computer programming, or something like that. But it's a big step, having a life change.'

I have to smile at that. A life change at his age; he's just a baby, he hasn't begun. I look through the cards on display, and bang this touch-screen thing that shows you what jobs are available and in what areas. But nothing seems suitable. Either the money is too low or it's more like a bloke's job – joinery, plumbing, that sort of thing. There's this one post, though. A school for the visually impaired wants a teaching assistant. I take down the details for that.

'You'll be good at that, Lisa. You should apply,' Sheila says.

We're sitting on my patio one evening, sharing a bottle of wine. It's a lovely evening. It's been a scorcher today – the whole week, really. Heatwave weather. I've spent a lot of time in the garden, sunbathing, reading. I wouldn't have done that if Derek had still been here – I wouldn't have given myself permission to do it. I wouldn't have done this either, invite a friend around to sit on the patio in the evening, drinking wine.

'No, really,' she says.

'I dunno. I've had no experience of that sort of thing.'

'Well, you'll never get it either if you don't try.'

'Well, maybe. I suppose it wouldn't hurt to apply.'

It's funny, I've been thinking of doing lots of things these days that I'd never thought of doing before. The other day, I was flicking through the local paper and I read this small ad from this person offering tarot readings and I thought, Why not? Why *not* have a tarot reading? Perhaps because of what the woman in the cafe had said.

You're very psychic. But you know that, don't you?

Do I know it? I know I get these feelings about people. I know I have hunches sometimes, and very often they turn out right. I know I've seen Laura. I've seen her several times. They say everyone's got a gift but I never wondered what mine was before. Maybe I thought I didn't have one; I probably didn't feel that special. But if it turns out that my gift is being psychic, that'll make me special. I'll be pleased about that.

The tarot reader is middle-aged and the worse for wear. Yellow-bleached hair showing its roots and a lived-in face too heavily made up for a woman of her age. The front room of her house is cluttered with bric-a-brac. Useless stuff, really: crystals and fairies and dragons and rubbish like that. Not tasteful stuff, like that medium bloke had. Just tat, really. She gets me to shuffle these cards then spreads them out in a big fan on the table.

'Pick ten. One at a time. It sometimes helps if you move your fingertips over them slowly. If you feel a tingle in your fingertips that's the energy drawing you to a card.'

I do feel tingles, but it could be just blood circulation. She puts the cards I've picked in a certain order then turns them over when I've finished.

'You're at a crossroads,' she says. 'You're not sure which direction you should go in.'

But I'm thinking, Isn't that true of most of the people she sees? Else why would they want a tarot reading?

'You'll have to sort out your finances. There might be legal dealings later in the year. You'll be getting a new job. It'll be a better job for you; it'll enable you to explore your hidden talents.'

Maybe some would be impressed, but I want the details. Where would the money come from? How much would it be? What kind of job would I get, and when?

'Someone close to you will have health problems later on in the year. But it'll be OK. It's nothing you really need to worry about too much.'

But what about the big stuff? *Your only child died on the seventh of November last year in a car accident.* Something as big as that, and she doesn't even mention it. But the first card I picked was the Death card. It had the word 'death' written on it. She placed it in the centre and put the Judgement card sideways over the top of it. When she turned the two of them over did she not see the look on my face?

'Don't worry,' she said. 'It doesn't mean an actual death. In fact, it's quite a positive card. It means you've undergone a big life-changing event. Your old life has fallen away. The Judgement card often means transformation. You'll become like a new person. Many of the things you used to care about won't seem important anymore.'

If she'd really been psychic she wouldn't have said that. She wouldn't have said, 'Don't worry, it doesn't actually mean death.' Because it did; in my case it did. There *was* a death, and my whole life was ripped apart.

Sheila sips her coffee. She looks at me thoughtfully.

'But the Death card doesn't mean real death. Not physical death. It's more on a spiritual level. Your old way of life will die. You'll have a rebirth.'

I get a bit angry then. It's like when the bereavement counsellor talked about moving on.

'What kind of rebirth do you think I can have, Sheila? My only child has died, my marriage has broken up, my home is up for sale. This time next year I don't know where I'll be living. I don't know anything.'

'None of us do, really. It's just in your case, you can't pretend,' she says quietly, her eyes fixed upon me steadily.

That's what I like about Sheila; there are no faces on her. She tells the truth.

I never go to the cemetery. I know it's supposed to give some people comfort, visiting the grave, putting flowers on it. But I can't bear to think of you under all that earth, buried in the dark. You were always afraid of the dark, even up to the time you died you had to have a night-light by the bed. But it's your birthday and I tell myself you'll expect it, I must put flowers on the grave.

Sheila comes with me. We park up the road and walk down to the entrance to the cemetery. My feet feel like lead. I don't want to go. I don't want to see you there.

'Isn't that Derek?'

A man walking briskly out into the road from the direction of the cemetery. He doesn't see us. He walks hurriedly away in the opposite direction.

I've turned to stone.

'I can't go, Sheila. You'll have to take them for me.'

I push the pink and white carnations into her arms.

I wait for her outside the cemetery gate. The sun is shining for you on your birthday. I'm glad of that.

It's all right, Mum. I'm here.

Sheila comes back and takes my arm, leads me up the road towards the car.

'It's covered with flowers. Fresh ones. It's very pretty.'

'That'll be her father,' I say. 'He'll keep it nice for her.'

But I don't regret not seeing it. You're not there, buried in the ground. You're out here with us, in the warm air, in the sun.

Three people interview me for the job in the blind school.

'What do you feel you have to offer us?' the woman asks. She's the only woman out of the three. She has long fair hair and an open straightforward face.

I don't know what to say. So I tell them the truth. A year ago I wouldn't have done that. I would have said what I thought they wanted to hear. Instead I tell them my only daughter died eight months ago, my marriage has broken up, and now I can't think of a better thing to do with my time than help other people. Because when you help other people, when you think of their needs before your own, you can step outside yourself; you help yourself as well. They just look at me, gobsmacked. The woman – the one who'd asked me the question – has tears in her eyes.

We have to wait outside in the staff room. I feel quite flippant because I think I don't stand a chance; one of the other candidates has been a teaching assistant in a school for deaf children for three years. It's bound to be her; surely they'll offer the job to her. So when they call me back in to tell me the news no one is more surprised than me. Some people might think it's nothing; it's just a low-paid job assisting teachers in a school for the visually impaired – we're not allowed to call them blind any more, I'm told – but to me it's special. My new direction. My new start.

Sheila pours me a glass of white wine to celebrate.

'It'll be great for you. Just the kind of change you need. You'll be so good at it too,' she says.

We clink glasses together. The sun shining through the kitchen window sends shards of light flashing from the glass in our hands. Outside in the garden I notice Sheila's roses are out. Soft creamy pinks and deep scarlet, the occasional milky white.

'To your transformation,' Sheila says.

'My what?'

'Remember? The Judgement card.'

'Oh, that. That was a load of rubbish.'

But Sheila just gives me that little smile of hers, raises an eyebrow.

'Why don't you come with me on the twenty-eighth to the spiritualist church?'

'Where?'

'The spiritualist church. They have a special guest evening of clairvoyance then. The medium that's coming is supposed to be really good.'

'I don't know. Sounds a bit spooky, mediums and that sort of thing. What do you have to do? Sit around in a circle holding hands?'

Sheila laughs. 'It's not a seance, not like in the films. They just stand up on the platform and talk. It's very ordinary, really. Nothing spooky happens at all.'

'I don't know. I'm not sure I agree with all this getting in touch with the dead stuff, Sheila. That Martin Clows bloke was OK, but a spiritualist church . . .'

But there's this voice in my head, *your* voice. *Go on, Mum. Why don't you go?* And I know that I'm just pretending I don't want to. Because you might want to talk to me, talk to me more clearly than just these odd words in my head, and if I'm not there how will I hear what you want to say?

'Think about it,' Sheila says.

19

'When Graham died I felt as if I'd lost a limb. Had a leg amputated or something. I would wonder how I could walk around at all, with only one leg.'

My mother laughs drily at herself down the phone. But I know what she means.

'If was a bit like that when we fell out. Like part of me was missing. I missed you so much, you know.'

My mother would never have said something like this before. She would have been too proud. Not only has my mother lost her husband, I think, but she's lost her pride too. It's as if she has no defences. Suffering softens you up. But there's a kind of strength in there too.

'You are looking after yourself? You're eating OK?'

'Yes, Mum. I'm fine.'

'I worry about you, you know. You're so far away. Can't you take some holiday and come and see me?'

'I am, Mum. I'm coming next week. I'm not working at the moment.'

There's a pause. I hear my mother catching her breath.

'Oooh, darling, are you really! I'm *so* looking forward to seeing you.'

I think, How long has it been since I've heard my mother calling me darling? Did she ever before?

I ring Sheila and tell her I'm going away for a couple of weeks.

'By the way, you know you mentioned that spiritualist church? That special medium who's coming?'

'Yes, July the twenty-eighth. The Evening of Clairvoyance.'

'I should be back by then. Maybe I could come.'

'Yes, of course you can. Give me a ring when you get back.'

What was the row about? I don't even remember. I'm not even sure there was a row, and if there was, it was the sort of row that isn't about anything really. That's just a vent for all this stuff that's been accumulating slowly for years, all this resentment, all this hate even, waiting to explode. Like a vent in a volcano. The pressure builds for years. Suddenly, something gives.

Was it something that I said, or didn't say, at Graham's funeral? Something that happened afterwards – some thoughtless word? Some comfort I did not give? Looking back, I think I was an awful bitch. When my mother had Graham behind her, shoring her up, when her foundations were strong, I just went along with things, I let things be. But when Graham died and her foundations crumbled, when she was weak and needed me most, I took advantage. I skewed some word, some thought, some look from a grieving woman out of shape, made it my excuse to dump her. She lost her husband, her daughter and her granddaughter all in the space of six months. For four years I had kept the cold war going. Not even bothering to send her cards on her birthday, or Mother's Day cards. At Christmas I'd condescend; it would be going too far, not to send one then. But I'd just grab one out of those cheap jumbo boxes. Some boring picture of Victorian children sledging or a cartoon-like Father Christmas, and I'd scribble in it, *Many Regards*. Not even, *Love*. I couldn't even bring myself to say that.

I don't deserve for her to forgive me, really. But she does. There's nothing fair about this world, it seems. You're either loved, or you're not. You don't earn it, you don't have to deserve it.

I was thinking all this on the train up to Sheffield, letting the scenery slip past me, the miles of terrace houses of those grim Midland towns giving way to open fields and farmland, to rolling hills. I was thinking about you, wondering if you're now in a world that's fair, or at least makes sense. Where you can see the whole pattern, the entire tapestry, instead of an isolated stitch of it, so that even a child dying suddenly can make sense, can have about it a certain fairness. Or maybe the world you're in is beyond fairness. Maybe fairness is just an idea we've invented when we grumble and complain about the things that make no sense.

It's all right. Everything's all right. Everything's all right in the end.

Your voice in my head. Or maybe my own thoughts. If they are my thoughts, I don't know where I get them from.

Before you died, I hardly had a thought in my head beyond what's for dinner tonight, what's on the telly. Now you're gone, these strange thoughts jump into my head all the time.

My mother's not at the station. I'd told her she must stay at home, she mustn't trouble herself to come out; she doesn't drive after all. So I get a cab. I give the cab driver my mother's address, and think how strange that I don't know the way, that I won't be able to tell when we're getting near. My mother has moved from the house where I grew up, the house where she lived with my dad, where my dad died that day in the garden, mowing the lawn. Then she had married again and brought another man into the house, his presence taking over from my father, driving me away. After I had moved down to London, then met Derek and married, I'd come back quite regularly, bringing Derek sometimes, and then Laura after she was born. Sometimes my mother and Graham would come to stay with us. My mother, a doting grandmother, loving Laura. The feel of her, the smell of her, the weight of her in her arms. Even when she was far beyond the baby stage, loving her, lighting up like a candle in Laura's presence. I used to wonder if she'd ever been like that with me. I used to feel almost jealous, watching them, the pleasure they had in each other.

But after Graham died, the house suddenly grew too big for her. She sold it. She phoned me up and told me of her plans. It was during that time we were supposed to not be speaking so I hung up on her, not wanting to understand, seeing it as another betrayal, cashing in on the family home.

Selling off a part of my father – the place that contained for me all the memories I had of him. But that was just me being selfish, acting like a kid, wanting to punish her still. Now of course I can see that she had to sell; the house was too big for her, the maintenance too much for an ageing widow on her own. For me, a house that contained memories viewed from a distance was something manageable, even desirable, but when you live in the midst of it, when the memories are all around you, crowding you like ghosts, that's a different thing. I should know. Aren't I selling up too?

The taxi stops outside her block of flats. They're modern, purpose-built, with a clean, classic grey-and-white façade; the ones on the upper floors each have a balcony and coordinating white-painted railings, looking over the neat communal lawns. I glance up and there's a figure on the second floor, standing on the balcony gazing down at me as I climb out of the taxi, and I know instantly, although the figure is some distance away and I can't clearly see her face, it is my mother waiting. She raises her arm to wave, and I can sense her smiling, although I can't see it, and the thin sound of her voice drifts down to me, calling my name. I look up, squinting into the light, and I wave back, and just for a minute I sense you are standing next to me, looking up with me and saying, *That's Granny. That's Granny waiting for us.*

Now that she's not alone, my mother's ravenous for this thing she has missed – company, and conversation, and just the sense of someone being there, in the room with her or busy in another part of the flat, having a shower perhaps, or preparing something in the kitchen. Even at night when we lie in our separate rooms I know she has this sense that she is not alone; there is someone else there with her now.

But it's as if my being there brings to the surface the pain of all those times when there is no one, and every so often she drifts away from me, losing herself in her own thoughts, or gazing wistfully out of the window. Or she looks at me, looks beyond me, her gaze slightly unfocused and says, 'It's so nice to have somebody here. It's such a shame you can't stay.' And I'll tell her again the reasons why I have to get back, about the new job I'm starting, the house I'm trying to sell. But I know that she isn't really listening; she's thinking fearfully of the time when I will be gone and the loneliness will crash back in, like rubble falling upon her.

'Do you go out much?' I ask. She says yes, she has these groups at the Over-Fifties Club she goes to twice a week. A keep-fit class and a watercolours class, and sometimes a young woman comes in with photographs or slides of past times and they talk about their childhoods in the war, the rationing and the Anderson shelters, and family holidays at Grimsby or Skegness, and how strict schools were compared to now, and how well behaved they were as teenagers, knowing their place, not like they are these days, wanting everything at once, and getting into drugs and debt. There's a small group from the club who phone each other during the week and arrange to meet up sometimes for lunch, or for an outing on a Saturday evening to the British Legion where they have a man with a keyboard who sings all the old songs.

'So it's not too bad,' I say, cajolingly. 'You do get out a fair bit.'

'Sundays are the hardest,' my mother says. 'The others have families living close by they can go to for Sunday dinner. I have no one. The days seem very long then.'

I say nothing, tendrils of guilt wrapping around me, thinking of the past four years of silence, when my mother didn't even have the comfort of talking to me on the phone, her only child, or the pleasure of my visits. And then I do what I've never done before. I get up and walk over to where she's sitting, and I put my arms around her. She leans into me, her white hair against the crook of my elbow.

'I'm sorry, Mum,' I say. She says nothing, just reaches up with a thin, veined hand and pats my arm, and I think how old her hand looks, how frail, the hands always betraying our age, no matter what effort we make elsewhere.

Of course, we talk about you. Not in the sense of missing you, of your not being there, but as if you're still amongst us, the memories of you woven into our lives. We talk about what a perfect baby you were, sleeping through the night from only a few weeks of age, the rhythms of your sleeping and waking synchronized into predictable cycles. About how happy you were, how placid, not grizzly and fretful and demanding like some babies are but always ready to hand out your smiles; you'd light up the room with them. My mother told me how one day she'd taken you in your pushchair into town and she'd stopped in a square by the church and a pigeon had flown down to alight on the ground in front of you. You spread out your arms wide with delight. 'Oooh!' you said. 'Oooh! Oooh!' – as if seeing a pigeon was something miraculous, something wonderful to behold. I said yes, you were always like that. As if each day unfolded something fresh and surprising. And I told my mother about your first day at school, trotting along the road next to me, so proud in your grey pleated skirt and blazer (grey then, in the infants, not royal blue). I said goodbye to you inside the classroom, wrapping my arms around you and hugging you and saying, 'I'll see you this afternoon.' And you saying, as if the thought had just occurred to you, as if it hadn't dawned on you what a first day at school was really like, 'Am I staying at school for lunch, then, Mummy?' I said, 'Yes, yes you are,' and you said, 'Do teachers know how to cook, Mummy?' We laugh together, thinking of you and your childish wonder at the age of five, discovering the world and the way it worked like a series of revelations.

'Sometimes I feel she's still here,' I say at last, the laughter dissipating now, threatening to turn to tears.

'I'm sure she is, dear,' my mother says quietly. We sit together, feeling no need to talk anymore. The silence enters us like a blessing.

I hire car and take my mother for outings. We drive into the countryside, stop for lunch at quaint-looking pubs. We visit a craft centre, turning the ceramic pieces, the turned-wood bowls and other artefacts over in our hands, sharing our comments on them. If we have to walk any distance from the car my mother takes my arm, and I feel her slightness, the uncertainty of her steps, and I think this is it now. The roles are reversed; I'm the mother now. Back in the flat I'm the one who notices the passing of time, who will turn and say, 'What shall we have for lunch?' 'What shall we have for tea?' She will look slightly startled, as if she hasn't realized time has passed at all and say, 'Oh, are you hungry, dear? Is it time to eat?' I'll go into the kitchen and rummage in the fridge and make her an omelette with salad, a pork chop with some green beans and new potatoes, or whatever we've remembered to get in, and lay it out on a tray for her and give it to her on her lap, and I'll wonder what she bothers to make when I'm not there. If she bothers some days to eat at all?

In the last few days of my visit my mother is tetchy with me, distant, but I know it's only because she's preparing herself for when I'll be gone; she's trying to make it easier for herself. Then the day comes, and I stand there in the hallway with my suitcase and the taxi is waiting down below and my mother hugs me, tears in my eyes, and says, her voice small like a hurt child, 'You will come again, won't you? You won't leave it too long?' What I hear inside my head is, 'You won't make it four years again, will you? You won't do that again?' And I hug her back and reassure her, telling her I'll come up as soon as I can. I'll come during the half term when I'll have a week's holiday from the blind school. She asks when that will be but I don't like to say, because it'll be in October and this is only July. She'll think that's too long, an eternity away.

The taxi driver loads my case into the boot and I get into the car and as we pull away I look back and up at the flat on the second floor, but it's not my mother I see on the balcony this time waving. It's Laura. She is wearing the baggy red T-shirt I bought her for her thirteenth birthday and light blue cropped jeans. Her chestnut-brown hair is flicking in front of her face in the breeze. She is smiling. I yell out to the taxi driver to stop the car. My heart is racing. The taxi pulls over. The driver turns to me, his face confused, full of questions. I jump out, run over the gravel forecourt towards the entrance that leads to the lift, but as I run I can see that she is not there. There is nobody there.

Just wait, darling, I say to myself, turning back slowly to the taxi. *I'll be back*.

20

When I arrive home there is a message from the estate agents on the answerphone. We have an offer on the house. A couple who want to relocate from Birmingham with their teenage daughter came to view it whilst I was away. The offer is five thousand short of the asking price.

'But there's no chain,' the estate agent tells me, when I phone him back. 'They've already sold their house. It should be a quick sell.'

I phone up Derek at work. He sounds short-tempered when he comes to the phone, as if he can't be bothered to talk to me, as if I'm some irritant from his past that he's already forgotten. But perhaps I'm just being paranoid. Perhaps he's just having a bad day.

'I don't know,' he snaps at me, when I tell him about the offer. 'Every fucker's out for what they can get these days. If you want a quick sale, then take it. Otherwise you could try pushing for a little more.'

'But they might back off. They might look elsewhere if I do that. The estate agent said the market's not at its best.'

'I don't know. It's your decision.'

'I'll accept it, then.'

'Do as you please.'

'Derek, can I see you? Come for dinner tomorrow.'

Why did I say that? I felt a surge of panic, a sense that my world is slipping away from me too fast, a sudden urge to hold on to just one small part of it before it goes.

The next day he rings the doorbell like he's a visitor, enters like a stranger enters somebody's home, self-conscious but slightly curious. I offer him a glass of wine and he refuses, says he prefers tea. He speaks without looking at me, as if he has something to hide, and I think as I make the tea, He's not looking after himself, he's not taking care. Derek who used to be so clean and tidy, who would scrub his nails so hard the oil from the cars hardly showed, except as a thin line at the quick, in a faint soiling of his broken cuticles. Now his hands are cracked and dirty. He's wearing a three days' growth of beard. His hair needs a wash.

'Where did you say you are staying?'

I place the white mug of tea in front of him. When he picks it up he will leave soiled fingerprints on its glazed surface. A quick flick of his eyes towards my face.

'I didn't.'

'But I should know, Derek. So I can send on your post.'

'No need. What post do I get anyway? Only junk mail. The bills are in your name, aren't they?'

'Yes. But I should know where you're staying. There'll be stuff about the house.'

'I told you, phone me at work if you've something you want to say.'

I'm quiet for a moment. He sips his tea. He looks uncomfortable, edgy. Maybe he thinks he's gone too far; it wasn't necessary to be so curt and secretive.

'I'm all right,' he says, more gently now. 'I'm staying with a mate. It's an informal arrangement. He wouldn't want me to spread it around.'

I think, What mate? Derek had no mates. He has acquaintances from work maybe, sometimes he'll go to the pub with one or two on a Friday. But not mates. Not anyone who'll say, 'Come and stay at my place till you sort yourself out.' No one that close. But I say nothing.

'You managing all right? You're getting the housekeeping money I send you OK, aren't you? It gets into the bank on time?' His voice has shifted down a gear, is softer.

'Yes, it's fine.'

'Good.'

'Dinner will be ready in a minute. It's shepherd's pie.'

Your favourite, I think, but I don't say it. I made it for you the day you proposed to me. Remember? The day you said, 'Would you like to be another Mrs Jenkins?' A funny way to propose – no tenderness, no romance. We weren't into that, were we?

He sits there in silence, gazing towards the kitchen window. I turn my back to him, open the oven door to check that the topping on the shepherd's pie is browning nicely. Derek used to like it brown and crunchy on top. Can he see the workshop from there? Is he wondering if I've taken the

217

newspaper clippings down? All those words in bold text: **killed, maimed for life, fatally injured.** The heat from the oven sweeps into my face, makes me blink, makes me cough. I close the door, stand up, wipe a tear from my eye.

We make small-talk while we eat, polite formal conversation like two people getting ready to be strangers, getting ready to go their separate ways. He tells me things are busy at work; there's talk of moving to a new premises, a bigger one. Expansion. I tell him about my new job and he says it'll be good for me; I'll be good at that. I tell him I've just got back from visiting my mother and he raises an eyebrow, knowing how things used to be. 'How is she?' he asks and I say, 'She's fine, she's softer now; something in her has changed.' His mouth tenses when I say that but he won't ask what I mean. Then I say, 'But she's lonely.' I want to ask, Are you? Are you lonely now we're apart? But I don't, of course; it wouldn't be fair. I was the one who asked him to leave, after all. Not that we'd been together really before that much, not that we'd been together for years.

'Maybe you can go and live with her,' he says, very matter-of-factly. That startles me a little, him saying that, because I'd thought it myself. Once the house is sold, once I've got my share of the money – which will be quite a lot, considering how much property's gone up since we bought it – I'll be a free agent, I could go anywhere.

'I don't know; there's this new job I'm starting.'

'There's jobs like that in other places too.'

'Well, maybe later.'

What will you do, Derek? I want to say. When you've got your share of the money, what will you do with it? What will you do with your life? But I say nothing. He wouldn't tell me anyway. And if he did, I'd be too frightened of what I would hear.

Afterwards, when we've finished eating and had coffee and I've cleared the things away, he looks at his watch, says it's time to go and I think, Why? What do you do with yourself these long evenings on your own? Who do you see? Is there another woman in your life? Or do you still walk the streets for hours, in all weathers, in the rain, looking for God knows what? For some girl who reminds you of Laura? For that man, that Jack Philips? Then suddenly I want to ask him, Do you see Laura too? Has she come to you too, like she's come to me? But I don't ask. I tell him I'll let him know how the sale is going. I hope things work out for him, I say. He shrugs then, mumbles something like, What's there to work out for me now? But I don't take him up on that. I show him to the door. Like he's just a guest, a visitor; he's not my husband, not someone who had carried me over the threshold all those years ago when we had just got married, when the future was something that had a shape in it waiting to be discovered, not the loose thing it is now. I watch him walk down the path, go through the gate, get into his car and drive away, and I think, He won't come to this house again. We'll never be together in this house again. It'll be sold and we'll take the money, half each because that's the fairest thing, and go our separate ways, and there'll be no place left, no place that's solid, that contains all the memories we have of Laura. She'll fade into thin air, between these walls where other people will live. They won't even notice she's there.

What surprises me most is how like a real church it feels. Not from the outside; you'd hardly know it's a church from the outside. It's like those prefabs where the Scouts meet, or where the WI holds its bring-and-buy sales. But there's an altar inside, covered with a blue satin cloth and decked with flowers, there's an organ in the corner. The floor is laid with a blue plush carpet that feels thick and spongy and swallows the sound of my footsteps. The chairs are solid and wooden and arranged in rows, and each one has little ledges in the back where prayer books and hymn sheets can be placed by the person in the chair behind. There is a sense of hush, a silence. As if something sacred happens here. I wasn't expecting that.

We arrive early. 'We've more chance of being picked sitting near the front,' Sheila whispers. What will I do, I wonder, if I'm picked? Giggle, faint, burst into tears?

The church fills up quickly. Soon it seems that almost every available chair has someone sitting on it. There's a shuffle at the back and more chairs are being fetched so that everyone has somewhere to sit. I sneak glances around me. There are fat people and thin ones, old and young, men and women, and even a few children coming in with their mothers. I look for a mark of suffering on their faces, some sign that says we have all been bereaved; we all have that in common. Isn't that why we are here? But I can't see any. People are smiling and chatting to their neighbours and generally looking normal, except for a few that sit quietly with their eyes closed.

What am I looking for? Suffering isn't something that shows, like a scar on the face. If people look at me they'll see me sitting talking to Sheila, looking normal. They wouldn't think, That woman has suffered, that woman has been bereaved. Perhaps the medium might, but she's supposed to be psychic, to see things other people can't.

I'm on the verge of leaning over to Sheila, to whisper to her that I've changed my mind; I'll just slide out now quietly before it starts. She needn't come; she can stay and enjoy the service, but perhaps it isn't for me after all. But then this woman with a tight perm and glasses tied to a cord around her neck starts to play the organ. Everyone shuffles to their feet and starts to sing, 'In the great by and by we shall meet on that beautiful shore,' and it's too late. I'll have to stay.

A fat lady with a wobbly throat is taking the service. In spite of her size, her voice is tiny – high and squeaky like a small child's – and it seems so odd coming from someone so big that I start to giggle. I take my handkerchief out of my pocket and snuffle into it, trying to turn the giggle into a cough. Sheila shoots me a look but I look back at her helplessly and start to giggle again. The woman is talking about 'Our Friends on the Other Side'; it makes me think that they've all emigrated somewhere. They're across the sea, on the other side of the world. Maybe they're Down Under, having a better life somewhere. *We shall meet on that beautiful shore.* It's beautiful, isn't it, in Australia? The Great Barrier Reef. With all its coral and tropical fishes. Is that what heaven is like, Laura? I think. Like a barrier reef.

But then instead of giggling I'm starting to feel irritated, even angry. This fat lady in a too-tight floral suit is talking in a squeaky voice about 'Our Friends on the Other Side', as if they'd just gone on a bloody holiday somewhere, smiling as she talks in a sugary sweet way, and there is Laura now inside my head, in that time that stands still, in that time that never moves on, far out at the edge of her life, bleeding to death in the rain. I want to get up and go, I feel sick. But something keeps me on my seat, and we're on our feet again singing, *Lord, make me a channel of thy peace*, and I think, What would the Catholics think if they could see us now? Isn't this one of their favourite hymns? We sit down again and the fat lady with the squeaky voice introduces Janice, Our Guest for Tonight, who is going to help us talk to Our Friends on the Other Side.

The atmosphere changes then. Just like that. Janice stands up and walks out to the front. She's been sitting in the corner behind the altar, waiting. Sitting quietly with her eyes closed, as if she was praying. She's in her forties, with shoulder-length dark hair and a pale face. She looks ordinary, she'd pass easily in a crowd, but when she walks out to the front of the platform and begins to speak, she comes alive. As if an energy has suddenly seized upon her, is running through her veins.

'I want to come straight to this lady in the front. The one in the green jumper.'

I don't realize for a moment it is me she means. I don't realize I'm wearing green. Sheila gives me a nudge.

'Y-you m-mean me?'

'Yes. God bless you, my dear. I have a child here, a young

girl. Twelve, perhaps. Thereabouts. She passed last autumn. A very sudden death. Can you take this, my dear?'

I can't answer. My throat's seized up. The room has fallen away.

'She was wearing her school uniform. She was running. She didn't look where she was going. She didn't see the car coming.'

Everyone has fallen away. All I hear is the medium's voice and the sound of my heart pounding.

'She wants you to know she didn't suffer. She wants you to know she wasn't alone. The man who was driving the car in the accident, he held her hand, he spoke to her gently. She wasn't frightened. This man is in trouble, she says. He needs help.'

21

'Why don't you stay tonight?' Sheila says.

'Thanks,' I say. 'I think I will, if that's OK.'

I don't want to be alone. Not tonight. Sheila's opened a bottle of wine and we're sitting in the garden. It's my favourite time of the day. The air has cooled and the colours have deepened, are burning with an intensity before the light fades and dusk falls. We sit for some moments saying nothing.

'Put it out of your head if it upsets you,' Sheila says suddenly.

'It doesn't upset me,' I say.

The medium said other things too, apart from the bit about that Jack Philips. She said I was going to be embarking on a new direction at work. She said I had gifts I never knew I had. I would be doing things in the future that I would never have thought possible; Laura was going to help me with this.

After she had finished with me she moved on to other people and she told them ordinary mundane things, things I wouldn't have thought the spirits on the other side would bother themselves about. One woman had been worried about her cat and was told by a cat-loving friend in spirit it would get better soon. Another person who was moving house was told by his father to check the central heating because it might be faulty. A young woman who had just gone on a spending spree she couldn't really afford was told she needed to be more careful with money. Surely spirits are beyond all that trivial stuff? Why would they bother coming back for that?

'At least Laura didn't come back to tell me she liked the new shoes I had bought, or ask why had I changed my washing powder. At least she had real things to say. Things that matter.'

'What do you think it meant?' Sheila says.

He held her hand. He spoke to her gently. This man is in trouble. He needs help.

'I think it's something to do with Derek.'

'What do you mean?'

'I don't know. He's not been himself, since Laura ... since the accident.'

But when was he ever himself? I think. Perhaps he was always weird, always unhinged, but I hadn't noticed. I had been looking through holes all the time, like the ones cut out of the papers, only seeing what I wanted to. The rest screened out.

'What are you going to do?' Sheila says.

The dusk has fallen now, has leached all the colour from the garden. I can feel Sheila looking at me but I can't see her eyes. Her face is in shadow.

'I'm going to go and see Jack Philips. I'm going to see if he needs help.'

*

225

I thought there would be loads of J. Philips in the directory, or maybe, being a cop, extra-careful, he'd be ex-directory. But there's only about a dozen listed and I start to phone each one in turn. The first 'J. Philips' I phone is answered by a woman. The next one's a man but he sounds old, much older than the Jack Philips I'm looking for.

'No, love, I'm a Joe Philips, not Jack,' he says.

The next one is a John Philips, which of course is sometimes known as Jack, but he says he never is. He's always John, never Jack, and he doesn't sound right anyway; I know he isn't the one. The fourth is answered by a man. In his thirties, or thereabouts. His voice vague, distracted.

'Is there a Jack Philips living there?'

'Yes, speaking.'

I put the phone down quickly, my heart racing. I ring the address in the book with a pen. *22, Beaumont Road.*

That's the one, I hear you say in my head.

On the way the next day I drive down the road where it happened. I pass by the bus stop where she'd been getting off that day, where she'd run out into the road, where she'd been hit and lay in the road and died.

I have passed this way before a few times – it's hard not to; it's difficult to drive into town from my house any other way, other than weaving through dozens of streets, going several miles out of your way. In the early weeks, months really, I did just that. I would have given anything not to drive by this place where it had happened. I would wonder, if I stopped the car and got out and walked over towards the middle of the road and peered down closely, would I still see a stain of blood? Some stain they had not been able to clean out with their special detergents. (Is that what they do? Send some man around afterwards to clean up the stain? Who would want to do a job like that?) Of course, it would be very faint and faded, discoloured to a barely perceptible brown. What would I have done if I'd seen it there? Would I have knelt down on the road and touched with my fingers that faint bloodstain where my daughter had lain dying? But this road is not connected with Laura anymore. She's somewhere else. A better place? Maybe. Not here.

An ordinary road with 1950s semis. The kind of house a policeman would live in. Neat and well maintained. I am surprised it's so close to me. Only seven minutes' drive away. The curtains are still drawn and I think, Maybe they've just forgotten to open them; they can't still be in bed at this time, at eleven in the morning. I walk up to the front door and ring the bell. I hope he's out. I hope no one answers the door. I'll be able to think, At least I tried; I can leave it to fate now. At first no one answers. I ring it a second time, and a third, and I want to walk away but something tells me not to.

Stay. Try again. Keep on trying.

I count ten between rings. I ring again, and again, and again.

Footsteps running downstairs. The door suddenly opens. He's there, blinking into the daylight, his eyes full of sleep. I can hear the blood pounding in my ears. But my voice sounds calm.

'Mr Philips? Mr Jack Philips? I'm sorry – it must be a shock, me coming round like this out of the blue, but I really need to talk to you.'

He's pulled on a T-shirt and tracksuit bottoms but he looks dishevelled, the muscles of his face collapsed and soft, as if he hasn't yet woken them up. Funny hours this policeman keeps, I think, and then I think, No, something doesn't feel quite right. There's an emptiness in the house behind him, and the look in his eyes is more than just sleep; it's a yearning, a loss. He stares at me, as if he's not seeing me really, and his jaw is working up to speak but then he changes his mind. It suddenly occurs to me that he might not have a clue who I am.

'I'm Mrs Jenkins – the mother of – you know – Laura.'

'Laura. Yes of course, of course I know who you are.'

He seems to wake up, as if suddenly snapping out of a dream. He sweeps his hand up to push the hair away from his forehead, shakes his head slightly, as if to shake the cobwebs away and take in this person standing on his doorstep, startling him into the day.

'I'm sorry, it's just that I wasn't expecting – I mean, I was expecting someone else.'

'I didn't mean to alarm you,' I say. I feel a fool. What must he think? The mother of the girl he accidentally killed standing here at his doorstep, saying she needs to talk. Perhaps he thinks I have a knife hidden under my jumper, in my handbag, tucked into the belt of my jeans. If he asks me in, will I suddenly produce it, stab it into his heart?

'I'm sorry, you must think me rude. Please come in. I'm afraid you haven't caught me at the best of times,' and then he flushes red and seems to catch up with what he's said. Strange that he's the one who seems in a state and I'm so calm and composed.

He steps aside to let me in and for a moment we stand together in the hallway, only a couple of feet apart. If revenge was what I wanted, if that was what I was after, now would be the time. I would slide that knife out from under my jumper, slip it out of my bag, pull it from the belt of my jeans, and stick it into his chest.

'This is for Laura,' I would say.

'Let's go into the kitchen to talk,' he says, and he turns and walks in front of me to show me the way. I stare at his back and realize that it hadn't occurred to him at all. That I might have a knife hidden somewhere, that I was here hell-bent on revenge. I feel guilty then. How could I have imagined he would think such thoughts, and yet been so far from the truth that he could turn his back to me and be that trusting.

'Would you like a coffee?' he says, filling the kettle. 'Excuse me. I'm afraid I've just got up. I'll be human again in a minute, when I've had some coffee.'

I notice that he is standing on the tiled floor in his bare feet. His feet look white and vulnerable.

'I'm not usually like that, sleeping in to this time in the morning. I do apologize. Things are a bit out of sorts at the moment.'

'I should apologize for coming around like that, without warning.'

He throws me a glance, but says nothing. He spoons coffee into the cups.

'Milk? Sugar?'

I tell him yes and no and then after a few moments of awkward silence the kettle comes to the boil and he pours the water into the cups and stirs it, carefully, slowly, as if this ritual is giving me time, time to compose my thoughts, to think what to say. But then he suddenly turns to face me, the coffee steaming on the work surface behind him, and I see the mask has slipped now and the muscles of his face are fighting against each other.

'Mrs Jenkins, I don't know why you're here. You say you need to talk to me but I can't understand why you would want to. How you can bear to sit in my house and even look at me. I'm so, so sorry about your daughter, Mrs Jenkins. I'm so sorry about Laura.'

Is that what you wanted, Laura? For us to sit together and talk like this? He tells me about his wife leaving, her affair with his best friend, how much he misses his children. (Going careful here, looking at me all the time, gauging my reaction.) He tells me about his mother's suicide and his father he hardly knew and a counsellor called Tom Swift who is saving his life.

I talk about you, mainly about you, and he winces as I talk but carries on listening. I tell him I have seen you. Several times. He tells me he saw you too, twice, standing outside his house with your father in the weeks following the accident. That shocks me, him telling me that. I'm almost jealous; I don't want anyone to see you. Only me.

I tell him then what the medium said in the church that night, and about Derek too – the shrine he built in the shed. He doesn't flinch; he's seen too many things I guess, when he was a policeman, to be shocked by this. I tell him about the old life that's slipping away from me and the new one that hadn't yet fallen into place. We talk as if we are old friends, as if we have known each other for years.

An Accidental Light

I hope this is what you want, in that place where you are that's a better place than this. I hope it isn't the knife, revenge at any price. That's not the memorial I want for you. Something has changed in me. Something has opened me up, so that I'm not living the half life I was living, but a whole one. Even though you were in my life, it was still a half life – not the bit that had you in it – but the rest of it. Now I feel things more. I feel the hurt, but it's bittersweet. The silt has cleared from my veins.

22

'Do you think this is wise, Lisa?'

Sheila and Jack have come for supper. She is standing close to me in the kitchen, tossing a green salad whilst I spoon pasta carbonara into warm dishes. Outside on the patio Jack is sitting alone, sipping a cold beer.

'There's no harm in him. You can see that.'

'Lisa, I'm not saying he's a bad person. I'm just thinking of you. Considering the circumstances, and that.'

I give her a small wry smile, but I'll not try to explain. Sheila does not know that in the past two weeks I have spent hours in this man's company. I have walked in woods with him, I have knelt in small village churches with him, he has visited me several times here in my home.

After we have eaten, we sit together outside on the patio, three people, all with separate lives and disconnected, but close in a way that I never was with Derek, talking together of small safe things – the weather, the fading summer – and we watch as the colours in the garden, the green of the grass, the deeper green of the laurels and the conifers, the pinks and mauves of the gladioli and the dahlias, the scarlets of the roses, deepen as dusk grows near, deepen until they are almost luminous, before they fade into the night.

Jack talks about his childhood. About his aunt and uncle in Plymouth who brought him up, the letter his uncle sent him that was written by his father, the visit to his father's sister in Bristol, the warmth she showed him. Sheila watches him quietly as he speaks. She's taking him in. She's beginning to understand why he's here.

'What will you do? Will you get in touch with your father, Jack?'

'I don't know. So much has happened since then.'

He falls silent, and we leave him musing with his thoughts into the deepening dusk. Sheila tells me about her own plans to move. She is thinking of going to live in Scotland, to be close to her daughter who has had a baby. A boy. Sheila's first grandchild. She shows me the picture. He's crumpled and wizened like all newborns are. Sheila strokes his face in the photo gently with her thumb. For her right now there is no other baby in the universe but him. This will be something I'll never have, this sense of life going on in a grandchild, looking for my face in his. Sheila reads the look in my eyes and puts the photo away.

'He's beautiful,' I say, because she needs me to say it. 'I'll miss you, Sheila. You've been the best friend I have.'

'Scotland is not on the other side of the world. A five-hour train journey. You'll be able to come up during your school holidays.'

'You've made your mind up, then?'

I have a feeling suddenly like I'm falling. I'm falling in slow motion through my known universe. But there are people in this universe who will throw me a lifeline. People I love. Sheila, my mother, even you, Laura, from that place where you are. They won't let me fall forever. They won't let me go.

'I've made up my mind to sell. But it'll be ages yet.'

Jack stands up to go. We both notice how weary he suddenly looks, his face pale under the dim patio lights.

'Thank you for a lovely evening, Lisa. So good to meet you, Sheila. Hope we'll meet again.'

He stoops over me, kisses me lightly on each cheek. Does the same to Sheila.

'Take care, Jack,' I say. 'Drive carefully.'

He flinches. Very slightly, but I notice. Why did I say that? I think. I'm glad of the darkness that hides my blush.

We listen to the sound of his car fading into the night.

'So what's been happening between you and Jack? This isn't the first time he's been here, is it?'

Sheila, bless her. Always perceptive.

'I can't explain it, Sheila. I hardly understand it myself. But he needs my help.'

Sheila raises an eyebrow. 'Isn't he the one who should be helping you, given the circumstances?'

'But he is. Having him here is helping me.'

And it is. Although it's hard for me to say why.

Jack comes around several days later. He brings a DVD. It is a strange sad story set in Vietnam about a taxi-cyclist who falls in love with a prostitute. Afterwards we sit together quietly in the half dark.

'Why did you marry Derek?' he asks.

'I'm not sure. I think because I saw in him the father I had lost. Someone who'd take care of me. Not the right reasons, I suppose.'

'Who's to say what the right reasons are?' he says. And I think, Yes, maybe they were the right reasons then. That's what I needed then.

I take him down the garden and into Derek's workshop. We stare at the plain plasterboard walls and I tell him about the newspaper clippings that had covered the entire surface of one wall. I can still see the small holes where the thumb-tacks had been.

'That's when I knew I couldn't live with him anymore. We had become like strangers,' I say. 'I didn't know what he was capable of.'

'Where are they now?' he asks, and I go over to Derek's desk and open the drawer and take them out. He takes the clippings from me and spreads them over the floor and kneels down and examines them.

'What is he capable of?' he says.

'I don't know,' I tell him.

We stand together looking down at the floor littered with clippings, the words of death leaping at us from the headlines.

Your voice in my head again. *Tell him*, you say.

'Laura wants you to take care, Jack.'

He flinches at the sound of your name.

Later, sitting together in the living room, having a cup of tea before he leaves, he reaches over and strokes my face, and I think for a moment he is going to kiss me. But he doesn't. Although the thought that he might have stays in my mind even after I've gone to bed, so that I can almost feel his lips there, their pressure on my mouth.

23

JACK

When I was a copper the cases that intrigued me most were the missing-persons ones. I'd turn up at the house, equipped with notebook and pencil. *No, officer, I haven't a clue why they went*, they'd say. A son, or a daughter, a husband or wife. *They seemed perfectly fine the day before.* They went off to college or work or whatever quite happily; they were getting on with their lives. They mean it. They haven't a clue. Their faces collapsed with the shock, that blur in the eyes. Sometimes when you dig a little deeper you discover some stresses lurking in the background. Money worries, troubles with a boy or girlfriend. In the case of a couple, some marital strife. But then they seem to rally around. They cheer up. That's the dangerous time, I learnt in the job. That's when they make their minds up, when they're resolved. They disappear, vanish into the ether. Sometimes leave a note but often don't. Even if they do it says nothing, leaves no clues. *Don't worry.*

When I get home from Lisa's there is a message on the answerphone from Aunt Susan, her voice strange and wobbly.

'Your Uncle Keith has died, Jack.'

Suddenly he's become a missing person. He walked out one clear bright day and has gone to live somewhere else.

He'll never be found again. I'm left with the questions. Why now? That stunned mismatch of memory. But when I saw him last he was OK. He was happy, getting on with life. Why now, when we have found each other again? The resentfulness of those silly teenage years, the misunderstanding of a screwed-up young man, falling away. Seeing him clearly again for the hero he really was. He had done his best. He had tried to save me. He had made a mistake. Don't we all?

I stand next to Aunt Susan at the cemetery, and feel her leaning against me, frail like a twig threatening to break. He's being buried. It's what he had wanted. An old-fashioned man. He didn't believe in crematoriums. He wanted the weight of the earth on him. He wanted this plot here up on the hill, where his forebears were buried. Overlooking the ships as they pass on the Sound. All men of the sea, woven now into the salt-laced soil.

I'm surprised by the turnout at the funeral. His cronies from the merchant navy days, drinking mates from the British Legion. Men with the sea in their eyes, faces furrowed by years of salt breezes, with their wives at their side. Friends of my aunt's, from the WI, from the League of Friends where she pushes trolleys around hospitals, even now in her late sixties, twice a week. The funeral is in the Methodist chapel, where my uncle and aunt attended Sunday services almost without fail every week, for years and years. They used to take me with them when I was a boy, until I got to the age of thirteen or so and announced I was an atheist now, so they saw the futility of forcing me and left me at home, but would go alone and pray for me anyway. Nearly the whole congregation turns out for him now. I feel them around us at the graveside as the coffin is lowered, their silent support bearing us up, as my aunt and I throw handfuls of soil to clatter on the lid of the coffin. The weather has turned, squalls threatening as they often do from this sea-battered town. It spits rain from a stormy thunderous sky and the gulls scream at us overhead, drowning the minister's words.

'*Ashes to ashes, dust to dust.*'

My aunt shivers, leans into me. I stand there, a man of over six foot who feels like a small boy burying his father.

'Come back with me.'

The wake is at the church hall. No room in my aunt's tiny bungalow for all these people, all these friends.

'I can't, Jack. My life's here.'

'I don't like leaving you alone.'

She squeezes my arm.

'I'll be all right. I don't think I'll be short of visitors.'

She indicates with a gesture of her head the people around her, standing around sipping their tea, and munching sandwiches and swapping stories about Uncle Keith.

'If you change your mind, you will phone?'

'Of course.'

She looks at me steadily, placing a frail, veined hand against my cheek.

'You're OK, aren't you, Jack? You forgive him, don't you? That thing about the letter. He was sorry about that. He – *we* – made a mistake.'

'No need to forgive him.'

'He loved you very much, you know. Your uncle did.'

'You mean my dad.'

Tears springing in her eyes. Now they're in mine. How easy it is to cry these days.

Sam's on the doorstep wearing a pale lemon linen suit, a jade-green blouse underneath. Her face is set for the battle-ground she is expecting.

'Didn't you get my messages?'

'Yes. I've been away for a bit. I was going to phone you later tonight.'

She looks slightly puzzled. There's no anger in my voice. There's no anger in me. I haven't the energy for it.

'We need to talk.'

'Fine. How about now? This a good time for you?'

Sam steps in and follows me down to the kitchen.

'Tea, coffee – or perhaps something stronger?'

'Tea will do fine.'

While I'm making it I can feel her eyes looking around, checking things out. Am I letting the house go? Are the work surfaces reasonably clean, the cooker, the floor? I'm grateful I had that spell of cleaning yesterday, when I got back from Plymouth. If she'd seen it before I went she wouldn't have been too impressed.

I put the cups down on the table and sit down. I notice the nervous pulling of her right hand on the lapel of the jacket.

'My uncle Keith died. I've been to his funeral.'

She wasn't expecting this. I've disarmed her.

'Oh God, Jack! I'm sorry. What was it?'

'He had a heart attack. I suppose it had to happen sometime. He was popping pills for everything, really.'

'Yes, but still. It's a shock. How's your aunt taken it?'

'Badly, of course. They were everything to each other.'

She flinches. Where in between my words did she hear, *Not like us, Sam. Not like us.*

'I'm sorry,' she says, stumbling now, faltering, looking down at her cup. 'Maybe it's not the right time for me to be here. Maybe I'll come again later.'

'No, it's all right. I'm all right.'

I need to get it in first, I need to say it.

'The other night. I'm sorry about that. It was out of order – I had no right.'

She blinks at me, a double-take.

'N-no, Jack. It was our fault. We should have said something to you, when it started. I wanted to – I was scared, I suppose.'

The million-dollar question. When did it start? I don't ask it. Instead, 'You've every right to see who you want to. We're not together anymore.'

By the look on Sam's face I'd guess she would almost prefer it if I got up angrily, threw a few plates, yelled a few words of abuse.

'It didn't start when I was still with you. There was nothing going on then.'

My turn to look surprised. Has she been reading my thoughts?

'Dave used to pop around sometimes for a coffee, if he was in the area. You know that. You were here mostly. Sometimes you were out – at your counsellor's, or maybe just walking. We used to talk about you. How you were doing. He was worried about you – you know – after the accident. He thought you might do something.'

'Doing something' – euphemism for suicide. If suicide is 'doing something' then carrying on living with the pain is doing nothing. That's what I did then. Nothing.

'So nothing was going on?'

'Not really. Not while I was living with you. I liked Dave. Of course, I did – he's a great guy. Wouldn't be your best friend if he wasn't, would he?'

I try not to react, but her hand shoots quickly up to her mouth as she realizes what she's just said.

'Sorry.'

'It's OK.'

Maybe now's the time. I go for it.

'So, when did it start?'

'Which bit. The falling for him, or the sleeping with him?'

'The first.'

'That was gradual. I can't pinpoint a time. I just felt myself getting more and more attracted to him. He was so supportive – and you – you weren't there anymore.'

'Those evenings, when you got back late after yoga – you were seeing him afterwards, weren't you?'

She lowers her eyes. 'Yes. But nothing happened. We just talked.'

But everything was happening. Like with me. Sneaking off to see my aunt Vera, telling Sam lies. Everything was happening.

'We're over, aren't we, Sam,' I say quietly.

*

Of course we are. The house is being sold. No going back.

A couple come round to view the house. They have a two-year-old, red-faced and grizzly from the heat. The wife is heavily pregnant. I think, Seven years ago that was us. Sam and I. All that hope and expectation. Where's it gone now? They've brought a tape measure to measure up room sizes, to see if their furniture will fit. I don't know if I should let them at first – they haven't made an offer yet, it seems a cheek. Then I think what the hell.

The offer comes. It's too low. They always are – the first ones. The second one's accepted.

'What will you do when the house is sold?'

You're back from Tuscany. You're wearing dark blue cotton trousers and a cream short-sleeved shirt. Your tan has deepened. I'm thinking, So many changes. So much stuff. How much longer will I continue coming here to see you?

'We've agreed I'll get a third of what's left over from the mortgage, and Sam the rest. She needs to buy another house; the kids will be living with her. When I'm earning I'll start paying maintenance.'

'Where will you live?'

'I dunno. Maybe I'll try and find somewhere to rent. A flat, I guess.'

'You're doing so well, Jack. The way you're adjusting. The way you're sorting things out with Sam.'

'Yeah, well, no point in letting it get into the clutches of the solicitors. It always costs you that way.'

But how much is this costing me, coming to see you?

How much longer can I afford to do this? Can I afford to at all? Time, isn't it, to move on.

You must be a mind-reader.

'Maybe we need to talk about how much you still need this support, Jack. How much you feel able to carry on this journey by yourself.'

'Give me a few more weeks,' I say.

One woman moving out of my life and two moving in.

Aunt Vera phones me once a week, usually on a Sunday evening.

'How are you, Jack?'

'Fine, I'm fine.'

'What's happening with you and Sam?'

She knows about the split. I've told her.

'It's over. There's somebody else.'

'Oh, Jack! I'm so sorry. We all are.'

'I'm OK. It might be for the best, in the long run.'

Do I believe that really?

'We think of you all the time, Jack. Come and see us whenever you want.'

'Thanks. I'll remember that.'

'I hope you don't mind, but I told your father about your troubles when he phoned the other day. He wants to phone you, Jack. He wants to know if you'd mind.'

What do I feel? The cold landscape between us shrinking, the snow beginning to thaw? A little bit of hope in me, sprouting like a green shoot from frozen soil. I squash it down.

'I don't know. I'm not sure yet. I'll let you know.'

'Don't be a stranger. Take care.'

And Lisa. That's a turn-up for the books. Who would have believed that, nine months ago, six? We meet up several times a week. We go for walks in thick woods, hushed like cathedrals. We meet for a coffee, for lunch sometimes, in little bistros tucked away down side streets. Once we even go to the theatre. The play is about two sisters growing old in this house together, reliving their past.

'That'll be me,' Lisa says. 'Old and batty and all alone.' But she laughs.

'I don't think so. Not you. You'll never be alone.'

She looks at me. A strange light in her eyes.

'Why do you say that?'

'Everyone that knows you loves you. How can you be alone?'

Pink spots in her cheeks. I want to touch her face. I want to kiss her. But it would be stupid to. We both know that.

'What's going on between the two of you?' you say.

'Nothing's going to happen. Nothing sexual, if that's what you're thinking.'

'Be careful, Jack,' you say. Like a father warning his son on a first date.

'Careful of what?'

'Need and guilt don't make the best bed-fellows.'

That shocked me, you saying that. Using that word, guilt.

I hadn't thought of myself like that for a while. Guilty. I hated you for days for saying that.

Strange, but we seldom talk about Laura anymore. We talk about our plans for the future – the new jobs we are waiting to start, how the house sales are going, whether she's seen Derek recently, how things are working out between Sam and me and the kids. It's as if Laura's name is becoming some kind of taboo, and to mention it would be to evoke ghosts again. But her shadow is always between us, the shadows of the questions Lisa cannot bring herself to ask.

What was it like, Jack, watching my daughter die? Why was it you that was there, and not me?

One Sunday, walking through the hush of a wood, the ground damp from years of fallen leaves cushioning our feet, I risk it.

'She didn't suffer. It was quick. She looked at peace.'

But she didn't answer, just shuddered, as if a chill wind had blown through her.

There's a nip in the air in the evenings now, a sense of the days drawing in. We sit in her garden. She's telling me about the group she's joined at the spiritualist church. Psychic development, she calls it. She's learning how to meditate, how to open her chakras. She knows who her spirit guide is; she's been on guided visualizations and had conversations with him. I worry she's going barmy.

'You sure this is wise, Lisa. All this spirit stuff?'

'But it makes me feel alive, Jack. It gives me such hope.'

And no one can deny the light in her eyes, how it transforms her face.

'D-do you ever – you know – see Laura when you go on these journeys?'

There. I've said it again. The 'L' word.

'No. Not really. But she's with me all the time, anyway. In here, and here.'

She touches her forehead with the ball of her fist, she touches her left breast, where her heart is.

A slight frown between her eyes. Then she says it.

'When you saw her, Jack – those two times, standing across the road looking up at the house? How did she look?'

I take her hand in mine.

'She looked fine, Lisa. She looked great. Happy, normal. No blood. Nothing.'

She smiles. 'I knew she would. I knew she'd look like that,' she says.

Maybe it was talking about those other times that made it happen, I don't know. But two days later, on the Saturday night, I can't sleep. The kids are staying over – one of the weekends when it's my turn to have them. They're fast asleep in their beds. But I'm restless. I get out of bed to close the window. Maybe I'm chilly, maybe that's why I can't sleep. I look across to the empty house next door. I've got into the habit these recent weeks of looking over there, checking for signs of life. Sometimes I see a torch flickering in the room upstairs, or sometimes downstairs, a blur of light beyond the drawn curtain. I've given up thinking the owners have come back. It's probably squatters, but it isn't really my business.

Whoever it is, they aren't there very often from what I can tell, and it doesn't seem they're doing any real damage, and squatting's lawful anyway, up to a point. I'm not too bothered. The light is there again this evening, flickering in the upstairs room. I gaze at it for several moments and then let my gaze drop, and there on the pavement outside my house, standing directly under a street lamp, a girl in a blue blazer and skirt. No, I am making that up. I can't see the colour blue; it's not light enough for that. But it could be blue. There's a dark shadow smudging the front of her chest that could be blood, a dark curled shadow leeching down from her head that could also be blood. Her eyes are staring up at me and I see her face quite clearly under the street lamp. I see Laura's face.

Time stops. Then it restarts and I run downstairs and out of the front door. But she's gone. Something pulls my eyes towards the upstairs window of the house opposite. The light has gone out. Did I see a curtain twitching? The shadow of a face for a minute peering out?

24

I didn't tell her. I couldn't. How could I tell her?

You know we were talking about Laura the other day, how we both think she's all right. She's at peace. In the spirit world, wherever that is. If there's such a place. Well, we were wrong. She's not at peace. I saw her again the other night and she's bleeding, she's still suffering. After all these months, she's still suffering.

How could I tell her that?

But I had to tell someone. I was going out of my head. I told you.

'You say it's months since you've seen her? Before this, that is?'

'Yeah. Months. Last February I think it was, the time before this.'

You look at me quietly. You're not thinking I'm losing the plot, not judging me. None of that.

'Jack, I don't know what I think about ghosts. Whether they're real, and if they are, what they are, and what they want. But I am inclined to ask why now? Why after so many months have you started seeing Laura again, and seeing her in that distressing state when you didn't before?'

I look back at you, waiting, but you're expecting me to give the answer.

'Have you thought about this before? Have you wondered whether you've seen her again like that – the blood you think you saw – because it's reflecting something that is going on inside you?'

'Like a projection, you mean?'

I'm learning the lingo; I've been reading the books.

'Yes, maybe. Something like that. You have been under a great deal of stress. What's happened with Sam, then your uncle dying. Maybe there's a bit of you that's like a suffering child, that needs looking after.'

She was standing there under the street lamp, staring up at me, a fixed intense look in her eyes. Like alarm, almost like fear. The light was touching her face – her cheekbones, the bridge of her nose. Shadows pooled under her eyes, on her throat; blood pooled in dark shadows on her chest and curled from her hair. It wasn't conjured from out of my mind. It was real. It was out there.

'No, that's too glib. I don't accept that.'

An edge to my voice, an energy. It takes him by surprise.

'If you're sure about that, Jack, then we may need to consider the other possibility.'

'What's that?'

'Maybe Lisa is right. Laura is trying to tell you something.'

At first it feels strange to be setting my alarm, getting up early, going out to work every day. How long has it been?

Nine months nearly. But after a week I feel an old hand, I've broken its back.

'Work's a habit,' my uncle used to say. In the winter time he'd be laid off sometimes for weeks. Would mope around the house, feeling sorry for himself. 'Bad thing to get out of the habit of work.'

'If work's a habit then you can get back into the habit again,' my aunt would say. She's right. It doesn't take long. In my case, a week, that's all.

Funny to be working this side of the fence. To see the origins of those criminals I've stuck behind bars. How they start out. The struggles they're up against, like life's a ledger book and the side they're on is all loss and no profit.

I'm working alongside a woman called Jo for the first few weeks. Jo used to be a shop detective and then she got this calling to the other side. Like me, I suppose. We have a case list of kids – mainly young males aged fourteen to eighteen, though sometimes the odd girl as well. They've usually been in trouble with the courts. Mostly petty crime – shoplifting, vandalism, joy-riding, that kind of thing. Sometimes they haven't got that far, but they're in danger of it. Persistent truanting, antisocial behaviour at school. The idea is we go around their homes and talk to them, talk to their parents, try to build a relationship with the kid, develop some trust, dig out the real issues.

I thought I was going to get some arsey, attitudinal kid, like the kind I ran into time and time again in the force, wearing the uniform. Mouthy, lippy kids, fronting me with their chests stuck out, sticking their faces into mine.

What you fucking looking at, wanker? What you fucking want?

Hackles up, their defences in full play. But it was the uniform that brought that out.

These kids aren't like that. No need to be. I'm just some guy coming to help them, to try to keep them out of trouble. We turn up at their houses to keep an appointment. Council houses normally. Single mothers normally – not always, but often. She'll look at us pinched, harassed, her face set into lines from years of having to fight her own battles. Or sometimes the kids are in foster homes, after a history of being in the care system. The foster parents again at their wits' ends, another failure looming large.

Our calls are usually in the morning. No matter what time it is, the lad – it's usually lads – is still in bed, bedclothes pulled over his head, shutting out the world. The mother calls up the stairs, 'Come on, wake up. Those people from the Social are here to see you.'

Eventually he makes an appearance, comes down, tousled hair, sleep in his eyes, some grimy sweatshirt pulled on in a hurry. He mumbles incoherently at me, but quite polite, bashful really, and I think, He's just a kid. Not too bright perhaps in the upper storey, easily led. Not the lippy mouthy things I used to arrest, high on drugs and drink.

Fucking pigs, you're all the same.

Wearing the uniform, there was no room for caring. No room for sitting across the kitchen table saying as he shoves toast into his face, 'How you doing, son? What's going on for you right now? Why aren't you at school? What's the problem?'

In my great-uncle's day – maybe in my dad's day too, but he wasn't around to tell me – kids like that weren't expected to be at school. Working-class kids, out-growing their strength, hormones rampaging. They'd be apprenticed out, putting in the hours, learning a trade. Wearing themselves out with physical work so that at the end of the day they were too tired to go out onto the streets up to no good. But then it was a different world. They'd have fathers around, working hard, showing them the way to be a man. No drugs then, no films with sex and violence, no computer games to fill their heads.

The girls are more difficult. They close up moodily, go into themselves, hide behind a curtain of hair. I let Jo take over more then. She's gentle with them, not pushy; that never works. They sit there with their thin white arms exposed, daring us to see the sores that they endlessly pick at, the white criss-cross of scars on the insides of their forearms. Later, when they get to know us a bit, come out of their shell, Jo will ask, 'What did you use the last time? A razor? A knife? What was going on for you then? How did it make you feel?' And later still, show them the ice cube she'd got the mothers to make in the fridge: 'Try that next time. It burns, it hurts, but it won't harm you. It'll leave no scar.'

The worst scars are the ones you can't see. I should know.

But I like the job. I don't know what good we do to the kids, if what we say or do makes the slightest difference to their long-term risk of offending, but it makes a difference to me. I come home feeling tired but sort of happy. Funny to use that word, but it's true. Happy in a way that I never felt in the police.

A lot of it is about the parents too. There was one woman in particular; she made an impression on me. She'd been brought up in care, then at seventeen she'd married the first bloke who'd come her way. A no-hoper with an alcohol addiction, who eventually left her five years later with four kids, the youngest not even born. She was tiny, thin, still looked like a kid herself really, these wide nervous eyes. Her eldest, Kevin, was only twelve but already into the truanting game. He wouldn't go to school and he wouldn't say why, and then he'd been caught stealing a book from a shop. That's where we'd come in. Normally it's clothes, computer games, CDs the kids start stealing. Hardly ever books. It was a book on martial arts he'd stolen, he eventually told me, and later, weeks later, he told me he'd been bullied at school. Had his dinner money taken off him every day, his school books emptied out of his bag and crumpled in the dirt, his home-work torn to shreds before his eyes. And then they'd started the head-ducking down the toilet stuff, and that's when he'd refused to ever go again.

'Why didn't you tell your mum?' I asked.

''Cos she's got enough problems of her own.'

I knew that was true. The third child – a girl – was a bad asthmatic, had to go to school with one of those ventilator things, and the youngest, a boy, had autistic tendencies. Asperger's, they called it. The council house they lived in was badly in need of updating – peeling wallpaper, damp patches, an old boiler that kept breaking down. No carpets in some of the rooms, just floorboards. Money always short, no matter how much she tried to budget, and she – no wonder – had problems with her nerves, was under the doctor for depression. They were potentially the kind of family you might read about in the paper one day. Mother who puts all the kids to bed with a hot drink laced with a heavy overdose of pills and then herself as well, and they're all found dead in their beds in the morning. Then the questions falling like a ton of bricks. Why did she do it? *How* could she do it? What kind of mother is that?

'Why couldn't you tell a teacher, then?'

'What could they do? That'll only make it worse.'

Grassing. Nobody likes a grasser. No matter what, you don't grass.

His bottom lip was trembling and there were tears in his eyes, and I wanted to put my arm around him, to give him a hug. But I couldn't; that would be inappropriate behaviour. I'm not his dad. I'm just some geezer who'll be in his life for a couple of months, then out of it for good when the job ends at Christmas. And anyway, we've been warned: no physical contact, don't leave yourself open to risk. Some kid might turn around and say you've been interfering with them, get off on the attention it gives them. Don't get emotionally involved.

As if we're automatons. As if we haven't got hearts. Wearing another kind of uniform – a less visible one. Fuck that!

I didn't hug him, but I did get emotionally involved. Life is getting emotionally involved. We eventually got him back into school, into a special school. A place where they've time to build him up, raise his self-esteem, give him some survival skills before returning him at a future date to the jungle of the comprehensive. I got some extra benefit sorted for the mother too, for the disabilities of the other two kids. Made sure the Asperger's kid was getting the extra support he was entitled to at primary. I feel good about all that. Really good.

'Because you can make a difference,' you say.

'Yeah.'

'It's right for you, this kind of work.'

'Yeah. I think so. I think I'm good at it.'

'But it's only temporary, isn't it?'

'Ends at Christmas. But something similar will come along. And I've decided to apply for a social-work degree. Starting next September. I've already sent away for the application forms.'

You smile at me.

'You're getting it all sorted, aren't you, Jack. I think the time's come now, hasn't it? You don't really need me anymore.'

A quick flutter of anxiety. But then it passes, and I know you're right. The time has come.

'Whenever you think you need to, please feel free to get in touch again. But I think you'll be all right now. Don't you?'

I nod, say yes. But I'm grateful for the safety net.

When I get up to leave I start muttering stuff like thanks for all the help you've given me; I don't know how I'd have got through without you. You smile, dismiss it with a gesture. And then it comes home to me. It was just your job. Maybe for me, for a time, it was a lot more than that, it was a lifeline, but for you it was just a job. I wanted to hug you, like men do sometimes, if they're brave enough, but I don't. We shake hands.

'Good luck,' you say.

The house sale is going through quickly. We've exchanged contracts; in ten days I'll be moving. I'm feeling like a displaced person. A sense of breathlessness catches me sometimes, but I'm all right. I've arranged to put most of the furniture into storage for Sam; she'll need it when she buys her new house. I'll just take my possessions, a few small items of furniture. I've put a deposit down on a two-bedroomed flat in a cheaper part of town. It'll feel cramped after what I've been used to. But the rent's affordable, and there's a room for the kids when they come over to stay. Sam and I are civil to each other, the girls are adjusting. I still have a life, of sorts.

I miss you, though. I miss those weekly sessions in that room in your house. I miss the space it gave me. Time standing still. But I'm all right.

Lisa comes over to celebrate my exchanging contracts. To help me say goodbye to the house. Why don't we have 'house-leaving' parties? I think. Isn't leaving just as important as arriving? She brings a bottle of wine. I'm cooking a meal; I'm getting good at this cooking lark. She tells me the couple who'd made an offer on her house have pulled out – they couldn't raise the mortgage in the end.

'I've already found someone else, though. They've actually made a better offer. Three thousand more,' she tells me. 'This is good, Jack.'

'Yeah, I'll make someone a good wife one day,' I joke. She blushes. Only slightly, but I notice that. Still a copper.

I look at her across the dining table as she dips her head towards her food, candlelight gleaming on the raised planes of her face. She's becoming beautiful, I think. This last year has metamorphosed her into something else, not the mousy, nervous, broken woman I saw standing with her husband outside the court that day, the two of them looking lost.

The food is good tonight. Braised lamb shoulder steaks, that have been marinating for hours in red wine, with plenty of garlic and rosemary. Served with couscous, and a mixed-leaf salad with olives and feta cheese. Afterwards I put on that Andrea Bocelli guy, the one who's blind but sings like an angel, and we sit outside with our coats on, sipping cold char-donnay, and Lisa points up to the stars. It's a sharp October night, a touch of frost in the air; the stars are like crystal.

'Did people used to tell you when you were a child that when people die they turn into stars?'

'I don't know – no, not really.'

'My dad did. When my grandmother died – I was about seven and didn't understand death at all, didn't understand why she wasn't coming back. He took me into the garden and pointed out the stars, told me the names of some of them. The Plough, the Archer. And there was this bright one on its own and he said that was her. That was my granny shining and looking down on us.'

We gaze up silently at the stars together. I have that feeling that gives you a buzz sometimes – how small and unimportant we are, how insignificant our lives. 'Which one's Laura?' I want to say. She must be reading my mind.

'That one. To the left of the Plough. It's a bit faint. I've never noticed it before. Maybe that's her. That's Laura.'

We gaze up silently. The cynic in me is thinking, If dead people all become stars, Lisa, the sky would be a great pulsing mass of light, with no dark spaces left in between. We'd be blinded by the stars, there'd be so many of them. But I say nothing. Her lips are moving slightly. Who is she praying for? I start praying too. I pray that Lisa will find the peace she deserves. I pray she'll be happy. I pray she'll never hate me again.

When she leaves, I see her to her car. She stands on tiptoe, kisses me lightly on the cheek. Her lips are cold. That light again, flashing against the downstairs window of the house opposite. I see it out of the corner of my eye. Lisa sees it too.

'That house, Jack. Is someone living there?'

'I dunno. I thought it was empty. I think they might have squatters – I should tell the police . . .'

The torch snaps off. Lisa shivers slightly. I have my hands on her shoulders.

'Lisa,' I say, 'if things were different . . .'

She puts a finger on my lips.

'Sssh, don't say it. I know. But they're the way they are, Jack; they're not different.'

She moves away from me, gets into her car and drives away. I have a feeling that something is falling away from me. Or maybe I am falling. I'm falling like a pinpoint of light through space, a falling star. I've no idea where I'm going to land.

25

Were we both thinking of it that night? The seventh of November, only a fortnight away. That rhyme that kids used to sing about Guy Fawkes' night goes around in my head. But it's changed for me now. *Please don't remember ... Please don't.*

Some things you can't change. That's what she meant. No matter how much forgiveness, how much grace, Laura still died because I was driving down a road one day on the seventh of November, when the light was fading fast, the edges of shapes bleeding into a blue gloom and a light rain falling. There was a little alcohol in my system, but not too much. And maybe I should have had my lights on but didn't, and maybe I could have braked sooner, but didn't, and maybe she was in a hurry and didn't look where she was going. Maybe it was a bit my fault and a bit her fault, and maybe neither. Maybe we were just two players in a cosmic drama someone else was writing. I don't have any answers; I don't even ask the questions anymore. But that's why Lisa and I can never be anything else. We're two people moving away from each other, locked into our own dark universes and that's just the way it has to be.

But that night in the garden, sipping chardonnay, wine and the night sky going to our heads, it was there all the time. November the seventh. When our universes collided.

The days tick down to it like a time bomb.

'I've decided that I would like to ring him. I'm ready to ring him.'

'I'm so glad, Jack. He'll be over the moon to hear from you,' my aunt Vera says.

But I'm not doing it for him. I'm doing it for me. Because I need to.

It's got something to do with those kids. Those kids hurting and hating and missing their fathers, hiding in bed with bedclothes pulled over their heads when they should be at school getting on with their lives. Or off their heads on glue or dope or worst of all, the older ones maybe, injecting, getting involved in car theft and break-ins and pushing drugs on the street. Giving up, not caring. It's got something to do with them. With realizing how much kids need their dads, even when their dad's a no-hoper, not able to keep off the drink or the drugs himself, in and out of prison. Even dads like that, better than the dad who's never there. Maybe I was always like that, hurting and hating and missing my dad because he wasn't there. One part of me, hiding in bed with the bedclothes pulled over my head, pretending I didn't care. Maybe it's time to give that up. Time to change.

'Don't tell him, though. In case I change my mind.'

But I know she will. She won't be able to help herself.

Jack said he's going to phone. He didn't say when, but he'll phone. He's ready now.

Saturday night. A good time. I'm not having the kids this weekend. Time to recover if things go badly.

I work out Vancouver time is eight hours behind us. I want to phone him at the right time. About nine o'clock in the evening. When he'd have had his evening meal, maybe sitting down relaxing with his wife, something on the telly, a drink in his hand. I don't want to phone him when he's out at work, or getting ready to leave. I don't want to risk him being abrupt, dismissive. I don't want to risk what that might feel like, after all these years.

If I phone him at nine o'clock over there, it'll be only five in the morning here. I decide to go to bed early, and set the alarm for four thirty. When I wake I'll have a shower, several cups of coffee to wake myself up. Then I'll be ready.

But I don't sleep well, despite going to bed on two double Scotches. Maybe I'm not tired enough when I go to bed. Maybe I'm too wired up. I have weird dreams. I'm on the top of a mountain talking to my dad. He has a long beard like Grizzly Adams. His eyes are a pale light blue, as clear as glaciers. They crinkle around the edges.

'Hello, son,' he says. 'I wasn't expecting you to be here. Did you climb up the long way?'

When the alarm goes I've finally got into a deep sleep. It's crucifying to wake up but I do. I have a cold shower, turn my face up into the water to let it drill on my eyes. Two cups of coffee later, a cigarette in my hand. I'm ready.

Maybe it rings five times, maybe six. It feels like forever.

Then a voice, a male voice. He says the number. There's a space between his words and mine into which I'm falling. It's only seconds really, but it contains the Atlantic Ocean, the breadth of another continent. Vancouver, British Columbia. Where the Pacific is deep blue and cold as snow. If you want to start a new life, you can't get much further away than that.

'Hello?'

He's puzzled by the pause, but he doesn't hang up, he doesn't sound irritated. Does he sense something across those thousands of miles of telephone lines – is blood as powerful as that?

'Hello. It's Jack.'

I don't say, *Hello, Dad. It's your son, Jack*. Words like that are too intimate. But I take a risk. He might have said, *Jack who?* What would I have done then? Hung up? The kid in me at the age of four, whose father walked out one day and never came back, taking over. But he doesn't. He knows who I am straight away. As if he has been waiting for me to call. Sitting there in that house in Vancouver waiting for this son he hasn't seen or heard of for thirty years to phone.

A pause again. He's taken aback. But he knows who it is.

'Hello, son. It's so good to hear from you.'

Grown men say 'son' to kids all the time. Shopkeepers say it, when they go in with their grimy fists full of coins.

Hello, son. What can I do for you?

There's a warmth wrapped around the word. It's what boys need from older men. Coppers say it all the time.

What's up, sonny? What have we here, then?

When he said that, *Hello, son*, I was a kid again. The

263

warmth of that word wrapping itself into my belly, into my heart.

We don't talk long. Him trying too hard, I guess, sounding earnest, me holding back, defences still up. He tells me Vera has told him I'm a policeman and I say I used to be, but not anymore; I'm thinking of going to university next year to train in social work. He doesn't ask why, and I'm glad, because if he had I wouldn't have told him. I wouldn't have told him about Laura.

'Vera says you've been having some marital problems, Jack. I'm sorry.'

I don't want to talk about Sam either.

'Things are working out OK. We're still friends.'

'I'm glad to hear that.'

Then he asks about the girls. Their names, their ages, what they look like, what they like doing best. I can hear the pleasure in his voice, the pride. I'm a granddad, he's thinking. I have two granddaughters. I close up a bit then. The unspoken words getting in the way. *You weren't there when I was a kid; why should I let you share my children now.* Then another voice – Tom's – chipping in. Get over it, Jack. Don't let what happened in the past spoil what you can have now. So I force the feelings down, I put the thoughts on one side. When we say goodbye and hang up, a pathway has opened up between us, pushing its way underneath an ocean, across a wilderness of a continent, clear and wide. He has my phone number now, my address.

'Don't be a stranger. Keep in touch. It's been so good to hear from you, son.'

*

I move a week later, on the third. Another Saturday. The sky is like World War Two, alive with explosions. Nobody seems to wait until the fifth anymore. It goes on for days nowadays, for weeks it seems. Kids in the street, underage kids, getting their hands on Catherine wheels and Roman candles. Wet splutterings in back gardens. Throwing bangers into the road for kicks. But the night I move, the Saturday, is the official night. The display at the cricket ground nearby sends huge golden fountains into the sky over our heads, rockets screeching. A neighbour lends me his transport, his time too, and we trudge up and down the path carrying the spoils of my life, stacking them carefully into the back of the van. Two trips in a Ford Transit, that's all it takes, for my life to be picked up and put down somewhere else.

For the whole of the next day I sit like someone shell-shocked amongst the boxes and bags, or I lie in bed in a heap of unwashed sheets. When the dark comes, the fireworks start up again. Thousands of brightly coloured stars exploding all over town. I watch them drift in fiery tails beyond the grimy bedroom windows. And then the next day it's cleared; something's cleared in me. When I get home from work I'm up till nearly two, unpacking boxes and bags, re-arranging my life into cupboards and drawers.

'Jack?'

She's going to ask me a favour. I can tell by the tone in her voice. Where is she? At her parents? Around his? Is he there when she phones me, eavesdropping in, listening to the tone of her voice, thinking, *Is there anything between them still?*

'Bethan's got a dance class on Wednesday after school. It finishes at five. I can't make it – I've something on at work and Mum's got to take Jessica to the dentist. Nothing special. Just the standard check-up. Any chance you can pick her up?'

'Yeah, of course. Shall I bring her back here and give her tea before I drop her off?'

'That'd be great. Thank you.'

I put the phone down. Sam and I being grown-ups, sorting things out. And the girls adjusting to the situation, not suffering too much because of it. Things are working out. Things are OK. I have a feeling, a shadow of a thought at the back of my mind, that there's something I should remember about Wednesday, but I can't quite be bothered to.

A feeling of dispossession still follows me around a bit. I have stuff on my mind for days. I need to fix up the kitchen. Give it a coat of paint if the landlord doesn't mind. Maybe ask if I can have the gas cooker taken out and wiring put in for an electric one. I don't like gas cookers. Never have.

The smell of gas. It catches at the back of my throat.

I have stuff on my mind on Wednesday when I go to pick up Bethan from her after-school dance class. It's held in the school hall. Some dance teacher comes in and teaches the girls tap, a bit of ballet, choreographs some moves. Sometimes they present a piece to the school in a special assembly. Bethan loves it. I can see her neat slim body toning up, delineating, the muscles on her limbs becoming taut and sinewy. I've picked her up a few times from the after-school club. It gives me a chance to see her on her own for a bit, to have the kind of talk with her that I couldn't have if Jessica was there. I take her home and we cook spaghetti bolognaise together – the proper kind, not out of a tin. Or if I've not got much in or I'm not in the mood, or it's special-treat time, it's cheeseburger and fries down the big 'M'. We sit there together, a lone father and his seven-year-old daughter, enjoying each other, like we're the only ones that matter in the world to each other, which for that time we are.

But tonight we're cooking at home. Not spag bol. I've bought a special pizza-making kit. There's the bread base, a small jar of tomato paste for the topping. I've got various things in the fridge to chop up and put on top. Mushroom, bacon, olives, mozzarella and cheddar. She'll love it. She loves that sort of thing.

I park the car opposite the school. I'm early. I leaf through yesterday's paper, left on the back seat. Someone drives past me in a dark grey Mondeo. Moments later, the same car coming towards me from the opposite direction. It must have turned around at the roundabout half a mile down the road. It stops, pulls up against the kerb about twenty yards away. Whoever's driving leaves the parking lights on but doesn't get out of the car. Maybe it's someone waiting to pick up their daughter too. I wonder briefly why they haven't parked closer, but my attention flits back to my paper.

More cars now, the area filling up. Some of the cars pulling into the school car park. It's nearly empty; most of the teachers have left by now. I can see movement going on at the side entrance to the school. Girls in anoraks and duffel coats coming out, sounds of giggles and chatter spilling out into the dusk. I get out of the car. Then all of a sudden she's there. She's on the other side of the road. I raise my arm.

'Bethan.'

The road is a quiet road. There isn't much traffic that passes through it, other than the people coming to the homes in the avenues and closes of the private housing estate the school backs on to, other than at times like this, when parents gather to pick up their children. She looks right and left, but quickly, casually, stepping out from the kerb, stepping out into the dusk, stepping out towards me. Maybe she notices the grey Mondeo has started its engine, has put on its headlights, is pulling away from the kerb. Maybe she notices, maybe I do. But there seems no danger. There's nothing else on the road.

Then within a second, everything changes. The whine of the car revs, the screech of its tyres, as it suddenly catapults towards her, its headlights full on, dazzling her, making her freeze like a rabbit caught in the glare, her scream, my shout, breaking the still November air. That's when I realize in a flash what day it is. November the seventh.

Then in an instant, shooting out into the road in front of me, as if she'd been there all the time standing by my side watching. A girl in a royal-blue uniform, running fiercely into the path of the car, pushing Bethan violently backwards onto the pavement. The car skidding, swerving, out of control, careering up onto the pavement, crashing into a lamp post, coming to a halt, its wheels still spinning.

I expect to see her there again. Laura. On the road, lying mangled perhaps in a heap. Blood welling from her chest, from her head. But there is nothing. Only the empty road.

My child is sitting on the pavement. I am helping her up to her feet. She is sobbing, stunned and shocked, but safe and whole and alive in my arms.

26

People have gathered around us.

Christ! Did you see that car?

What was he thinking!

He must be off his head or something!

A couple of men have run over to the Mondeo. I can just make out the driver, a dark shadow slumped over the steering wheel. I know who it is. I know what day it is. One of the men is speaking on his mobile. He's phoning for an ambulance. Flashback. That other time again. Fragments like broken leaves caught in a whirlpool.

The headmistress is hurrying across the playground towards us. Someone has gone into the building to tell her what happened. She puts her arm around Bethan, gives her a hug. She guides us back into the building, takes us into the office. Someone is offering me a cup of tea, is offering Bethan a glass of milk and a chocolate biscuit. She's sitting close to me, her head leaning on my shoulder, she's stopped crying.

'A terrible thing to happen, Mr Philips. Thank God your daughter jumped out of the way in time.'

I can hear the ambulance arriving in the distance. It was Dave who called the ambulance that day. I was kneeling on the road. The road was gritty and damp beneath my knees. Her face was pale. Her breath, a faint warm fan of air against my cheek. I saw her eyelids flutter for a moment. The noise of the siren getting louder, then it stopped. I remember the paramedics jumping out, bringing the stretcher. I remember the way they had slid her small still body onto the stretcher, lifted it up. I remember the rush of cool air as I knew she had gone. I look over towards my daughter. The blood has returned to her cheeks. She is warm and breathing and alive. She sips the milk, takes a small bite of the chocolate biscuit. There are crumbs clinging to her lips.

Thank you, I say, silently, the words building in my chest. *Thank you.*

We wait until the ambulance has gone. I don't want Bethan to see anything. Blood? A dead body? Who knows?

Two police constables enter the office. They want to talk to me about what's happened. I don't know them. They're from the other station. They're young. New recruits? They have earnest serious faces.

'Is he all right – the driver?'

I am standing talking to them outside the headmistress's office. The door is pulled shut so my daughter won't hear.

'We're not sure how seriously he's been injured. He's been taken to Shrodells.'

He's not dead. I feel a surge of relief.

'I need to take my daughter home. I'll call round the station afterwards.'

*

In the car, driving home. I glance sideways at Bethan. She looks OK, she looks fine.

'You OK, sweetheart?'

'Yes.'

How much should I ask? How much should I say?

'Daddy.'

'Yes, sweetheart.'

'It wasn't like they said. I didn't jump out of the way.'

Time stops. My heart stops.

'What happened, then?'

'It was like I was pushed. I could feel something pushing hard on my chest. Then I fell backwards out of the way.'

Time starts again. My heart starts again. I breathe out slowly.

I take Bethan straight home. The pizza will have to wait until later. She needs her mother now and there are things I need to do. Sam is home from work. For a moment she panics when I start explaining what happened but then when she sees Bethan's OK, is not hurt, she calms down.

'What do you mean, the car just started speeding towards her? Who would do that? Is he some kind of monster?'

I don't remind her what day it is. The seventh of November.

'They've taken him to hospital. I don't know how serious it is.'

'Have you told the police what happened? You must tell them the truth.'

'Yes. I'm going round there now. They'll probably want me to make a statement.'

I walk into the living room, where Bethan is sitting next

to her sister on the floor, engrossed in something on the telly. As if the events of the last hour hadn't happened. As if a miracle hadn't intervened to save her life. I lean down and drop a kiss on the top of her head, on Jessica's too.

'Bye-bye, sweethearts. I love you.'

'Love you too, Daddy,' they say, without turning their heads, their eyes still fixed on the television.

Sam sees me to the door.

'Thanks, Jack,' she says.

But what is the truth? What will I say?

I think I know the man that was driving the car. I think he is the father of the child I accidentally knocked down and killed last year on the seventh of November. The time was about the same. Just before five in the afternoon. He must have followed me. He must have been waiting for us.

But I can't say that because I'm not sure. It could have been a stranger in that car. Maybe something went wrong with the car, or with him. An epileptic fit, a seizure, his foot sticking on the throttle, out of control. Maybe the date was just a horrible coincidence. Has Lisa ever mentioned what car Derek drove these days? Did I see a Mondeo outside the court that day? But that would mean little – people change their cars all the time.

I pull up outside the station and toy with the idea of ringing Lisa on my mobile, asking her right there and then. Lisa, what car does your husband drive? Is it a dark grey Mondeo? But I don't. It would worry her, it would panic her. Christ knows today must be hard enough to get through without this. Anyhow, I can't be sure.

I tell them only what I know, what I can be sure of. The car was parked about twenty yards down the road, on the same side as the school. It arrived just after me. I assumed it was another parent waiting for their daughter to come out from the dance club. My daughter saw me across the road. I was intending to walk over to join her but she stepped out to walk across to me. It happened so quickly I had no time to warn her. One minute it was parked there quietly, then the next it was screeching towards her. I didn't notice the driver start the engine, put the lights on. It just came out of the blue.

'Are you saying the driver appeared to be intending to run your daughter down, Mr Philips?'

'I don't know. I'm just telling you what I think happened. I don't know what the intentions were.'

The sergeant is middle-aged, greying hair. He is taking this seriously, I can tell. I wonder if he has children. How old are they? Are they safe? Has anything bad ever happened to them?

'We've taken statements from other witnesses. They say the same thing. That all of a sudden the car started speeding towards her as if the driver was intent on hurting her. Then just before impact your daughter appeared to jump backwards out of the way. Rather miraculously, it seems. Then the car went out of control, careered up onto the pavement and collided with the lamp post.'

'Yes,' I say. What else could I say? *Well, actually, officer, that's not exactly what I saw. I saw the child who I killed on this date last year speeding across the road towards her, pushing her violently out of the way.* How could I say that?

'How is he, the driver? Is he going to be all right?'

'He hasn't regained consciousness yet. He's in intensive care.'

'I see.'

The sergeant looks up from his paperwork. He looks at me very seriously and steadily.

'Mr Philips, the driver's name is Mr Jenkins. Does that mean anything to you? Have you any idea why a Mr Jenkins would want to harm your daughter?'

I'm thinking, I need to phone Lisa, I need to tell her what's happened, she needs to know.

I look him straight back in the eyes.

'Maybe because I killed his daughter.'

Lisa's voice on the answerphone when I get in. She sounds wiped out.

'Jack, it's Lisa. Please phone as soon as you get in.'

She knows. Of course she knows. She would have been the first one they contacted. I dial her number. She answers straight away.

'Oh, Jack, I'm so sorry.' She sounds on the edge of tears.

'Don't be silly, it's not your fault.'

'How's Bethan. Is she all right?'

'Bethan's fine, she's all right.'

'What the medium said that night – about you needing help. It was a warning. Laura knew.'

'I don't know, Lisa.'

A cold feeling in my belly. Suddenly I'm remembering the torchlight in the house opposite. The feeling of being watched. Seeing Laura that night, standing outside the house, staring up at me. Lisa's voice resonated in my head.

Laura knew.

I phone the estate agents the next day. The ones who have their names on the board outside the house opposite our old home. A woman answers the phone.

'It's still for sale, then?'

'The owners are considering taking it off the market. They're thinking of returning to live there themselves in a few months. They've instructed us to show nobody else around until they've made up their minds. Mind you, the market's not picked up yet. Wrong time of year at the moment too. We haven't had a great deal of interest for some time, to tell you the truth.'

I tell her I'm interested in a viewing if the owners decide to keep it on the market, make up an address but give my phone number. After I've hung up I drive over to Beaumont Road. I park outside my old house. I walk across the road to the house opposite, go through the small front gate and across the front garden, up along a path leading up the side of the house into the back garden. I'm not nervous now. I'm fairly sure that whoever was there on those nights, flashing a torch inside the rooms, is not there now.

The back door is fitted with a mortise lock. I peer closely. There are shreds of aluminium around the edges of the lock-fitting. Maybe it's been changed. Maybe he broke the lock the first time he broke in, then fitted a new one. I try the kitchen window, the dining-room window. Double-glazed. Both locked. But at the side of the house I'm in luck. A smaller window with frosted glass that seems to belong to some kind of lobby, a downstairs toilet perhaps, is on the latch. I slide my hand in and take it off the latch, open the window wide. There's not much room but probably just enough. But I need something to climb on. I fetch a dustbin and clamber on top of it, pray that no one can see me. I need to go headfirst, wriggle my body through afterwards. There's no other way I'll fit. I get wedged in the window, half in and half out, but manage to thrust my body forward until eventually I slide through, just missing cracking my head on the basin. I pick myself up from the floor. I close the window, then slowly open the door. It leads out into the hall. I listen for a moment. But nothing. There's no one here. The house is empty.

First the kitchen. Kitchens are where you can find signs of human activity. When a coppers enters an empty house, looking for something, for someone, that's where he'll go first. Into the kitchen. A rinsed cup on the draining board, or better still a dirty one, dregs of coffee sitting cold in it still. Crumbs on the table. On work surfaces. A frying pan, the fat still warm in it. But nothing much here; nothing out of place. The kitchen is very much like I'd expect a kitchen to be in a house waiting to be sold. No cups or plates on the draining boards, no food stains or crumbs to be seen. If this house has been harbouring a squatter, then it must have been a very tidy and fastidious one.

Just one thing. Years of being a copper sharpening my instinct. If I'd put my house up for sale, then gone abroad, leaving the keys in the hands of the estate agent, I wouldn't have left the fridge on. This fridge is on; I can see a red light at the top. And the door is closed. Why would the fridge be on if it's empty? Which it should be if I'd gone away, if I hadn't lived in my home for months. I would have unplugged the fridge, emptied it, cleaned it out, left the door open to prevent the growth of mould. Why use up electricity for nothing?

It isn't empty. There is food there. Not much, but the kind of food that someone would use to snack on when they're having their main meals out. A packet of opened Kraft cheese slices. Half a loaf of bread. Margarine, and a jar of meat paste. Three eggs left in a carton. And milk. I take the milk out, screw off the top. It's full-cream milk. Only men buy full-cream milk these days. It smells fine, like milk should smell. I tip a little into my hand and lick it. Creamy and fatty, but not rancid.

Upstairs is where I find the evidence. There's not much of it. This man, this intruder, is very careful and meticulous. He's not here to vandalize this property, or to steal from it. He's simply here to use this place because of its location, because of the lookout point it affords him. What if the estate agent were to bring viewers round? He doesn't want to leave evidence that would alert people to his presence. The police might be called in to inspect. New locks might be fitted. Hasn't he already had to change the mortise lock on the back door? He had to break the old one when he broke in, he had to fit a new one quickly. Of course that would have been quite easy for him. Wasn't he a mechanic, after all? But he is a careful man, a fastidious man. Not the sort to leave things out of place, to take unnecessary risks.

The only evidence, apart from the bits of food in the fridge, is in the front bedroom, the one that directly overlooks mine. I find it under the bed. A rolled-up rubber mat like the sort used for camping, a sleeping bag, a large lantern torch. There're things wrapped up in the sleeping bag. They feel hard and stiff through the quilted material. I unroll them. Two scrapbooks. I've seen ones similar to these in Smiths. Their covers are hard-backed, covered in a brown grainy paper with images in sepia of Victorian people. Scrapbooks to record nostalgia. Scrapbooks for the memories you can't let go of. I pick up one of them, the cold snake of fear in my belly. Time's stood still again. All my attention focused on opening up someone else's secrets.

Newspaper clippings. Pages and pages of them, like the ones Lisa showed me. The ones she spread out for me, like a sea of accusations, on the floor of his workshop that day.

BOY, 10, MOWN DOWN BY HIT-AND-RUN DRIVER

TEENAGED GIRL KILLED BY DRUNKEN DRIVER

CHILDREN KILLED IN ACCIDENT CAUSED BY RECKLESS DRIVER

Different ways of saying the same thing. Over and over again. I am guilty. I am to blame. A child is dead because of me. Pictures of smiling children in old school photographs, hazy and faded like time has blown its breath on them, wiped them out. There's Laura here, smiling and pretty, her hair bobbed, her school tie sitting in a neat knot against the collar of her white blouse. She looks younger, barely older than Bethan is now. They nearly always use out-of-date pictures of victims. Not hard to do – children change so fast, their innocence falling from them like leaves from a tree. She looks younger than she was when I leaned over her pale face as she lay dying on the wet tarmac of the road. The seventh of November. A year away from yesterday. I am in awe of this man. For his meticulous scheming, for his patience, for the beautiful symmetry of his attempt at revenge.

I've seen enough. I close the book up and slowly pick up the other one. I turn it over a few times in my shaking hands. What secrets will I find in this one? What could be more shocking than the first?

Inside the pages, photographs of my life. He's an artist, this man Derek. He has chosen the medium that artists often use. Minimalist. Black and white. No colour to seduce the senses, to throw us off the essential truth. Colour lies. It makes life out to be better than it is. This is a candid-camera peep-show of my life. Not the posed, ready-for-the-camera pictures I am used to. It's the fly-on-the-wall treatment.

In this one I'm coming out of the house, Bethan and Jessica in tow. I look harassed, preoccupied, the children are pouting. In another I'm in the supermarket with Sam; I'm behind her, lost in my thoughts. Another. I'm walking through the park on my way to see Tom Swift, winter trees skeletal above my head. I'm caught in glimpses through windows – sitting at the table, talking on the phone, in my bedroom, my head turned away, a smudged shape through the glass. There're pictures of Sam with the girls getting in and out of the car, at the school gates, in shops. Pictures of her and Dave. Going into his house, sitting together in cars. Another, caught through the hazy glass of a cafe, their faces leaning towards each other, earnest and absorbed. Pictures of me alone with the children. Bethan sulking. Pushing the trolley in Tesco's, staring at the print on packaging, Jessica grizzling. Walking through the park with the girls dawdling behind me, at the zoo smiling at monkeys. At a funfair, the children's faces buried in candyfloss. Even pictures of Lisa. Pictures of your wife, Derek – what are they doing in my life? Lisa knocking on my door. Lisa and I getting into her car, going in and out of her house. Walking through the park, a picture taken of our backs. It surprises me, this picture. Our shoulders are almost touching, my head is turned down towards her, listening to what she is saying.

How did he take these pictures and manage not to be seen? A powerful zoom lens? A reliance on disguise? Whatever, he has a skill in the art of stalking that I hadn't given him credit for. And of course a position here, right here in the house opposite, a bird's-eye view of my life and the people that entered it. He must have been following me for months, almost from the time of the accident. Following me and recording me on film, entering into the routine and texture of my life, and those whose lives were a part of mine. Sam and the children, Sam's parents, Dave and Sam. Even Lisa. They are all here, caught in grainy hurried moments, unaware of the drama they were playing out in the head of this man who is hiding behind a camera lens. I am in awe of his skills in the art of surveillance. He would do well as a private investigator, trailing around after wives and husbands, waiting to expose on film moments of indiscretion, moments of adulterous intimacy. Like this one: Sam with Dave in his car kissing, seen through windows misted with rain. I can make out only the dark outline of his head, but her face is turned a little towards the lens of the camera. Her eyes are closed. She is kissing him, and her eyes are closed. I want to shake the image from my eyes but I stare at it instead, until it has burnt its way into my memory for ever. Why do we take ourselves to these unbearable places, when it's easier to run away, to pretend we haven't seen?

I keep staring. Until the images are burnt into my mind. Burnt into it and then until they are burnt out of it, dissolving into nothing. Then I close the scrapbooks, push them back into the quilted sleeping bag again and slide them back under the bed.

27

Lisa looks exhausted. Her face is shadowed by the light in the room, so that I can't make out her eyes, can't see the movement of her mouth. She speaks quietly. I have to lean forward to catch what she says.

'He's conscious. He's out of intensive care. He had a bad concussion, a couple of broken ribs where he made impact with the steering wheel. But he's going to be all right. Not that he deserves to be.'

If I could see her eyes more clearly maybe I could read what they say. Does she still love him? Why do I want to know that?

'I tried to talk to him.'

I lean further forward, till my ear is close to her mouth. I want to turn my head and kiss it.

'What did he say?'

'He said nothing. He wouldn't talk to me. He turned his face to the wall and said nothing at all. I asked him what had happened. What he was trying to do.'

'And he said nothing?'

'No. Nothing.'

Something catches in her throat.

'Then ...'

'Yes?'

'I said, did he think that would bring Laura back, another child dying? Did he think that would bring our daughter back to us?'

She is crying. There are small strangled sounds of pain. I can feel the movements of her shoulders, jerking spasmodically through her thin jumper. I am an intruder in her grief; I have no right to be there. Even though she's sitting in my flat, curled up on my sofa, hugging one of my cushions to her belly. It could be a child she's hugging there, as she sobs quietly. That's when I turn my head. My mouth catches the sobs from her lips and swallows them. Her body shudders, as if a current is moving through it and she moves towards me, kissing me back.

When I make love to her as I do later, it doesn't feel like a betrayal. I thought it would. Not a betrayal to Sam – to Laura. Instead it's like something hard and cold and dead inside me opens up to her touch, to her mouth and eyes and breasts and belly. It's like I'm forgiven. No shadows, no ghosts.

The sun falls into my eyes through a gap in the curtain. A rare November sun. She's already up; she's gone. I stagger out of bed and cross over to the window. The sun is making my eyes water. A hard, slanting, cold November sun. But the kind of sun that makes everything clean, pierces through. Down there on the street, her white Citroën is gone. I go back to bed. It's a Saturday, no need to be up. I roll into the space her body has left behind, still feeling her, tasting her, smelling the fragrance she has left on the sheets. Inside I am smiling. I don't know how long it has been since I felt like this. Despite the mess and the pain and the whole bloody business of being in this world, I am smiling again.

When I eventually get out of bed it's nearly eleven. I suddenly remember Sam is dropping the girls around at twelve. I shower, shave, catch my face in the cabinet mirror and startle myself. Is this what I look like? I'd forgotten. I stroke my hand over the lean curve of my jaw, the slightly hollowed cheeks. There is a look in the eyes like something has walked into the light, has surprised me. I walk into my small, compact kitchen and make coffee and toast. All the time memories like sensations on my skin. Lisa's lips, hands, the softness of her body in the dark. I can't believe it happened. Was it wrong? Is she regretting it already? Putting it down to tears and too much wine, to sitting in the dark together on a cold November night and reaching out to the only one who happened to be there. Was that all it was? Was it that simple? Is that simple at all?

I suddenly have an urge to know what she is thinking or doing, like a scab demanding to be scratched. I go to the phone in my small hallway and ring her number. I know it by heart. How many numbers do I know by heart? Sam's, Lisa's, maybe my father's. Yes, even his, although I've only phoned him once. Funny expression, knowing things by heart. As if words and numbers could be scored into the red muscle, as if you could slice the heart open and find them inside, the letters raised like dots in Braille under your fingertips. The phone rings and rings, and then the answerphone cuts in but I hang up. I don't want to leave my voice etched like an afterthought, a message she'll pick up later, maybe hours later, and think listening to it – *Is that the man I went to bed with last night, a man who could sound like that*? The flat measured tone of a policeman still there in my voice. Some things you can't erase. Some things you're stuck with. DNA. The fall and rise of your voice on an answerphone message. Memories.

Then I can hear the girls at the door, the confident press of the doorbell, holding it a tad too long for a stranger, like someone who feels entitled, who almost lives there. I stand for a moment, re-working my face, smoothing out the small creases of anxiety. Does she regret it? Does she wish it had never happened? What is she doing? Where has she gone? I put on the mask of a weekend father who is greeting his children and open the door.

The girls are a blaze of autumn colour on my doorstep. The sun that makes everything clean again is flashing glints of gold light in their brown curls. They're wearing multi-coloured scarves wrapped around their necks, matching woollen hats and gloves and red duffel coats. Sam is trailing up the path behind them. She smiles at me. As the girls rush into my arms and I hug them for a moment it feels as if my life has begun again, everything's brand new. The sun and the cold air and Sam's smile and my children's faces like flames in the November light.

I spend the weekend with the kids doing small ordinary things. I hoover the flat and give them dusters and cloths to wipe over surfaces. I take them shopping at Sainsbury's and they trail behind the trolley helping me find things, whinge-ing after sweets and biscuits. I buy flour and eggs and maple syrup and when we get home we make pancakes and drizzle the syrup over them and have them for supper. I let them stay up late and we watch *Jungle Book* together which we must have watched a dozen or more times, but no matter how many times it's never enough. All the time I'm seeing her face. Lisa's. I'm feeling her body under the whorls of my fingertips. Where is she? Why isn't she phoning? As the evening wears on, the bubble inside me deflating, something like loss taking its place. Did it really happen? Did I dream it?

Finally I get the girls to bed. I phone her again; there's the same answerphone message in my ear, Lisa's voice, breathy, in a rush. *Sorry I'm not here to take your calls at the moment. If you would like to leave a message I'll phone you back as soon as possible . . .*

I want to say, 'Where are you? Why haven't you phoned? I'm worried about you. How dare you not be there?' As if it's a real voice I'm talking to, not just some trace her voice has left behind. An electronic imprint. And then I think, Am I crazy? What right have I, after just one night?

I go to the kitchen and forage through cupboards, find a bottle of Scotch, a half-finished bottle of red wine that I opened a week ago. It's slightly sour now, but I drink it anyway. I carry the bottle of Scotch into the living room and put on the television. There's the usual Saturday-night rub-bish. The fifty best comedy sketches, something like that. We're on number twenty now, and I drink the whisky right down to number one, then go to bed and sleep a disjointed troubled sleep, broken by dreams of being stranded on an empty railway platform watching as a train rushes past in the night, its windows lighting an interior of faces. Lisa's face is one of them, pressed up wordless against the glass.

Sam rings to say she'll call for the girls soon after lunch. They've arranged to go out for the afternoon. She doesn't tell me where and I don't ask her, thinking it's probably something to do with Dave. His mother maybe who lives somewhere in Oxfordshire. A Sunday afternoon outing. Her and Dave and the girls, the new family outing that doesn't include me. The girls are cabin-fevered shut up with me in this cramped flat with the sun turned to dark clouds of rain outside and me irritable and tired with a hangover I can't get rid of, despite the orange juice and aspirins I chucked down my throat this morning. We make spaghetti bolognaise for lunch. Jessica accidentally pushes her plate off the table onto the floor, and I have to lean down to mop it up so that my eyes are screwed into knots of pain. I shout at her, tell her to be more bloody careful. She starts to cry and then I feel like a heel, and think I'll lose her too if I'm not careful. I put my arm around her and give her a cuddle, kiss the curls of her head.

'I'm sorry, honey.'

She snivels into the back of her sleeve and takes long draughts of air.

'Why are you miserable today, Daddy, when yesterday you were happy?' Bethan says, knowingly, wisely, and I think, That damn kid, she's too clever by half. Then I think, They don't need this; none of this is their fault. I feel a quick stab of anger towards Lisa. It's her fault, this bloody awful Sunday we're having. It's her fault I've a headache. It's her fault it's raining. Then the anger's over in a flash and I laugh.

'Next time you come I promise I'll be happy all the time.'

'You don't have to, Daddy. We love you just the way you are.'

And I have to grab her then with the other arm – the one that's not around Jess – and give her a cuddle, and eventually I cuddle them both so hard they slide off their chairs and land on top of me on the floor, and we roll around helpless with laughter in the mess of Jessie's spaghetti bolognaise.

When the children are gone I jump in the car and drive straight around to Lisa's. I wasn't going to. I was going to wait. For the phone call, for the chance to retain my pride. But what was the use? If I'd stayed at home I'd be too preoccupied to do anything. I would have paced from room to room. The phone would have crouched there on the sideboard, shouting its silence at me. Better to be doing something. Anything.

She isn't in. I know that immediately because her car isn't parked on the drive. Of course, she might have put it in the garage, but I know she hasn't. She never does. But in spite of this, I get out and walk up to the front door. I'm going through the motions but I have to do it. I ring the bell three times. I stand there shivering, waiting. I want to go home, I want to pretend I don't care. But I can't. I'm thinking, If Lisa is trying to avoid me then she's going to a lot of trouble over it. She isn't even coming home. She's gone Christ knows where. Was it that bad? Was it fucking that bad? I've had enough. I turn to go. It was a mistake; it shouldn't have happened. Got to forget about it. Get on with my life. And then it comes down on my head like a ton of bricks. I sit in the car and burn the heels of my hands into my eyes and shout out loud. Fuck! Fucking hell! So that anyone walking outside and overhearing me would think, Christ! He's off his rocker, or something. *What* life, I think? I used to have one, and then some fucking shit happened last year, this month last year, the seventh of November last year. Some woman's kid that I've never seen before runs out in front of my car and that's it. The kid dies. The 'what ifs' begin. And I can't even imagine 'what if' it hadn't happened, because my life has changed beyond recognition since then. In only a year. The person I used to be died along with that kid on the road, in the dusk, with the rain on his face. I can't do the fucking job anymore and that's over and gone, and my wife's gone off with my best mate and the kids will soon be calling the fucker *Dad*. The house is gone. I'm paying through the nose for a rabbit hutch and now some woman I fucked last night and thought was beautiful doesn't want to know me anymore and why should she anyway? Why *should* she? Since she's the mother of the kid I killed. And there's this other kid called Tyrone I'm visiting twice a week at work – *Tyrone*, for God's sake, who'd give their kid a name like that, some fucking film star's name, for God's sake! He's killing off his brain cells with glue and is never at school. His mother is comatose on booze every night and who can blame her, having a life like that. Life's shit. Everything's fucked up and the only thing that makes it worthwhile is love. Like in all those corny love songs the whole world over. Having someone to love.

Suddenly I'm thinking of my uncle Keith, the way he looked at me the last time I saw him, in the British Legion that Sunday lunch time when he slipped me that piece of paper. I'm thinking of another man's voice calling me 'son' over thousands of miles of snow. That's when I realize what I've got to do.

28

A nurse shows me the way.

'Mr Jenkins is in the bed over there, by the window.'

Her dark hair is pinned up high on her head. She has a lovely neck, a neat oval face. I watch her slim body in the dark blue uniform walk away. I wonder for a moment what she's like in bed. The patient by the window is lying down, his head propped up on thick pillows. There are visitors around all the other beds but none around his. None till now. Inside me there is a place that feels like ice. Ice is dangerous. Ice can kill. I don't know what I'm doing here but I know I have no choice. I walk slowly over towards the window. The man lying on the bed is about fifty, maybe a little older. Dark thinning hair, a five o'clock shadow over a chiselled chin, a long narrow nose. His eyes are shut. There is a slight contusion on his cheekbone under his left eye, the faint yellow tinge of old bruising. Slight filaments of scratch marks across his cheek. Small signs of damage, I think, considering the accident. I have an image inside my head of the car wrapped around the lamp post, the front bumper smashed, the bonnet caved in. His eyes are shut, slight stirrings of movement under his eyelids, his breath pulsing in slight puffs. I stare down at him for a few moments, and think, Why am I here? Have I come just to stand here and stare at him, to see what he looks like? This monster who has carried such a torch of hatred for me that he could plot to harm my child. Did I expect to see the mark of Satan on his face? No, I know they're not like that. These monsters look the same as anyone else. If anything, they look more ordinary, except for the lack of light in their eyes. This man's eyes are closed. As I stand there looking at him they flicker open, as if he can feel me looking at him. What do I see in his eyes now? Fear?

'It's you.'

'You know who I am, then?'

'Of course.'

'How do you know who I am?' As if I don't know.

He doesn't answer. He doesn't need to.

'Your girl – she's all right?'

'Do you care?'

He turns his head away from me towards the window. What did I see in his eyes?

'I shouldn't have done it. It wasn't her fault.'

What am I doing sitting here, by the bedside of a man who tried to murder my daughter? Why don't I wrap my hands right now around his throat and throttle the breath out of him? Why don't I hate him?

'If it's any consolation, I wasn't supposed to be here either. I wanted to die. I still do. I wanted to be with her.'

With Laura. Her name is between us now, a prayer that neither of us can articulate. Too sacred to put our breath to.

His head is still turned towards the window, so I can't see his face. His hand is lying outside the bedclothes by his side.

The quicks of his nails are cracked and stained with black. Thin line of black under his nails. The hands of a working man, of a man who understands cars. How the precision parts of an engine fit together, rotate together. How they are subject to wear and tear, to stress. How they need lubrication. I slip my hand over his. I do it without thinking.

'I'm so sorry about Laura. I'd do anything to bring her back.'

Funny. I'd come here to hear him say that word. *Sorry*. I was supposed to drag it out of him, to watch him grovel.

When I get back to the flat the silence hits me like a wall. Suddenly I miss the kids, I miss the urgency of their presence, how they keep me in the here and now. There's a message from Lisa on the answerphone. I listen to it, several times over.

Jack. I've gone to my mother's. She's been taken ill. She's had a stroke. I'll phone when I get back. I'm sorry.

It's funny, last night with her in my bed already seems such a long time ago. Almost like it hadn't happened. I go to bed early and sleep the sleep of the dead.

The week keeps me busy. Tyrone is off school again. I call round the house and his mother is sitting on the sofa, her face puffy and red with tears and drink.

'I don't know where he is, Jack. I don't know. I haven't seen him since last night. We had these words, and he gave me this mouthful of abuse. I can't cope, Jack, I can't.'

Her face crumples, and she bawls into my shoulder like a baby. I hold her hand.

'I know,' I say, 'I know.' And I do know. 'We'll sort it out,' I tell her. 'We'll find him.'

It turns out he was around his mate's house. I fetch him home, I talk to him. He spills all his anger and hurt into my ears. I know I'm just papering over the cracks, but I paper over them anyway. Who knows, maybe one day he'll listen to me, something I'll say will sink in. If not this kid, one of the others. There are thousands of Tyrones. There always will be.

On Friday evening I'm stretched out on the sofa, unwinding, when the doorbell rings.

It's Connor. I ask him in. He looks even taller than I remember, standing in my cramped hallway. He follows me into the lounge and sits down on my second-hand sofa. He dwarfs it. He dwarfs the room.

'How you doing, Jack?'

I feel like saying, How d'you think? Can't you see how I live these days? But I don't. I don't have that kind of anger in me anymore.

'I'm OK. How are you, Jim? How's the family?'

The name tastes funny in my mouth. Jim. I would never have called him that before, when he was my boss. Now he's just some tall guy in a uniform I used to know.

'They're OK. The youngest is off our hands, away at university. Mary and I, we've got the house to ourselves now. We're getting out more these days. Takes some getting used to, but we're enjoying it.'

A time of rediscovery for them. For me too, I think.

'We're so sorry to hear about you and Sam, Jack.'

He looks embarrassed, but I don't react. I keep my voice steady, my eyes looking at him steadily, levelling at him.

'I guess these things happen.'

'Any hope there? That you two might get back together?'

'I don't think so.'

He doesn't know, I think. *He doesn't know about Dave.*

'I'm sorry, Jack,' he says again. His face looks empty.

'It's all right. I'm adjusting well.' I give a hollow laugh. 'But that's not why you're here, is it?'

'No. I thought you ought to know. The Jenkins man. He's been into the station. He's made a confession. Said he meant to harm your daughter, drove the car towards her on purpose. He said he'd planned it for some time. He'd chosen the same date – the anniversary of his daughter's death.'

His voice drops. I can feel him looking at me intently.

'Did you know that, Jack? About the date?'

'Yeah. I knew.'

'So you must have suspected?'

'Suspicion isn't evidence, is it,' I say, quietly.

'Well, we've got the evidence now. Signed and sealed and delivered by himself. He just turned up at the station and confessed on the day the hospital discharged him. Dangerous driving, attempted murder.'

'Is that what he said in the statement? That he attempted to murder her?'

'That's what he said. It may be converted to attempted assault in a prosecution. I suppose a car isn't the most foolproof murder weapon.'

I wonder if he sees me flinch. It was good enough with

you, Laura, I think. Although murder was never part of the plan.

Connor is looking at me strangely. He's thinking I'm too calm, too neutral. Aren't I suppose to be pleased? After all, we have a chance to nail the bastard now?

'What'll happen to him?'

'We'll go for a custodial sentence, of course. The fact that he made a voluntary confession might make a difference, and what the judge thinks of mitigating circumstances.'

He means Laura, I think. He means the fact that Jenkins was off his head with grief.

'At the very least it might be a spell in the loony bin. The defence could go for diminished responsibility. There will have to be a psychiatrist's report, of course. You'll probably be called as a witness in court.'

It was like I was pushed, she'd said. Like something pushing hard on my chest.

'Did he say – in his statement – did he say whether he saw anything? When Bethan jumped back out of the way. Did he say whether he saw anything?'

He's still looking at me strangely. He's taken off his hat and laid it beside him on the sofa. He's scratching at his crinkly grey-haired head, probably thinking, What does he want me to say? What *do* I want? Some confirmation that I'm not crazy, not having delusions? And if I am, that others have them too?

'There was something he said, something a bit strange. He said he aimed the car right at her, full throttle, and then just before he thought he'd hit her, something like a blue shadow seemed to rush between the car and the child. I don't know, something like that. Maybe he suffers from some kind of epilepsy. Whatever it was, be glad of it. It saved your girl.'

After Connor leaves I get in the car and drive around the streets. I need to clear my head.

They discharged him yesterday and he went straight to the station. Can people have a change of heart that quickly? Is that what he's had – a change of heart? *Turned over a new leaf. Become a new man.* So many metaphors in the language for it, it must be true. It must happen.

I think about that message for me from Lisa on the answerphone. She was sorry. That had been the last thing she'd said.

Sorry that she'd slept with me. Sorry that she'd started something that we could never finish. Sorry, because that wasn't meant to happen. Was that what she meant? I'd listened to the message quite dispassionately, already feeling what had happened to us that night had happened in a different universe to the one I lived in now. In the short space between her leaving my bed that morning and returning from the hospital and her message in the late afternoon, something had changed. *I'd* had a change of heart.

Then I get to thinking about everything. Everything that had happened since the seventh of November last year. I think of Tom Swift, and that room with its cream walls and biscuit-coloured carpet, the landscape in oils on the wall and the tree nudging against the window. A room in which anything could happen. I think of my trip to Plymouth and my visit to the house with the sloping eaves where I'd hidden for years and built Airfix models in grey plastic of planes to fly away in, and my uncle's grave up on the hill now, with views out over the sea. And my aunt with her stories of pushing small spoonfuls of food between my mother's lips to keep her alive. I think of my aunt Vera and her houseful of children and grandchildren all lined up to say hello to me, and the letter from my father, and the miles of ocean and wilderness that lay between us, a stepmother and a brother I've never met, and the snow now thawing, the ice now melting. I think of Sam and Dave, and the girls and I trying to build something of a life together in a shabby flat, a life that has to find room for stretches of time when we can't be together. I think of Lisa, the strange friendship we've salvaged, and that night together that maybe shouldn't have happened but was beautiful for all that. I think of Laura who I never knew. Laura, derived from Laurel, meaning victory. Who has watched my house and sent me messages from beyond the grave and saved my daughter's life. What am I supposed to make of it all? Where can I go from here?

'So you're going on an odyssey?' Tom said, when I told him about my planned trip to meet my aunt Vera.

I looked it up when I got home. *An eventful journey; a crusade*. It seems the whole of the year had been that. *What if* again. What if it had never happened? A child had never run out in front of me that day, had never died? Would I still be back in my three-bed semi with a wife and two kids, going to work every day in my uniform, keeping it all buttoned up inside?

'You're not my father!' I shouted that day, fifteen years old and not knowing my own strength. Off my head on cider and cheap beer. He hung on to me as if he was drowning, and I was the lifebelt that would save him. Then I ran away, and all the years of silence, the wasted years, until that weekend, in that small bungalow pelted with rain and storms, when we'd really talked to each other for the first time. He slipped me the note with the phone number scribbled on it in the British Legion, sipping a pint of orange juice because of his heart. *He wasn't all bad, your father*, he'd said. *Sorry, son*, he'd said.

How long will it take to make that journey? The last part of the odyssey. How long?

29

LISA

They have put her in a special ward for geriatrics. I hate to see her in there, looking so lost amongst old women who wander around in their cotton nightgowns with unkempt hair, mumbling to themselves, shouting at ghosts, wanting to go home. She knows who I am. Her eyes fill with tears at the sight of me but when she opens her mouth to say my name no sound comes out.

'It's the language side of the brain that's been affected. The left side,' the consultant explains. 'Her memory's fairly intact, we think, but she's having difficulty accessing the words at present.'

'Will it come back? Will she be able to speak again?'

'Give it some time. I can't give you guarantees, but in my experience it normally gets much better even after just a few weeks. Although her speech may always show residual difficulties.'

But I want certainties. I want to hear her naming things. I want to hear her say my name again.

Alice, who lives in the flat next to my mother's, had phoned me with the news. After I get back from the hospital, I call around there to pick up the key. She puts the kettle on and sits me down and offers me biscuits from a jar. She speaks to me gently as if I'm a small child, a girl, not a grown woman who's had a child and lost her. Who's been through all that.

'I found her in her chair by the fire. She was tapping on the wall with her stick. We always keep each other's keys, just in case there's an emergency.'

'Thank you for everything you've done, Alice. You've been so kind.'

'What else was I to do, my dear? Your mother and I, we always look after each other. That's what you have to do when you get to our age. It keeps you going, that does.'

I know she doesn't mean anything by that, but the words hurt me.

'I should have been there,' I say. 'It should have been me that found her.' I'm on the edge of tears. I'm tired. Alice looks horrified. She takes my hand.

'Oh, my dear, I didn't mean *you* don't care. It's just that – you live so far away. And you've had so much to cope with yourself.'

Her voice trails away, and her eyes flicker away from my face. My mother no doubt has told her about Laura. She doesn't know how much she should say.

'Well, thank God you were here. Thank God my mother has a good neighbour like you, Alice.'

I retrieve my hand, wrap it around the hot cup of tea. The warmth revives me, makes me feel human again.

'Did they tell you how long she'll need to be in hospital?'

'Not really. Perhaps a couple of weeks.'

'And how long will you be able to stay? You have a job, don't you, dear?'

'I'd like to stay as long as it takes.'

Letting myself into my mother's flat I have a strange feeling like I'm coming home. There's a book lying open just under the chair where my mother usually sits, as if it had slipped off her lap, perhaps when the stroke had seized her. I stoop and pick it up and put it down on the small side table by the chair. A historical romance. Then I find myself staring for some time at the pictures on the mantelpiece, then over on the sideboard. There are pictures of me when I was a child. One of me in my pram, wide-faced and smiling. Older, dressed for school, wearing braces and pigtails. Older still, dressed in black with a white unsmiling face. My goth phase. Was that before my father died or after? Then a picture of me on my wedding day, hanging on to Derek's arm, in that cream linen suit because he'd said we don't need the white wedding thing and all that fuss. I'd wanted it really but I'd given in – hadn't I always? He was older, a man of the world, someone who'd take care of me. He knew best.

I pick the photograph up in its frame and look at it hard, as if I hope to see what I was really feeling. I was just a girl then, in my early twenties, smiling into the camera, into the future, not having a clue what lay in store for me. How many of us would have the courage to live each day if we knew that? But I don't find any answers, and think it looks like the picture I've seen of Derek's parents on their wedding day. Two people dressed in their smart clothes but nothing special.

Just making do. Derek was frowning in it a bit; that surprises me, I didn't remember that. Perhaps the sun was in his eyes. Perhaps he could see something I couldn't.

There are several of Laura too. A baby one: Laura sitting on a rug, dimpled and smiling and open to life, not knowing too what it had in store, how short it would be. Several more when she was older; the last when she was about nine, just before the rift when my mother and I didn't speak for years. She's wearing her school uniform, Alice band in her hair and freckles over her nose. I pick it up and look at it closely. How could we go on living from day to day, living and smiling at small things, if we knew the future? Would Laura have? Would I?

It occurs to me later that evening, after I'd rooted through the fridge and found something to make a meal of – some cold ham, potato salad, limp lettuce leaves – I should phone Jack, I should tell him at least where I am, what's happened. Although last night seems like it had never happened, like I had dreamt it. Because Jack can never be part of my future. Partly because of you, Laura. But not out of a sense of blame or unforgiving. But because his part in that has made him belong to another country. I was only visiting; I could not stay. Last night was a mistake. Yet I can forgive myself now for making mistakes. For not being there to pick up my daughter that day after school, for not holding her in my arms when she died. For leaving a stranger to find my mother, half conscious and distressed in a chair. It's like grief has entered my heart and then left it, softer now and more permeable. Emotions seep through me more easily now and do not stay.

You've done that to me, Laura. You've changed me.

But I'm relieved that there's no one there when I ring. No voice with that slight veil of accusation.

Where are you? Where have you been all day?

One night in someone's bed, one night and the chains start to enclose you. Vague and malleable at first, but still there.

I leave a message, careful of what I say. He will hear my message, listen to it perhaps several times, note where I pause, where the intonation rises and falls. He will make conclusions, read for signs. Judge me.

Jack. I've gone to my mother's. She's been taken ill. She's had a stroke. I'll phone when I get back.

I try to keep my voice neutral. I won't mention last night. I'll try not to give him any hint that I wish it had never happened, nor any promise that it might happen again. It has already faded into insignificance, become part of my dream world, a mistake I made in the past that is already forgiven. But then before I hang up, *I'm sorry*, I say.

I don't know why.

My life slips into an easy routine. I visit my mother twice every day, in the afternoons, and again in the early evenings. I take her flowers, grapes, read her paragraphs from the papers, missing out the awful things, the things that might upset her. Another terrorist attack, another insurgency outbreak in Iraq. The Middle East crisis is growing worse. What good will it do for her to know that? The world is full of people dying, of children dying every day. Isn't it enough that she has suffered, lost two husbands, lost her only granddaughter? Isn't it enough that we have had our own worlds ripped apart, our own hearts broken? Isn't that enough to bleed for? You can't bleed for the world. So I pick papers that are not too serious, the *Daily Mail*, the *Express*, select bits of gossip about the stars. Who's getting married, who's split up or had a baby. I read her horoscope, tell her the weather forecast. She looks at me with interest as I read, she smiles and nods. After a few days she can say my name now. It is warm and familiar and easy in her mouth.

The consultant tells me she is making good progress. She is seeing a speech therapist already for the aphasia. I am there one afternoon during the session. The therapist is just a girl, slender and pretty. She shows my mother pictures of everyday objects. My mother glances over to me, her eyes sharp with fear. The words seem to swim at her as if through water. Sometimes my mother catches the words in her mouth like a fish, and then releases them. They swim out again, whole and clear. The speech therapist praises her enthusiastically for her efforts.

'Have you made any plans for when your mother's discharged?' the consultant asks. I know what he means. I know what is implied.

Of course I will do it. Have I any choice? But it's not even that. It's what I want to do. My life has narrowed to this point. To this flat here in Sheffield, not many miles from the house where I grew up. To taking care of my mother, here where the photographs surround us. My father grinning into the camera with his arms around me. Laura with freckles and an Alice band. My mother, frail and old and sitting by the fire with memories like mists in her eyes. All the people I love are here.

I phone work. I tell Alison the headmistress what has happened and I can hear her heart in her voice.

'I'm so sorry, Lisa,' she says. 'You take as long as you need to. We can put it down as compassionate leave.'

But I tell her clearly, no doubt in me now, that I'm sorry but I won't be able to come back. That my mother needs me and for now I'm going to stay.

'If you change your mind, Lisa, if the situation changes, you must get in touch. We'd love to have you back working for us. You've been wonderful. We'll all miss you. The children will too.'

When I put down the phone there are tears in my eyes. How kind people are. I'll miss them. I'll miss the staff, I'll miss the children. I think of Polly, one of the kids I've been working closely with at school. Polly is thirteen, the same age as Laura when she died. Polly is dying too, but slowly. She has a genetic disease that is destroying her. She was born normal, was a healthy little girl until she was six or seven, running around, her eyes full of light. Then bit by bit, the light faded. Her nervous system is being eaten away, her muscles wasting. The light in her eyes, disappearing, chink by chink. She can hardly see at all now, is finding it difficult to walk, to pick up a spoon and release it. Soon, she will find it difficult to talk. Finally, when she's barely out of her teens, her breath will stop. Her mother lives with the fact that her daughter is dying, day by day. Goes on doing all the small things for her. Cuts her food up, puts pretty grips in her daughter's hair, buys tops for her to wear in pink, her favourite colour. How brave people are, I think. How kind and how brave. Compared to Polly's mother, for me it was easy. At least the light fell quick.

The hospital tells me Derek's been discharged.

'Did he leave a forwarding address?'

'I don't know, my dear. But if he did I wouldn't be allowed to give it to you. Data protection, you see.'

I could say, 'But I'm his legal wife, does that make any difference?' But I don't. Because I don't feel that it's true. He hasn't got anything to do with me anymore. He's just a man I once married. We had a child, and the child became someone who belongs to me and always will, but he doesn't and he never will again. Anyway, I was a different person then. Not this person with this soft and permeable heart, where emotions seep through so easily and are gone.

Then I think of phoning Jack, but I don't. What could I say? Jack, what happened between us makes no difference. I'm not coming back to Watford. Not to live, not ever again.

I bring my mother home in a taxi one Saturday afternoon in early December. As the taxi drives through the city centre, the lights, at four o'clock already on in shop windows, display Christmas trees decorated with lights and tinsel. My mother is happy and excited to be going home. She clings to my arm as if I am the parent and she is the child.

'We can make a Christmas cake together,' she says. 'Just like the old days, when you were little. Don't you remember?'

My mother's speech is slurred, as if she's tipsy. The right side of her face still droops down a little, as if it has a mind of its own. I say, 'Yes, I do remember.' But I don't. I don't remember making Christmas cakes with her at all, lacing them with brandy and peppering them with shiny sixpences. I wonder sometimes if she inhabits a different past to me. Or is she confusing the child I was with the child she was. Perhaps it was she who made the Christmas cakes with her mother. But what does it matter? Don't we all go that way in the end, those of us who live long enough? Become the child we used to be again?

30

The solicitor phones to tell me the searches have been completed; we should be in a position to exchange contracts soon after the New Year. I tell him I'll be back around that time. I need to sort the house out. Go through papers, get rid of unwanted furniture, pack up my life.

My mother doesn't talk about baking Christmas cakes again. Or baking anything. I am grateful. I buy us two portions of duck and put them in the freezer, and a sherry trifle from Marks and Spencer's as neither of us care for Christmas pudding. I will buy my mother some embroidered handkerchiefs and a new cardigan, and because there is no one else to do it, I'll buy myself a gift as well. I will wrap them and put them under the small artificial tree that I will set up in the corner of the room. We will eat the duck with sprouts and roast potatoes and orange chutney, and we'll have a bottle of Blue Nun, my mother's favourite. Although I can't let her have more than a glass, because of the pills. After lunch we'll open the presents and then settle down to watch the Queen's speech. Alice is going to her daughter's for Christmas dinner, but perhaps she will be back in the evening and will join us for a glass of sherry and a mince pie and we will watch the usual rubbish that's on the television at Christmas time.

We won't watch the news; we won't have the outside world breaking in on us at all. We won't want to know about wars and terrorism, children dying cruel and wasted deaths. Not on Christmas Day; not then.

Last Christmas was only a year ago. Yet it feels as if I lived in a completely different universe then, one where Christmas could never happen. I stayed in bed until two o'clock, the covers pulled up over my head. The rain was drilling softly on the windowpane. Derek had gone out walking. When I eventually got up, I sat on a chair by the living-room window and looked out at the rain and the grey skies and I held a glove in my hand, a glove you used to wear to school. I put it on. I pushed my thick fingers into the small fingers of the glove and laid my hand against my heart. I felt as if I had become you, my hand pushed into your glove. I sat still for over an hour, and then Derek returned. He walked into the living room and stared at me, his hair dripping wet and his eyes wild.

'Would you like some chicken soup?' I said, and I went into the kitchen and opened a can of soup and made some toast, and we'd sat there together in the cold kitchen silently forcing ourselves to sip soup from spoons, like people with a terminal illness.

This year I can have my Christmas back. I can sit down with my mother over duck and sherry trifle, laugh over some nonsense on the television, and although I will think of you, Laura – and I will, I always will – you will be like a weft of thread in the tapestry of the day, not a hole ripped into its centre, that tears the thing apart.

After Christmas the cold comes in, as it always does. Christmas Day itself was warm and moist, with winds blowing from the west. My mother came down with a cold on Boxing Day, her immune system, from weeks in the hospital, softened and ready to succumb to the germs that bred so easily in the milder, moister air. She took to her bed for a couple of days and I busied myself with cleaning the flat and making lists of all the things I had to do. One of them was to contact a care agency and find my mother someone who could move in and look after her for two weeks whilst I went back to clear the house and sign the contracts and see old friends to say goodbye. Then Jack phoned. His voice took me by surprise.

'I hope you don't mind me phoning, Lisa.'

'No, of course not. I was expecting it. Sheila phoned me to ask if I minded if she gave you my number . . .'

My voice runs out. I wait for him to say, 'Why didn't you phone, why didn't you phone to wish me a happy Christmas? Why didn't you want to speak to me?' But I've been away so long the chains have faded, have fallen away. It was only one night, after all.

'How is your mother?'

I tell him that she's getting better, that she's walking with the help of a stick again, that she's regained some movement in her right hand, that her speech is coming back, the words for the names of things returning more and more.

'That's good news,' he says. There is a pause that we cannot fill. We cannot mention that night. We cannot admit that it happened at all.

'Will you be coming back to Watford?' he says, at last.

'The contracts will be ready to sign soon. I'm planning on coming back in the New Year to sort the house out. I'll only stay a week or two. Then I'm returning to Sheffield to look after my mother.'

'I thought you would,' he says quietly. Then: 'I'm leaving soon, Lisa, as well. I'm going to Canada to visit my father.'

A cold wind has blown between his words. It's as though he's already on his way, up there in the pale winter sky, the nose of the plane tipped westwards.

Rita is recently divorced. 'He exchanged me for a younger model,' she says, jokingly, over a cup of tea. But I know that beneath the humour there is pain as deep as the ocean. Don't we all carry that inside, no matter how much we pretend that we don't? But Rita comes from tough Grimsby stock. She can weather the gales, bear the brunt of the storm. She has sold the marital home, bought herself a flat. She has grown-up children who don't really need her anymore, so she seeks out those who do. She goes off for several weeks at a time to give comfort and companionship where it is needed, then returns to her flat in Grimsby to put her feet up for a while, before going off to do another stint.

'I love it,' she tells me. 'I get out all over the country, see places I've never been to before. I've met such lovely people.'

I tell Rita about my mother's speech therapist who visits

once a week, about the pills my mother takes. I give her all the important numbers: the doctor's, the pharmacist's, mine. Alice says she'll pop in every day to keep an eye on things, but I know it'll be all right, I know Rita will be all right. When I leave, on a morning of frosty blue skies, Rita and Alice and my mother are all around the kitchen table drinking tea together and sampling Rita's cherry scones. Their laughter over something Rita's saying about her husband's wayward ways follows me out of the door.

I enter the house that I have not set foot in for weeks and close the door behind me. It feels cold and musty because I turned the central heating off before I left, knowing that I'd be away for some time, knowing perhaps even then that I'd never really come home again. I turn it on now. The boiler leaps into life with its noisy roar. I go into the kitchen. There is a cup still on the drainer that I left unwashed. Outside in the garden, a stillness, a sense of nothing growing at all, as indeed there isn't, under this cold, leaden January sky.

Laura used to play in this garden when she was small. I can still see her there, in my imagination, in her cool cotton pastel frocks, turning cartwheels, showing the white flag of her knickers as she spins, or squatting on the grass threading daisies into chains. She would later bring one in to me, make me put my head through its noose.

Look, Mummy. It fits!

I would put my hand up and gently feel the fragile daisies, already wilted, their stems bleeding thin sap, dying as they lay like knots against my skin.

Tomorrow I will look through the Yellow Pages, choose a house-clearance firm to come and take away the furniture, the bric-a-brac of the empty life the house contains. I will order some packing chests, and when they come I will go about the house, opening drawers and cupboards, crawling under the attic eaves. I will select only those things I need to take with me into my new life. A few framed photographs of my daughter, the piggy bank with its swirled pink glaze she made at school when she was ten. Her swimming certificates, some paintings she brought home from nursery when she was little. Blobs of bright colours. *This is the sun, Mummy, and these are flowers. I painted them for you.* In them the sky is always blue, a bright blue band that hems in the white empty space. I'll take some of her books, and mine, and the teddy bear she could never bring herself to discard, that still sleeps in hibernation under the blankets of her bed upstairs. I will pack up some of my clothes, taking only those things I know I'll wear. I will pack away safely the jewellery box that I'll find in my dressing-table drawer upstairs, that holds my wedding and engagement rings, and a few other trinkets that Derek once gave me, to remind myself that it wasn't all dross. That love of a kind had once been there. The rest of the things I'll leave behind for the house-clearance people. They'll find their way into junk shops and car-boot sales, into the homes of other people who will need them more.

The next day, after making the phone calls, making arrangements for the house to be cleared, spending the morning sorting through stuff, I go and see Sheila. She is in the middle of packing too. But she's taking her life with her, not casting it away. In her living room a sea of chests, labels stuck on the outside detailing what each of them contains. I watch her pick up ornaments – a blue vase, a glass paperweight, a framed picture of her husband, wrap them carefully in newspaper and pack them away.

'Let's take a break,' she says.

We go into her kitchen and have coffee with jam dough-nuts, fresh from the bakery, where I stopped on my way here to buy them twenty minutes ago. I sink my teeth into one. Jam spills into my mouth, trickles down my chin.

Sheila shows me a picture of the house she intends to buy in Scotland. A chalet bungalow like most of them are. Firm and solid in red-brown stone.

'You will come and visit me won't you, Lisa?'

'Of course I will,' I tell her. 'You try and stop me.'

'It's only forty minutes' drive from the Trossachs. Oh, it's so beautiful there, Lisa, you'll love it. You can bring your mother up for a holiday when I'm settled – if she feels up to it, of course.'

'That'll be lovely,' I tell her. 'My mother's always loved Scotland. She'll love to go.'

We sit munching our doughnuts and drinking tea in Sheila's kitchen. Outside the window, shadows already lengthening, dusk already falling. Inside, in Sheila's bright kitchen, the light is already on. As they're going on all down the street, all over the town. Tessellations of light to offset the coming night.

'How long will you stay with your mother, Lisa?'

'I'm not sure. Not forever, of course. Until she's better.

Well enough anyway for me not to be there all the time. Right now, I think it's where I need to be.'

My unfinished business. A wrong I need to put right.

'And Jack? Won't you miss him?'

This question in her eyes. *What happened with Jack, Lisa? How far did it go?*

'Yes. But Jack and I are both moving on.'

What did she tell me once about love? *You carry them with you. They're with you all the time.*

'What about Derek?' Sheila says.

'What about him?'

'Have you seen him?'

'No. But he wrote to me. He must have guessed I'd gone to my mother's.'

'What did he say?' Sheila asks.

The letter arrived just before Christmas. I didn't recognize the handwriting. Or maybe I didn't look at it very closely, thinking it was a card, although I should have realized it would be from Derek – who else would think to send it to me at my mother's address?

Inside there was a card, a traditional one of the nativity scene, but then when I opened the card up the letter slipped out. Two sheets of pale-blue paper, folded neatly, so that when I opened it out each sheet of paper divided along its crease-lines into four symmetrical squares. Immediately I saw my name, *Dear Lisa*, in his tight, cramped hand. I read it slowly, sitting at my mother's kitchen table while she was taking her afternoon nap. Then I read it a second time. Then

I got up and went over to the sink and put a match to the corner of the paper. I watched the paper curl and smoke, and the flames lick up blue and then orange and finally I dropped it into the sink where only one small shred of it, charred and wet, remained.

Dear Lisa

I hope this letter reaches you. I've been to the house several times but you've not been there. I phoned up your work and said I was your husband trying to trace you. They said you had left, something about your mother being not very well. So I'm writing to you there.

I turned myself in to the police because I tried to do a bad thing. I tried to hurt that policeman's little girl, because I got it into my head he deserved it, that he deserved to feel what I had been feeling since Laura died. I tried to run her down with the car, but thank God she managed to jump out of the way in time. The car hit a lamp post and that's how I ended up in hospital.

I know you've been in to visit me. The doctors told me. I guess I was unconscious when you called because I don't remember seeing you. I had a couple of broken ribs and concussion, but I'm better now.

When they discharged me I went straight to the police to confess. I wanted to go to prison. I deserve to be punished for what I tried to do to an innocent child. I'm still waiting for the trial, but my solicitor thinks because I've never done anything wrong before and because I confessed I might be let off with a suspended sentence.

You've been a good wife to me. None of this is your fault. You couldn't have stopped me doing what I did. When this is all over I think I'll move to the coast somewhere, maybe up north. I've always wanted to live near the sea.

Meanwhile I go to a clinic and talk to a psychiatrist several times a week. He thinks I'm making good progress. I don't think about revenge anymore. I'm sorry about what I tried to do.
Derek

The house-clearance people have been and gone. They've taken everything. Left me here with a few packing chests containing the things I have chosen to take with me. I walk from room to room, surprised at how big the house seems now. So much space waiting to be filled. The couple who are buying it have two children. They will fill it with their noise and their clutter. Lives bursting at the seams, lives waiting to happen.

Yesterday I drove to the solicitor's office in town and signed the contracts. My hand shook as I signed the forms. But it wasn't fear. What can I ever be afraid of now? Haven't I died and passed through to the other side? Having died once, how can I ever fear it again? Isn't death the only thing we really fear?

Maybe it was excitement that made my hand shake. I like change – I like the fresh winds that blow in its path. I like the sense of momentum change brings. Moving forward, leaving little behind. What can we ever leave behind? Except our memories. Except love.

'A couple of weeks should do it, till we complete. I have your new number, don't I, Mrs Jenkins? So I can phone you when the transfer of monies is completed.'

He checked that he had it written down. I shook his hand.

I thanked him. Good luck, he said. He didn't know that good luck would never follow me again. But yet I'll be all right. Nothing as bad as losing my daughter will ever happen to me again.

Nothing to stay for. I walk around the house, checking the windows are locked, turning off the mains and the water. I take readings of the gas and electricity to phone in to the suppliers later. But one more thing to do. One more thing I have promised.

Jack's voice on the phone last week.

'Lisa, you're back in Watford, then?'

'Yes, but I won't be staying long. Another week at the most . . .'

'Will you still be around on the 16th?'

'I'm not sure . . . Why?'

'My plane leaves from Heathrow at 4.30 in the afternoon. I would like to see you before I go.'

'Who's taking you to the airport?'

'No one. I'll probably need to take a taxi.'

'I'll take you, Jack.'

'Are you sure?'

'I'm sure.'

He's ready when I arrive outside his small flat. The cases are packed and waiting in the hall. Jack steps towards me, kisses me lightly on the cheek.

'It's so good to see you again, Lisa. You look well, you really do. Changed your hairstyle, haven't you?'

'A new life, a new hairstyle,' I joke. 'You look well too, Jack.'

And he does. He's put on a little weight, but not too much. He's lost that haunted look. There's a light in his eyes I haven't seen before.

He loads the cases into the back of my car.

I wasn't planning to do it, but something tells me I have to. Just this once. It isn't too far out of our way. I pull up near the cemetery gates.

'Are you sure you don't want me to come with you?' Jack says.

He looks concerned. But he knows really it isn't his place to. I know it too.

'I'll be all right. I won't be long.'

I haven't brought you flowers. I hadn't thought of coming until this minute. But there are flowers on your grave anyway, fresh ones, I knew there would be. Carnations and a few red roses, still folded in their buds. Expensive to buy at this time of year. Your dad still taking care of you.

I stand by the graveside and try to find words to say to you. But I can't. You're still not here. All I manage is *Goodbye, Laura. I love you.* I turn to go.

The M25 flows all the way. It's a good time to be travelling to the airport, in the middle of the day, before the rush hour starts to build. I park in the short-stay car park and we go into the terminal.

'I've a while before I need to check in,' Jack says. 'Can you stay for a bit of lunch with me.'

I sit myself at a table next to the plate-glass window while he goes up to the counter. The weather outside is dull and dreary. One of those days when the lights indoors need to stay on all day. When it seems to be dusk all day. When nightfall lurks constantly on the edge of the day, waiting.

Jack returns with tuna sandwiches and coffee.

'This OK?' he says.

'Fine.'

I nibble on the edge of a sandwich. But I'm not that hungry. This strange excitement again. This shivering inside.

I hear Jack's voice as though he's talking from the other side of a pane of glass. His divorce will be through soon, he tells me. His wife is planning to get married again. To Dave, who once was his best friend.

'I've seen him a couple of times, when I've called to pick up the girls. I guess it's civilized enough. We won't ever be best buddies again, nothing like that, but I don't feel like garrotting him anymore.'

'How do the girls feel about you going to Canada for a while?'

'OK, I think. In a way, it's a good time to be going. They're all preoccupied – the wedding plans, and that. And maybe the next time I'll be taking the girls with me to meet their grandfather – who knows.'

He laughs at himself, at the irony of it all.

'So, Jack. We're both on the edge of a new life.'

He smiles, a quick, bittersweet smile.

'I guess.'

'How long do you think you'll be gone?'

'Not sure. One month, maybe two. Depends to some extent how it goes, meeting the old man and all that.'

'Of course. This must be hard for you.'

'Yes – and no. I've let go of stuff these last few months. We've talked a lot on the phone now. He sounds OK – nice, even.' He laughs. 'Christ! I never thought I'd hear myself say that.'

He pauses, sips his coffee.

'I've been told I may be called as a witness at Derek's trial. But I'll probably be back by then, anyway.'

A quick glance at my face, checking my reaction. I give him none.

I look at him, thinking, there's a distance already between us. He's someone I met on a journey I once made. Someone important, but I always knew I could not stay.

He is looking at me too. There is a strange working on his face, as if he is struggling with himself, daring himself to speak.

'Lisa, I'm not sure if I should say this – sounds stupid I know. I'll always regret the circumstances in which we met, always, till I die. But I can't regret knowing you. You've given me a lot. Thank you.'

His right hand plucks at the tablecloth. I place my hand gently over his.

'Good luck, Jack.'

That word again. What can it mean for the two of us, who have lost so much?

*

I leave Jack to check in and return to the car. I want to get on my way now, before the dusk falls. I edge out of the airport and back down the M4 to pick up the M25 again. Soon I will reach the junction for the M1 and head north, back towards Sheffield, towards that flat that will be warm and lit and where people will be waiting for me. I turn on the radio, flick it over to a classical-music channel. Classical music calms me, keeps me centred on a long journey. Since Laura died I have started to listen to it more and more. Something Sheila said once. *It's good for the soul*, she'd said.

The soul. Is there such a thing? At the spiritualist church, at the clairvoyance evenings, they certainly think so. They see dead people in the same sort of way that they see people who are still alive. 'People on the earth plane,' they call them. They can describe their hairstyles, what clothes they are wearing. They can tell whether that person 'in spirit' had a shortness of breath, a pain in the leg, an angry temper. There's little difference, it seems, between the dead and the living. They care about the same sort of things, pass on messages about cats and exams and whether it's wise to move house or not. I'm not sure I'll go to the spiritualist church, the clairvoyance circles, anymore. I needed to once, but I don't want to see her anymore; I don't want to see Laura. Not in that way, an apparition of something she used to be but is no longer. A child in a blue school uniform, in a pink anorak, a child threading daisies on the lawn. I don't need to see her like that anymore.

There's a request programme on the radio. People have written in to ask for a favourite piece, for a loved one, to celebrate an anniversary or a birthday. Someone has requested a hymn; it was his wife's favourite. She died at this time last year. We never forget the day it happens, I think. We never forget.

Be still, my soul, the Lord is on my side . . .

Why do choirboys' voices sound like the voices of angels? Why do they make us feel this yearning to be home?

Bear patiently the cross of grief or pain . . .

If there is a soul, it doesn't look like a person once looked. It's something more beautiful. Like the sound of a choirboy's voice, like a starry sky. I don't want to see Laura again because I want to believe she's somewhere beyond this, beyond this grief and pain . . .

Through thorny ways lead to a joyful end . . .

. . . beyond the tears. She had such joy as a baby, at the sight of a pigeon landing on the ground before her, the sight of the Christmas lights on the tree. Whatever the soul is, whatever she is now, it's like that. Like the joy of a small child.

All not mysterious shall be bright at last . . .

I don't think I need it anymore. The mediums, the spirit guides, the holding hands in a circle. The longing to see her again as she once was . . .

Be still, my soul, when dearest friends depart . . .

Because she's with me; she's always with me. She's in this car with me, driving up to Sheffield, to her grandmother's flat . . .

Be still, my soul, when change and tears are passed . . .

Perhaps the soul is just what is left, when everything that changes is gone. The love, the light.

All safe and blessed we shall meet again . . .

Outside the dusk is beginning to fall. Cars are streaming up the motorway in both directions. Later their lights will look like stars in the night, like moving constellations of souls . . .

Through passing clouds shall but more brightly shine.

The last note fades away, and in the silence it leaves I miss the beauty, I miss those angel voices. We *shall* meet again, in that place where you are, Laura, wherever, whatever it is. Meanwhile, I am travelling to start a new life with my mother in Sheffield. Later, when my mother is well enough to be left, I'll look for another job. Working with children again perhaps. Or maybe I'll take up studying, like Jack's planning to do. I could start with a GCSE in English literature, pick up the pieces of the life that got scattered when my father died. Go to university myself one day. What would I study if I did? Psychology? Or maybe nursing. Something like that.

I've reached the junction for the M1. I'm on my way now, one long road going north. On the radio a soprano is singing an aria by Puccini. It makes my heart soar. So much beauty, I think, in the world. Very soon Jack's plane will be taking off into the darkening sky, nosing its way westwards, towards the Atlantic Ocean. So many journeys to make.

Maybe one day I'll meet someone else. I can't think of it now, but maybe one day. Someone decent, someone like Jack maybe. Who knows? Meanwhile, my mother will probably be sitting down now with Rita by the fire, having her afternoon cup of tea, a slice of fruit cake perhaps on a plate on the arm of her chair. Will Rita be making her laugh again, telling her another story about the wayward husband? Will Alice be there? They'll have their eye on the clock. They'll be wondering what time I'll arrive. They'll be looking forward to my coming home.

ACKNOWLEDGEMENTS

Thanks to my agents, Lucy Childs Baker of the Aaron Priest agency, New York, and Arabella Stein of Abner Stein, London, for their faith and encouragement, to Maria Rejt for her kindness and support, and to all the team at Picador for their help and expertise. Thanks to New Writing Ventures, and to Arts Council England, South West. Also to Tim for his advice, Ben for his enthusiasm, and Lesley, Shirley, Hugh and other friends for their patience and for providing a listening ear.

Elizabeth Diamond's second novel

UNDERWATER

is published in hardback in
May 2009 by Picador.

What do you remember, Jane? How much do you remember?

Jane is living a solitary life, estranged from her husband and
son after her family is marked by a tragedy she cannot face.
As she recovers from a debilitating bout of treatment for a
serious illness, Jane is plagued by childhood memories and
strange, underwater dreams of her beloved brother, Paul,
who went missing as a teenager. Now he seems to be urging
her to remember her long-buried past.

Her mind desperately seeking connections, Jane begins
searching for Paul. But as she digs further into her brother's
disappearance, she realizes she must untangle the web of lies
from which she has woven her life and confront the devastat-
ing truth about her family . . .

Read on for an exclusive peek at the first chapter . . .

I

The dreams about her brother, Paul, started during those dark grim weeks when she was shuttered in the house, convalescing from the operation. The worst of them, the one that upset her the most, she dreamed on the night of the winter solstice. The same date that her father had died on. Thirty-three years ago.

She dreamed Paul was swimming in the Ouse, on the stretch not far from their home where the river curved smoothly. She was watching him from the riverside, under the shade of willows. He was swimming far out from the bank, his thin boy's arms spinning wreaths of white spray. He stopped suddenly, turned to face her, treading water.

'Come and join me, Jane,' he said. 'The water's lovely.'

The sunlight dappled the water, made it look inviting. She slid down from the bank, lowered her body into the water. Her limbs were young and tanned and slim. She started swimming slowly out towards him. She was surprised she could keep afloat, surprised at the rhythm of her limbs turning in the water, how easy it was. When she got close to him he suddenly disappeared from sight. She felt herself begin to panic, felt her limbs frail in the water, felt something wrap around her legs and pull her down. In the murky green her brother's face nudged up close to her. He was crying, he was laughing; she couldn't tell which. His arms were wrapped tight around her, holding her down. She heard his voice, as if it was inside her, in her head, in her chest.

Stay with me, Jane. Don't go. Stay here with me.

She couldn't breathe, she was drowning. Panic sharp in her chest, like a blade. She kicked and threshed underwater, his grip weakened, his arms sliding away . . .

She was sitting bolt upright in the bed, gulping back air, the sound of her voice sobbing, breaking in waves over her ears.

She had been plagued for several weeks by the dreams, coming from nowhere. Some seemed to come from the past, as if she was reliving real events. Things that had happened in her childhood. Things she had forgotten, or thought she had.

Usually Paul was in these dreams. The Paul that belonged to her childhood, her older brother. These dreams disturbed her, distressed her. Cast a shadow upon her thoughts all through the long mornings after waking. She felt riven with anxiety. It wasn't so much because of the illness, although of course that played a part. She didn't know what it was or where it came from. But there was a sense of danger, lurking continually beneath her thoughts, haunting her days.

The night after the dream about drowning, she phoned the Samaritans. She had never done anything like that before, never thought she ever would, didn't know why she was doing it now. The voice on the phone was male, in his thirties, perhaps. He told her his name was Simon. They talked for a while as if it wasn't some unearthly hour of the night, as if they were just two people getting to know each other, making small talk. She had a sense of the irony of it. *This wasn't real.* They didn't talk about Christmas, only days away. They avoided that.

At some point in the conversation he asked what she did for a living. She thought, briefly, about not telling the truth. Art therapists, after all, weren't supposed to be doing this in the small hours of the night. They were supposed to be the sane ones, the ones who helped others. The ones who never felt this kind of despair. But she thought it would feel immoral to lie to someone like this, who could have been at home perhaps, with his wife who missed him. Instead of sitting up through the night somewhere, listening to desperate people who couldn't sleep.

'I'm an art therapist,' she said. 'I work in a psychiatric hospital.'

He didn't flinch.

What did they talk about? Inconsequential chat, really. If she had any hobbies, where she liked going for her holidays, even her favourite food. The central heating had switched itself off; the room was growing cold. Josie, her Labrador, snored at her feet.

Then: 'Are you married, Jane?' The first serious topic of their conversation.

'Yes. Well, not really. We've been separated for over two years now.'

'I'm sorry,' he said. 'Any children?'

'One,' she said. And then in a way she was unsure again

about what was the truth, because she'd lost the child she'd had and been given another.

'I've two,' he said. 'A boy and a girl. Ten and eight. What do you have?'

'A boy,' she said. 'Dominic. He's nearly eighteen.'

'Ah, coming of age, then,' he said. 'I've got that to look forward to.'

She said nothing. Because what was there to say?

'Any other family?'

'My mother, I suppose. She's in a care home. She's lost her memory. She gets confused. '

'Father?'

'He died when I was a child.'

Did she say it too quickly, did she give anything away?

'That must have been difficult,' he said.

A softening in his voice, now. The silence of his listening was tangible, a different kind of silence to the one that had been pressing on her heart for weeks, making it difficult to breathe, to eat, to sleep.

'Brothers or sisters?'

'I've a brother. Paul. But I haven't seen him for years and years. He went missing when I was fourteen.'

And as she said it she felt strange. Like she was falling from a great height. She had never told anyone about Paul before.

'Tell me about your brother, Jane. What was he like?'

So she talked about Paul, for the first time ever. To a stranger, someone who'd never known him, never known her, was just a voice on the phone. And it was as if her words were bringing him back again. He could almost have been there with her, sitting across the room in the dim light, listening.

He was tall. Nearly six foot. He had red hair. Not ginger, never ginger. Auburn. Eyes not quite green, not quite brown. Sometimes a little more one colour than the other, depending on the light. He liked birds and fishing and dogs. He was in the Sea Scouts. He liked the sea, he loved it. He was a good swimmer. The best in his class. He could swim for miles.

'Are you a good swimmer too?'

'Not really. No, not at all. Like a stone,' she said. And he laughed, and she laughed too.

His voice dipped, softened again.

'Why do you think your brother left home, Jane?'

'I don't know.' She was telling the truth, she wasn't telling it. She suddenly felt a wave of tiredness. As if the words dragged up from some morass inside her had worn her out.

But because of the way he listened, in spite of her fatigue, she told him about the day her brother left.

It was a day in early March. A mild day, quite warm and sunny. She'd just got in from school. Her aunt and uncle – 'we'd lived with them ... since our father died ...' – hadn't got back from work yet, didn't get back till after five. She went upstairs to start her homework. Paul was home. She could hear him playing music in his room.

'He had weird taste. He didn't like the usual stuff that teenagers liked, back then. Adam Faith, Cliff and the Shadows, things like that. He liked Jacques Brel, this German songwriter, Kurt something ...'

'Kurt Weill.'

'Yes, that's it. I'm not sure how he got into that sort of music. Perhaps my mother introduced him to it – I think she liked it too.'

Jane didn't like it. She always thought it sounded depressing. She heard clattering noises coming from his room as well, and opened the door. Stuff, scattered on his bed. Small piles of clothing. A torch, a pile of coins, a penknife, binoculars. A rucksack on the floor.

'Aren't you ever going to learn to knock first?' He looked a bit odd. Flushed, guilty, as if she'd caught him doing something he shouldn't.

'What's all that stuff for? Are you going somewhere?'

'I'm just sorting things out.'

She shut the door and left him to it, went to her own room. An hour later he opened her bedroom door. She was sitting at her desk, doing her French homework. Trying to learn the past historic for 'to forget' and 'to remember'. He stood looking at her, like he'd forgotten what he'd come for. The light from the window in his eyes, making him squint.

'What are you doing?'

'Homework, of course.'

'What homework?'

'French. I've a test tomorrow.'

'Good,' he said.

She waited, wondering what was good about it, wondering what else he was going to say. He looked like he wanted to say something more.

'I might be late. I'm going round Stuart's. Tell them not to worry.'

'OK.' She turned back to her verbs.

'Goodbye, Jane.'

There was something about the way he said it. But she thought nothing of it at the time, was lost in her head with the past historic. Just a short while after, she heard the front door close she had an urge to go to the window. He was walking away down the road. He walked like someone who wasn't in a hurry, who had plenty of time. He had his khaki rucksack on his back, the one he used for his scouting trips. It looked full, all the little pockets and compartments bulging. *Why has he packed his rucksack to go to Stuart's?* She thought perhaps he'd changed his mind; he *was* going away, after all. He and Stuart had decided to go camping on the spur of the moment. She thought of opening the window and calling out, to ask him, but didn't bother. She turned back to her homework.

Jane paused. The past was stealing into her heart, was taking over. She was fourteen. She was looking out of her bedroom window, her hand on the catch. Then changing her mind and turning away.

'Funny, I can't remember them at all now. The verbs. I used to be good at French. I used to know all the tenses. The imperfect, the pluperfect. I can't even remember the French for "to forget" and "to remember" now.'

Oublier, se souvenir. Simon's voice, so soft it was like the imprint of a voice on her ear.

'The thing is,' she said, 'this stuff's been coming back to me. These memories.'

'Do you mean flashbacks, that sort of thing?'

'Yes, I suppose so. But in dreams, mainly. I haven't

thought of him for years, or dreamed of him. And now suddenly I dream of him often.'

'When did it begin?'

She told him they'd only recently started. They just seemed to happen, to come out of nowhere.

'I never used to be the sort that dwelt on things. I was always one just for getting on with things before.'

'Maybe that's part of the problem,' he said. 'Maybe you need to take the time now to think about the past.'

'I don't know.' This tiredness again, overwhelming her. Like something heavy on top of her, like the weight of water.

'The thing is, it doesn't help that I'm on my own a lot. I'm not working at the moment. I've been ill, you see; I've had an operation. I'm still convalescing.'

He didn't ask what kind of operation, what was wrong with her, but she told him anyway. About the breast cancer and the consultations with Mr Fazil. The lumpectomy, and the radiotherapy she was due to start in a fortnight.

'I could go back to work then, if I want. They don't mind you working during the radiotherapy, providing you feel well enough.'

'Do you think you're well enough?'

'I'm not sure. Perhaps not. I'm not sleeping well, and these dreams, sometimes they bother me. Sometimes I feel rather desperate. But then you know that. I wouldn't have phoned you if I didn't.'

'Have you talked to your doctor about the way you feel? It might be a good idea to do that.'

'Yes, perhaps. I'll think about it.' But she knew she wouldn't. She couldn't talk to her doctor the way she'd talked to him. Her doctor knew her. She'd have to see him again, whenever she went to the surgery, sit across the desk from him knowing he knew those things about her, had written them down in her notes.

'It sounds like you've been though a great deal these last few years. It would be surprising if you weren't feeling depressed, Jane. Anyone would, going through what you've been through.'

The sort of thing she would say to patients at work.

'Yes, I suppose you're right.'

'Do you ever think of suicide?'

It was said quickly, carelessly, like words thrown away, but it took her by surprise. She wondered if she had misheard him.

'I'm sorry, what did you say . . . ?'

Maybe it was a ploy. Maybe she was buying time.

'I said, do you ever think of harming yourself?'

But he had changed it now. Softened it. Made it sound more probable, more commonplace. *Aren't there a thousand ways to harm oneself?* she thought. *Don't we all choose at least one way?*

But she knew that wasn't what he meant. He meant the first word. The one she'd heard but pretended she hadn't. The one that sounded medical, like *sarcoma*. Dry, tearless. Conjuring the smell of antiseptic, the white coats of doctors, pills that stuck in the throat.

'No, not really.'

'Not really?' he echoed back. As if he didn't believe her.

'No, I haven't. Not seriously, anyway. I would never actually *do* anything. I mean, I may have thought about it, but only in a vague way. There's a world of difference between having a thought and carrying out an action, isn't there?'

'If there wasn't my wife would have divorced me for adultery a long time ago,' he said. And they laughed, uneasily.

'So you'll be OK? When we finish talking?'

'Yes, of course.'

'What will you do?'

'Go to bed, I expect.'

'You must be tired.'

'Yes. Yes, I am.'

She was. This weariness filling her head, like water.

'Well, if you feel like ringing again. Any time. Don't hesitate.'

She sat alone in the darkness for another hour. She was tossing the word over in her head. As if it was something she had suddenly found. An artefact. A stone with an interesting patina. She had heard the word so often. In the mouths of psychiatrists and nurses at case reviews. She had read it patients' files, had written it there herself. *This patient has suicidal thoughts. This patient is currently on suicide watch.* She had seen the morbid fantasies in their paintings and sketches. In the hospital, on the ward, in the claustrophobic confines of the art-therapy room where anything can happen in a painting, in a shape wrought from a lump of clay, it was just another word. Removed from the world outside, the normal world. Like *psychosis*, *schizophrenic*, *mania*. But now it was stripped of that context and given another. Handed to her by a stranger on the phone.

Have you ever thought of suicide?

Had she?

She wasn't sure. She didn't know.

No, not really.

Ambiguous, deceptive. The only kind of answer she could give.

She felt she was putting the word away now, as if in a corner of the room. On a shelf perhaps, hidden behind books. Tucking it away in a corner of her mind. Still there, but out of sight.

But that night she had a different dream. This time it didn't seem to come from the past. She didn't know where it came from. It felt like the future was spinning itself backwards into the present.

She was in a room crowded with people. A stranger was sitting in the shadows in the corner. She couldn't see his face. A blonde woman with an open, smiling face came up to her.

'Let me introduce you to someone. He thinks you may have met somewhere before.'

The woman had a slight American accent. She led Jane towards the stranger. Her heart was racing. As the man saw her approaching, he stood up, moved out of the shadows, and then she could see that it was Paul. His hair that had been auburn, russet like autumn leaves, was faded now, greying at the temples. He was older, a man in his middle years, not the boy of eighteen he had once been. But she knew without any doubt that it was him.

When she finally woke up it was late. Long past the time she would normally wake, weary from a night of broken sleep.

She got out of bed and drew back the curtains and she knew she was past the worst now. There was a hard, bright, January light. The grass sparkled with frost. The winter solstice was behind her.

She had always hated the depths of winter. The darkness would feel to her as though it was something physical that had the power to still her blood, and take her breath from her. Jane's aunt had died just after Christmas and her father just before. In all the years she'd lived with Adam, when Dominic was little, she had to force herself to celebrate the holiday. Put up the tree, the decorations, buy the presents and wrap them. Whilst all the time, this feeling of suffocation. This dread that ached in her bones.

But now, waking from a dream that seemed to come from some future place, a Paul she didn't know and hadn't met, she knew she'd passed her own personal nadir. The light was coming back, bit by bit.

He wants me to find him, she thought, a small bubble of excitement rising within her. *That's what he wants. He wants me to find him.*